THE PUCK DROP

JAQUELINE SNOWE

Published: 2021

Published by: Jaqueline Snowe

Copyright © 2021, Jaqueline Snowe

Cover Design: Dany Snowe

Editing: Katherine McIntyre

Formatting: Jennifer Laslie

All rights reserved. No part of this publication may be reproduced, stored in a retrieval system, or transmitted in any form, or by any means, electronic, mechanical, recording, or otherwise, without prior written permission from the author. For more information, please contact Jaqueline at www.jaquelinesnowe.com.

This is a work of fiction. The characters, incidents, dialogue, and description are of the author's imagination and are not to be constructed as real. Any resemblance to actual events or persons, living or dead, is completely coincidental.

THE PUCK DROP

Michael Reiner has the new start he's been craving, where no one knows about his past and he can finally figure out what he wants out of life. Because one thing's for certain—he can't play hockey anymore, and life without hockey seems daunting. But when he gets the chance to intern under the Central State Hockey coach, he couldn't be happier. Until he finds out the mysterious hottie he met at the bar is the Coach's daughter.

Naomi Fletcher-Simpson has always been the weird twin. She prefers spreadsheets and trivia nights while her popular sister is everyone's favorite. Things have been tense in her family, so when she gets a chance to pair up with the hockey team for a huge stats project, she takes it. She can repair her relationship with her dad *and* hopefully score her dream internship in the process.

Neither Michael nor Naomi expected to like each other. Complete opposites in every way, they slowly form a deep friendship that makes their chemistry sizzle, and friends with benefits is the only option to deal with their growing attraction. Michael can't afford to lose the internship, and Naomi can't afford to lose her heart to a hockey guy.

For the guy who's suffered enough loss, and the girl who's *always* left behind, they can't risk falling in love—not when they both know all things come to an end, right?

CHAPTER ONE

Michael

There was something about the way the cold air smelled in the rink. It cooled my lungs and settled my soul. Standing there and watching the younger guys skate caused a pang in my chest because that part of my life was over.

I wasn't a hockey player anymore.

After my whole identity revolved around that for so long, it was like losing a limb. Without hockey, who was I?

"Reiner!" Coach Simpson yelled at me from a few yards away. His sharp tone had me standing up straighter, and I shoved my hands in my pockets. I could daydream about being on the ice later. I had shit to do if I wanted a future, and that meant starting my internship under head hockey coach of the Central State Wolves. Not daydreaming about being part of the team. That ship had sailed.

"Yes, sir," I said, forcing myself to look away and focus on the man who I followed around all last year. Not in a creepy way but in an *I-need-this-internship-please-like-me* sort of way. It was my second year at Central State, and I learned a lot watching the team last year. The stern man had a winning reputation for a good reason. He liked to win, hated excuses, and ran a smooth hockey program. A little gruff, a little charismatic, and a little intense. I couldn't think of a better person to shadow for my last year of grad school. *Masters in sports management, here I come.*

"This is hard for you," he said, no bullshit in his tone. He stared at me, his dark eyes and almost-black eyebrows softening in understanding. His attention moved from me to the rink, and he nodded. "That'll never go away."

"The urge to play? No, I don't think it will." I sighed and looked at the ice again. "It feels like an amicable break-up where we still gotta hang out all the time. Hard to digest it or move on."

"It's in your blood, kid. You think I didn't call your old coach to get a reference? I don't accept just any goddamn intern." He barked out a laugh, and the sound echoed in the hallway.

God, I missed the Northeast. The Midwest was fine. Illinois had all four seasons, and I could experience *each one* within a five day span, but it wasn't home. Every time I thought about it, I wondered why I chose to attend school here. I could've stayed closer to my sister Ryann, closer to where we grew up, where I had friends. Something propelled me to move away from all the memories—the good ones and the bad. That was the thing about grief I'd never understood until it happened to me.

I wanted to grasp onto something just as fiercely as I needed to let it go. My past. My memories. The fact that our parents died in a crash when I was twenty, and ever since then, every memory back home held a twinge of sadness.

Here? At Central State? Clean slate. It was like a breath of fresh air most days, but once in a while, a comment would take me back. Like Moo U. I lifted my hat and ran my fingers through my hair before adjusting it. Coach Simpson arched one of his bushy eyebrows, and I tried not to look smug.

"I take it the call went well then."

"You're here, aren't you?"

I grinned. "Sure am."

"What's your take on Cal?" he asked, shifting gears as he jutted his chin toward the freshman stand-out. Cal Holt, often referred to as The Bolt, possessed more talent than I ever had, but the problem was that he knew it. I might've only been at Central for a year, but I researched the players, the culture, and the legacy. Even if I didn't get the internship, I would've followed the team because Coach was right. Hockey was in my blood and always would be.

I clicked my tongue and rocked back on my heels. "Is this a joke? Are you testing me right now to see how honest I'll be with you? Or is this a different kind of quiz?"

"You talk too much."

"My previous coach should've mentioned that," I said, snorting when Coach Simpson closed his eyes for a beat. "My take. Hm. Talented, clearly. Fundamentals are top-notch."

"And?"

My shoulders tensed. There was something about his question that had me pausing. I considered myself pretty emotionally intelligent. I had to be as an alternative captain, or the team dynamic could shift. But his question felt different. I cracked my thumb knuckle in my pocket and tried to figure out *what* he wanted. He was no-nonsense, gruff, and honest, so his inquisition didn't feel like a trick. The truth was the best scenario. With as much confidence as I could muster, I said, "Older leadership could have issues with him if he doesn't open up to the team. He refers to himself as The Bolt in third person. Not exactly encouraging brotherhood by acting like that."

"How would you fix it?"

"Fix it? Not sure one person could." I took a deep breath, the familiar smell of the ice easing the growing worry in my gut. Coach Simpson narrowed his eyes at me. This felt like a tryout.

Shit, maybe it was. I cleared my throat and told my *worries* to fuck off. I knew my shit on the ice, in the rink, and if this was an attempt to see what I was made of, then I'd give it to him straight. I met his gaze. "He needs instances where he relies on the team, and vice versa. He might not see other players as useful, and until he realizes that, there won't be a good dynamic on the ice. And, Coach? He needs to be on the ice."

"Sacrifice my morals for a win?"

"Ah, I would never say that." My ears heated, but the regret didn't last long when he grinned back at me. "Plus, you're the one making the dough here. You decide that call. I'm actually *paying* the school thousands of dollars to attend. Quite different scenarios."

He laughed and hit my shoulder. "Good insight. Lesson one of coaching a NCAA hockey team? Once the puck drops, your job is done. It's every single little thing that happens between games that's on you. Sure, Cal can have the best numbers in the league, but if I don't create a team culture that fosters togetherness, those stats are shit."

"Yes, sir," I said, nodding and wishing like hell I'd gotten a chance to play for him. My body hummed with adrenaline, the urge to lace up almost getting me to the point where my hands shook. I was a junkie needing my next hit of ice.

"I know you just showed up and never really left, but we do have to go over your requirements for the practicum. I need to hop on a call and get transportation ready for next week's away game, but meet me at a *Logan's* this evening. Seven pm. I prefer to drink beer if I'm looking over a goddamn syllabus."

"You got it. First drink is on you."

"Oh, you think you're slick." He grinned and pointed at me. "Don't disappoint me, Reiner."

"I wouldn't dream of it."

Logan's smelled like stale beer and peanuts, but damn, I loved coming here. It was situated in the heart of campus and was the perfect spot to have a beer and watch a game. Football season was underway, and blues and oranges covered every surface. Central State loved their football, that was for sure. While I was dedicated to my Moo U gear, I'd caved and bought a few Central shirts for team spirit. Competition was part of who I was, and I liked being part of a dominant school that won a lot.

My phone buzzed in my pocket right as I got to the bar, and I sat on a stool and eyed the text from my sister.

Ryann: How was the first day of the internship?

Michael: Still going. Coach wanted to meet me at a bar for a drink to talk.

Ryann: Wow. Right up your alley. Do you love him already?

Michael: Shut up.

I grinned and put my phone facedown. I missed my sister and even her shy boyfriend, Jonah Daniels. They were living up their senior year back home while I was here, relatively alone. I scratched my chest over my Central shirt and waited for the gut punch. It came and went as a cute bartender approached me.

"Hey there," I said, smiling and forgetting all about home.

She winked and tilted her head to the side. "Hi, handsome. What can I get ya?"

"312, please."

Her gaze lingered on my face then moved to my tatted arm, and my smile grew. Maybe that's what I needed. A distraction. Someone or something to occupy my mind from the fact I'd be back in the rink and *not* playing. A distraction from reminiscing about home. A way for my mind to escape reality because hockey had always been that for me and I'd lost that haven.

The pretty bartender wore short shorts as she got me a beer, which snagged my gaze. I was not prepared when someone ran into me on my right side. *Hard.*

"What the hell?" I gripped the edge of the bar to stop myself from falling off the stool as a woman put her hands all over my body.

Hints of lemon and cookies washed over me, and a petite person cussed a few times before pushing long dark brown hair off her face. "Shit, shit! Sorry. Wow. This isn't going well."

"No, not really," I said, reaching out to steady the girl. Her large brown eyes seemed worried, and a red blush painted her cheeks. She was cute. Small nose, big eyes, full lips. Not a knock-out like the bartender but still cute. "Do you always fall into people, or is this a special occasion?"

She chewed on her lip, frowned, and looked over her shoulder. Her pulse raced at the base of her neck, and I followed her gaze, expecting someone to be chasing her. Why else would she crash into me? There were just a few guys sitting in a booth. One of them squinted over at us, and recognition lit up his face.

I didn't know him, but Klutzy McGee sure did.

Her entire body tensed, and she snapped her attention back to me. "Hi, hello. We can do introductions later, but I need a huge favor. The biggest. I'll buy you a drink or two. Hell. Three!"

"This is getting more interesting." I smiled. "What's the favor?"

"I need you to pretend to date me, right freaking now." She scooted closer and swallowed so hard her throat made a clicking sound. She glanced over her shoulder at the guy approaching us, and her breathing picked up. "Please."

It took two seconds to think it over. She looked worried, and a protective instinct took root in my gut. Was this guy bothering her? Harassing her? Did she tell him no and he refused to accept it so she had to lie about having a boyfriend? Fuck. Guys could be the worst.

"You got it, Klutzy."

"Oh, thank god." She closed her eyes and moved onto the stool next to me, just as the large guy approached us.

"Fletcher," he said, his voice low and deep and weird.

Her name was... Fletcher? Interesting choice. She sat too straight to be at a bar, her spine like a steel pole as she made a fist with her left hand. "Gage," she said, the redness spreading down her face toward her chest.

Gage eyed her, then me, and lowered his voice like I couldn't hear him. I was two feet from him, and sound didn't work that way. I rolled my eyes. I already didn't like this guy.

"Could we talk, please?"

"I told you, *no*."

Yeah, I really wasn't a fan of *Gage*. "Bud, do you mind? We're on a date, and I prefer Fletch's time all to myself, no offense."

Gage winced and took a step back. "He calls you Fletch?"

Hm, was that a secret name for her that I shouldn't've have said? I put my arm on the back of her stool, not quite touching her but also sending a message to Gage.

Klutzy McGee—AKA Fletcher— reached for my beer and took a large swig. Her throat bobbed, and half my glass was gone, but I didn't mind too much. I couldn't figure out the dynamic between her and Gage, and I wasn't going to move until I did. I needed to make sure she was safe from beefcake Gage.

"Where's Cami?" my pretend-date asked, her voice gaining strength that wasn't there before. Maybe it was liquid courage, but I liked the way her voice sounded. Deep, smooth, no-nonsense. "Shouldn't you be talking to my sister?"

Oh, shit. Sister! *What did Gage do?* Fletcher's face hardened, making her petite features way more intimidating than I would've thought. She might've been frazzled before, but there was a fire in her now. I was into it.

Gage paled and ran a hand over his face. "It's not like that, Fletch. She's just... wild. You know that. It didn't mean anything."

"This conversation is over." Fletcher's tone had a finality to it that had me sitting up straighter. If this doofus didn't march back to his friends, I was gonna be pissed.

She turned her back to him, her left hand shaking, and I covered it with mine. I didn't know much about this chick, but whatever she was going through didn't seem easy or fun. Footsteps signaled Gage's departure, but I didn't care about him anymore.

Fletcher was way more intriguing. She had long brown hair and large eyes. Her lashes were extremely long which I appreciated. Girls with big eyes made me do stupid things—like pretend to date them at a bar. Plus, her t-shirt hung off one of her shoulders, showing off her slender collarbones—I had a weakness for those too. A trio of birthmarks sat right where her neck met her shoulder.

"So, girlfriend, we gonna talk about what just happened, or…?" I let go of her hand, and the strangest thought intruded. When was the last time I held someone's hand? I wasn't lonely by any means, but a connection that went on longer than an evening? Damn. It'd been…awhile. Plus, her hand was so small and petite under mine.

"Nope. I'm going to finish your beer, buy another one, and give myself some liquid courage." She did just that. She downed my beer and gave me the side-eye. "You judging me?"

"I would never."

That made her snort, and she finally relaxed into the stool. "You actually mean that, don't you?"

"Absolutely. We rarely know what people are going through. Who am I to make assumptions about you for running into me and then making me pretend to date you without an explanation as to who that Gage guy is?"

"Sarcasm came out there."

"Shit, it didn't, didn't it?" I said, my lips twitching.

She laughed, and the deep sound did something to my chest. It made me want to hear it again. "Okay, you're charming. What's your name?"

I didn't get a chance to answer. "Reiner, Naomi. This is perfect. You're both here. Two birds, one stone, you know the drill. Come on, let's get a booth. I hate sitting on those damn stools."

My pretend girlfriend had different names. That made her all the more interesting, but we stared at each other.

"Why are you meeting Coach Simpson?" I asked first, already moving off the stool and trying to read her face. What could this chick with three names have to do with the hockey team?

"Why are you meeting with *my dad?*" she asked, her eyes wider than before.

"Coach Simpson is your *father?*"

Klutzy McGee—Fletcher—Naomi slid off her stool and walked by me, her lemon scent infiltrating my thoughts and distracting me for a second. The feisty cute woman was the daughter of the hockey coach?

Well, shit.

CHAPTER
TWO

Naomi

My entire face burned after running into—literally—the guy named Reiner. His stare was so intense that my nervous system threatened to strike, and my rational, linear mind went AWOL. He was the most handsome man I had ever seen, and the tattoos covering his arms...I wanted to file each one away and study them like a spreadsheet. The dark blue color of his eyes was a mixture of the ocean and navy, and the way the Central State shirt fit him? The dude was buff.

Very fit.

Hockey playing fit.

Ugh.

My fingers twitched at the thought of sending a picture of him to my roommates. We could hang him up on the wall right in our kitchen just to stare at him every day. Totally appropriate idea to have *right* now.

"Come on, I need a drink." My dad grunted as he squeezed into a booth, manspreading so the hot hockey player and I got squished to one side. I went in first, holding my breath to not inhale Renier's clean scent, and pressed myself against the wall.

I had so many questions, most of them having to do with the great-smelling, gorgeous guy scooting next to me. Like, why was my heart hammering in my ribcage? I was logical. I knew he was attractive, but boy howdy, his body made my insides go wild. I tensed when his thigh hit mine, but he gave no indication that my touch bothered him. I swore I could feel his warmth spread through his jeans and into my very soul.

Reiner relaxed and leaned his elbows onto the table, and it took all my effort not to ogle him. Which, in a way, was uncharacteristic of me. I liked nerds. Skinny, unathletic guys who listened to hipster music and drank cold brew. The guys who hung out in the library and got excited over a used book sale. Growing up with a dad who coached hockey and a twin sister who flirted with all of the players, I stayed clear.

Plus, the *one fucking time* I tried dating a muscle-head, the dude played me.

So, *calm down libido*. I cleared my throat, adjusted my leg so it didn't rest against Reiner's, and narrowed my eyes at my father. "You asked me to meet you at *Logan's* to talk about the...thing. This guy's here too. Why?"

The thing in question was doing stats for the Wolves and completing my junior data analysis project on the results. Our junior class was competitive and boring—as my advisor so kindly put it, I needed to *stand out* if I wanted to earn an internship next summer. What better way than to combine my ingrained knowledge of hockey with data sets? Plus, maybe it'd help my dad see that we had something in common. I'd been trying to get even a sliver of his attention for years, but I always came in second place to hockey. My insides twisted up with bitterness. The missed quiz bowls. The birthday dinner he forgot about, even though he made it up to my twin sister. Despite being twenty-one, the baggage he created still caused a punch to the gut.

"Always to the point. That's Naomi for you." My dad's face warmed for a second, and he raised his fingers into the air, signaling the bartender. The woman made a beeline for us so fast she stumbled, the stars in her eyes shining a bit too bright. "Hey, darling. Could we get three 312s, please?"

"Sure thing, Coach." She curtsied before she strutted away, which made me roll my eyes. I hated this shit. It was ridiculous how people put hockey players on a pedestal—even my dad, a middle-aged man with a bit of a belly and eyebrows that seemed to have a life of their own. They were just people who excelled at sports. I was great at spreadsheets and pivot tables, yet there were no fans wanting my signature.

Which was a shame. Data analysts could do some pretty cool things.

"Naomi," my dad said, his stern tone telling me he saw my reaction. We both knew my thoughts on how people treated hockey players like royalty.

I raised my hands in surrender, and my face heated. Cami was a dancer at Central and seemed to get all the athletic and charismatic genes from my dad. They watched football together and had inside jokes that left them heaving with laughter. Everything I said or did around my dad made me self-conscious, yet I couldn't seem to stop the continuous eye-rolls when people acted weird about my father's profession.

"Sorry."

He leaned back into his seat and looked between me and Reiner. "Thanks for both coming here. As Reiner so kindly said, this first drink is on me."

"As it should be," Reiner replied with an easy lilt I envied. They were already buds. How fitting.

My dad slapped the table and laughed. "You two are going to be spending time together as my interns."

Reiner snapped his head in my direction, and his brows furrowed as his tongue wet his bottom lip. I had to squeeze my thighs together to avoid reacting to that movement. That little dip of his tongue had me wild.

"What are you interning for?" he asked, the deep timbre of his voice making me brush my hair out of my face. Guys didn't find me attractive—that was all Cami. She was long legs and sleek hair and curves and beauty.

I was...not. I was messy buns and ripped jeans, small boobs and zero coordination. I liked murder podcasts and 90s alt radio. I was under no illusions that Reiner would ever actually date me, but the fact he let me use him to get Gage off my back made him all the more appealing. "Data."

"Data," he repeated, making the word sound sinful. "What type?"

"Excellent question, Reiner. She's going to help with stats for the year, and as my intern, I want you to listen to the reports and make recommendations to me. How would you, as a future coach, use data to make decisions?"

"Sir, no offense, but stats are just one small piece of what makes a great team."

My stomach tightened like I was preparing for war. In a way, I was. Data was *my version* of hockey. "Excuse me, but data is transformational."

"Stats don't show the whole picture."

"Then you're not using them correctly," I fired back, my lungs heaving at the confrontation. Reiner frowned and ran a hand over the back of his neck, really making the bicep bulge. It wasn't even fair.

Thank god the bartender returned with the drinks, spilling some all over her hand as she set them down in front of my dad. I didn't even roll my eyes once.

Point to me.

"Thanks, doll," my dad said, his attention already back on Reiner. "No *one* piece of data defines a player, sure, but trends are telling. Common themes. Errors. Matchups. This will be a weekly assignment for both of you."

"I have to report my findings to him?" I asked, the edge of my tone more intense than planned. My chest tightened. Well, there went my shot at a real relationship with my dad. Not the awkward holiday hugs and catch-up we seemed to do despite living in the same town. My mom's new husband and three kids kept her busy, and my dad was married to his job, and through it all...I kinda got forgotten. I cleared my throat and sat up straighter, annoyed that Reiner threw a wrench in my plan. "I'm not going to be working with you?"

"You will, but you'll meet with him weekly."

"Why?" I asked, not caring that my unhappiness was clear.

"Because it benefits all three of us." My dad took a long swig of the beer and groaned at something on the TV. "Fuck, I put twenty down on Ohio winning."

"Oh, bad move." Reiner craned his neck to stare at the screen and whistled. "Their offense has been struggling."

Football talk. Of course. For a niche geek like me, this was a slow form of torture. Why couldn't we talk about true crime? Or 90s movies? I could rattle on about those topics for days. Weeks, if needed.

I had the urge to kick them both in the shin. Maybe this was why my dad got along so well with Cami. Hell, this was why Gage wanted my sister after I didn't put out. I was geeky and not an athlete in any sense of the word. I preferred iframes over the ice. That meant I was a weirdo in my family.

The brief connection I thought I had with Reiner when he put his arm around the barstool earlier slowly evaporated. The more him and my father gabbed about football and rankings and all things I didn't find interesting, the more I pulled away. It was Thursday night, and a new episode of MARRIAGE, MURDER, AND MYSTERIES dropped, a crime podcast I loved. My roommates had strict instructions to not play it until I got back, and if this was going to be sportstalk, it was time to go.

"Excuse me, I'll just head out," I said, doing the awkward stand to try and exit the booth.

Reiner's large, warm body blocked me though. I tapped his shoulder, and he spun to face me again. Those damn blue eyes and long lashes were a real distraction. I blinked and focused on his nose. It was slightly crooked and probably the only imperfect thing about him.

"Do you mind?" I asked.

"You leaving already? You barely touched your beer," my dad said, frowning as he looked at the glass and back to me. "We never talked about schedules."

"I'll be at every game and report to Reiner, right?"

"Well, yeah," he said, blinking a few times and giving me *that* look. The one where he pressed his lips together and his eyes clouded. It was the *how are you my kid* expression I'd seen all my life, and it hurt. Every single time. My chest felt too tight, like a balloon wedged in there, and my face flushed with shame.

"Then I'll see you at the games next weekend. Opening the season on the road," he said, disappointment dripping from his voice as per usual.

Reiner watched with his mouth slightly parted and a little line between his eyebrows. He probably figured I was a total flake, but it was better he knew now that I wasn't a sports girl.

Reiner took his time getting out of the booth, but I couldn't fault him for that. His massive frame and muscles were probably hard to move around. God knows, I got tired just by looking at his biceps.

"Thanks," I said, ignoring how my skin tingled when our arms brushed. "What time should I get on the bus?"

"We're leaving at noon. Friday."

"Great. See you then." I didn't look back and waved over my shoulder as I left the bar. My feet felt heavier than normal, like two cement blocks, and I hated how my eyes prickled with emotion.

The opportunity to work with my dad had gotten passed off to Reiner. The guy who already had a rapport with my dad in a way I never did. They laughed, they joked, and they had the easy-breezy banter I'd always wanted with my dad. I took a deep breath of the leftover humid air. Despite the midwestern summer changing to fall, the heat stuck around for a bit in October, and it warmed my skin.

I fired off a quick text to my roommates that I was heading back just as a familiar laugh caught my attention. Loud, cute, *Cami*. My stomach dropped like I was falling through frozen ice on a lake. *Damn it*. If my sister saw me—

"Naomi! Hey, hey!" Cami spoke in a singsong way that tended to charm even the grumpiest person. Seeing her familiar face sent a ripple of hurt through me. I *missed* my sister. The girl who had my back no matter what growing up. The girl who punched Peter J in sixth grade for me. The girl who would *never* hurt me.

We'd changed though. Life did that to people. She was now the girl who slept with the guys I was dating. How could I ever get over that?

She waved her hand in the air, causing all the bracelets on her arm to jingle.

I gritted my teeth together and forced a light-lipped smile as my sister approached me. She wore a tight CENTRAL dance shirt, all sequined out in orange, and bright red lipstick. While my hair was straight and often in a bun, hers was down and curly. Just looking at her made me feel less put together. She was the wild, pretty twin.

I was the nerd.

"Look at you in your cute as hell shirt and shorts." She laughed and wrapped her arm around my shoulders in an awkward hug. She smelled like expensive perfume.

"What? No." I scoffed and eyed my ripped jean shorts and shirt that said *I have a spreadsheet for that*. Not cute.

She grinned at me, her familiar features the same and yet so different than mine. "I love it. Seriously." Her face warmed, but her attention moved to someone inside the bar. She jutted her chin toward the door. "Want to grab a drink with me? I don't have to be at the party for another hour."

"No, it's fine," I said, taking a step back. "I gotta go. My roommates are waiting for me to start the episode of our murder podcast. You know how it is," I said, desperate to leave. Lilly, Mona, and Kellie would talk me through this and help me come up with talking points because while I *needed* to confront my sister, hard conversations weren't my forte. At all.

She stared at me a beat, her eyes flashing with hurt, and it pissed me off. She slept with Gage! While I was with him! She was the favorite daughter! She could have anything in the world and chose to go after the first guy I dated after my terrible break up last year. My throat felt like I'd swallowed an entire bag of cotton balls, and I took off.

Attending the same school as my sister where my dad coached seemed like an okay idea three years ago. Now, it brought a storm cloud whenever I saw them.

I could graduate in a year and eight months and be done with them. I just had to nail this final project. Even if it meant working with the guy who made my pulse race.

CHAPTER
THREE

Michael

Frederick Brady the IV might've been one of the best roommates I'd ever had, but he was the oddest study partner. We headed to the library together for a few hours, and during that time, I'd gotten to learn his odd habits.

When we had to do team studies back at Moo U, the twins would get into it, but that was nothing like watching Freddie line up his highlighters *and* Skittles.

"Stop staring at me, man. Makes me self-conscious."

"You're matching the Skittle color with the highlighter. I can't look away," I said, amused as hell. The guy was six feet tall, wore thick black glasses, and had the body of a linebacker. Yet, he'd never played a sport a day in his life. "So, when you finish three pages of reading, you eat the yellow Skittle?"

"Reiner," he said, staring at me with wide eyes. "I will smack you if you mess me up."

I grinned and let him be. We'd been living together for over a year now when I answered his roommate ad, and he was my first friend at Central. He knew enough about me to be friendly, and having a fresh start that wasn't clouded in grief was nice.

No sympathy looks. No cringe-y smiles. I put on my headphones and got my economics book out. I had assignments to do that weren't all based on shadowing Simpson.

I read a chapter and took notes, using red ink to jot down the key points. Someone told me back at Moo U that using red ink *and* chewing gum while studying helped trigger your brain to remember. I never looked into the validity of it, but I did both every time. As I organized my notes filled with definitions and applications of finance—when it came to athletics—I almost snorted at myself.

I always did okay in school. My sister was the overachiever, but this past year? I worked my ass off. Earning those A's meant more than before. I couldn't pinpoint how or why, but they did. My parents would've been proud of me. Sure, I liked partying and having a good time, but without hockey...I needed a challenge.

There was a soft thud to my left. Then another thud. Someone knocked over a large stack of books at a table. The hardbacks dropped in slow motion as a girl covered her face before sliding off her chair to pick them up.

Recognition flared through me. *Coach's daughter.* Klutzy McGee was at it again, and without overthinking it, I pushed out of my chair. The movement caused Freddie's Skittles to wobble, and he shot me a death glare.

"Shit," I said, reaching to reposition the sweets, but he swatted my hand.

"Don't even think about it."

I backed away from the table slowly and walked toward Naomi, or Fletcher, the moment she slammed her head under the table. It'd been four days since we got that beer, and she'd crossed my mind more than a few times. Her adorable nose scrunch and full lips caught my attention, but it was the passion she had talking about data that intrigued me. I was a fan of people who *loved* something as much as I loved hockey.

"You should come with a warning sign."

She rubbed the spot where her skull met wood and winced. "Approach with caution then."

I bent down to help her pick up her books, and charts and numbers jumped out at me. Made sense if she was going to do stats and report the trends to me. I set the texts on top of the table as she plopped into the chair. She wore a faded blue shirt that said GO TEAM, and she had two braids going on. Neither of those things drew me in, but the intelligence in her eyes, the smooth skin, and the damn lemon scent coming off her did. I pulled out the chair across from her and sat down.

She arched a brow. "Please, sit, join me. I'm at your leisure."

"I'm sensing a tone here," I said, unable to stop my lips from curving up. This woman was a puzzle, and I had questions.

"I'm not being subtle." She blew out a breath and played with the end of one of the braids. "What are you doing here?"

"At the library? Studying with my roommate. Or did you mean, life in general? Because I'm not sure. I have moments of clarity at times but then I feel purposeless, you know? Oh wait," I teased, blinking and putting a hand on my chest. "Did you mean *here* at your table?"

Her mouth twitched, and she shook her head. "Obviously the last one."

"I saw you and wanted to say hi."

"Well, hi." She waved, and a light blush crept on her cheeks. She chewed the inside of her cheek as she stared at me, and there was something about her that made me want to stick around. She had an air of loneliness that I understood, but there was no real way to explain how I knew that.

It was just a feeling. The way she steeled her shoulders and how she looked at her dad with hurt in her eyes. We all had our baggage, and while I never talked about mine, I wanted to ask about hers. Who was the girl who needed a fake date? The girl who bolted before taking more than three sips of a free beer?

"Since we'll be working together, I feel like we should get to know each other more, hm?" I said, leaning onto my elbows and getting an inch closer to her. She had a light dusting of freckles on her nose and a mole on her left cheek. I instantly pictured the trio of moles I saw on her collarbone.

She sighed and looked everywhere but my face. "Why? You seem like trouble."

"Well, I am." I winked and flashed her my best smile. "Have you ever helped out during a hockey season before?" I asked, chuckling at how she narrowed her eyes at me. "Lots of time together, you and me. What if you need a fake date again? Hell, what if I need a fake date? These are important questions, so we should probably be friendly."

"Did my dad make you do this?"

"Wait, what?" I recoiled. "No. We didn't talk about you after you left."

Naomi seemed to sink further into her chair. "Fine. We're friends."

"Doesn't work like that." I tapped my finger on the table, and she watched the movement. "Did that guy stop bothering you? Do you need me to help again?"

She blinked. "It's fine. I haven't seen him."

Okay, she was a tough cookie. A hard cookie, like a biscotti or something. Didn't make it less delicious, just a bit more effort to get to the good part. It was exhilarating and weird to struggle to get more than one-word answers with this girl. Flirting was as easy as skating, but Naomi had me questioning my game.

That wouldn't do.

"Okay, data girl, since I pretended to date you for ten minutes, do I get the story behind it? I think that's a fair ask."

"Nope." She swallowed and played with that damn braid again. Her big brown eyes seemed to stare through me as she said, "I appreciate you helping me, by the way. I never got to thank you."

I liked her voice and how it was a little deeper than I'd imagined. I flashed her another grin and leaned back into the chair. "You're welcome. I'm always up for pretending to date cute data nerds."

"Mm," she said, her mouth *almost* curving up at the sides in a smile. That tiny movement shouldn't have sent a thrill through me, but shit, it did.

"Okay, this one-sided conversation is going swell." I laughed at how much shit I'd get if the guys back home knew how much I failed at this. Was I hoping to harmlessly flirt with the woman who'd been on my mind the past week? Yes. Would anything happen? Nah. But she shot down every attempt. I covered my yawn with a hand as I started to stand up. The anticipation of being back in the rink during game time, not as a player, kept me up. I wasn't sleeping great with all the mental gymnastics I'd been partaking in. "Sorry, Fletcher, super tired today."

"Wild night?" she asked with a hint of judgement to her tone.

"I mean, watching a documentary about Michael Jordan and then tossing and turning all night isn't in my top five crazy nights, but sure. We'll go with wild."

Naomi fought a smile again but lost. She laughed, and it was like a wall crashed down between us, the tension in my chest fizzling away.

"I'm being rude. It's not you, it's me."

"Sounds like we're breaking up, which ironically, still makes this the second longest relationship I've had."

Her eyes crinkled on the sides, and she let out a deep chuckle. "Ah, and the longest would be?"

"Melanie Veroni. Third grade. Now that I think about it, we never ended things. So, this is awkward. I should probably call her, right? To make sure we both know?"

She snorted, and it charmed me. She swallowed as her gaze moved from my face to my arm with tattoos. The ink designs were all flowers, free-hand drawings from sick artists back home, and a large phoenix that covered my entire bicep. "Is your first name Reiner?"

"My last name. Michael William Reiner is my whole name. That was going to be your next question. I could already tell."

Naomi had a great smile. Straight white teeth, soft lines around her full lips. I liked how I could break down that slight grumpy exterior. Again, something told me she had a story there, but until I found out what it was, I'd settle for those little grins.

"Your turn," I said, jutting my chin at her. "Full name. You could also provide your social security number and name of your first pet. If you wanted to. No pressure."

She chuckled again. *Two points for me.*

"God, you are something else." She set her hands down on the table, and the lone silver ring on her middle finger caught my attention. "Naomi Fletcher. I'm not sharing my middle name because it's…well, you're a hockey player. You'll just make fun of me."

"Try me."

"Gordie. My dad made a bet with his buddy, and my dad lost. My godfather got to pick my middle name and went with Gordie. So yeah, Naomi Gordie Fletcher."

"Gordie as in… Gordie Howe? Mr. Hockey?" My eyes almost bugged out of my face. "That's pretty badass."

"Not as a young girl when we were bedazzling everything and getting monograms of our initials." She forced out a laugh and looked down at her hands. "My sister was Cami May, so you could imagine my envy."

"I don't know if I've ever given much thought about my middle name." I crossed my arms and tried to remember if my parents told me why they'd chosen that. Maybe it was a long-lost family name or a tribute to their favorite dog. I wasn't sure, and it was moments like these where my chest weighed a million pounds. I would never get to ask them for middle-name anecdotes. The paralyzing grief rippled under the surface, and I did the only thing I knew—deflected it. Distracted myself.

I could give my whole attention to a person, a sport, an assignment, just to avoid getting lost in my own thoughts or feelings. "Listen, I can see you have some bitterness about not having a cute middle name that looks good in sparkles, but that shit is cool. Not saying that because hockey is in my blood. It's unique, and anyway, who wants to fit in? I sure don't. My sister's name is Ryann with two N's, and she loves how different her name is. No offense, Klutzy, but you don't strike me as someone who was born to blend."

Naomi's entire posture changed. Her shoulders relaxed, and warmth flooded her eyes. "Thanks. I needed to hear that."

"I'm always good for a truth bomb and pretending to date you when guys like Gage come around." I winked at her, and Naomi blushed. The pink on her cheeks had my grin stretching across my face. She was damn cute. "So, speaking of names… Fletcher. Simpson. Why do you go by Fletcher?"

She nodded. "My official last name is Fletcher-Simpson. My mom never took my dad's last name when they married, and I just liked Fletcher better. My sister chose Simpson."

"Naomi Gordie Fletcher it is." I studied her again, feeling a natural closeness with her that I hadn't experienced in a long time. Kindred spirits, lost souls. It wasn't purely physical either. Sure, she was attractive, but the fact she was the boss's daughter put an instant *not going there* vibe around her. That made her live in a different part of my mind. One that didn't cross into more than friends.

Because this internship, working with Simpson, was the thing I needed to figure out my future. No matter how cute his daughter was, nothing could mess that up. Plus, I missed having someone to share stuff with. Freddie was great but distant. My sister and I spoke twice a week, but that was via phone. Once I got past Naomi's exterior, she opened up, and it like we'd known each other for months instead of days. I said her name again and winked when she met my eyes.

"Okay, you charmer, you're a hockey player." Naomi smiled.

"Was. Not anymore," I said, the edge of my voice a little sharper than intended. "I was. For most of my life, but that chapter's done."

"Not really. Sure, you're not *on* the ice, but you're interning with my dad. He lives and breathes the sport. This might be more intense than being on the team." She released a little sigh that had me frowning. Her dad's dedication to hockey apparently bothered her.

I wanted to ask why, but her attention shifted to my right where a very different version of Naomi stood. Same facial features, same coloring, but everything else was the total opposite.

The sister waved and smiled brightly at Naomi, who stiffened. *Interesting.*

"Hey, you!" the girl said, her gaze moving to me, and her eyes widened. "Oh, you're handsome. I'm Cami."

"Cami with the cute middle name. Nice to meet you." I smiled and winked before getting up from the table. Cami's grin grew as she checked me out from head to toe, but I didn't react with more than an arched brow.

"Talking about me, I see," Cami said, sitting next to me and not leaving more than a few inches between our arms. She smelled like an explosion of lavender and flowers, and I itched my nose. It wasn't bad, but it was a lot. Nothing like the subtle lemon of Naomi. "You on a study date with my sister?"

"No. This is *not* a date. He came over here to annoy me," Naomi said before I could even breathe.

"Well Ms. This-is-not-a-date," I said, laughing at how fast she claimed we weren't together. Her tone made it sound like I was the last person she'd be caught on a *study date* with, and a prickle of annoyance had me narrowing my eyes.

Which was dumb.

I didn't *date,* and hello! COACH'S DAUGHTER. That cleared up any weird feelings she caused, and I smiled at the sisters. "I should let you both catch up, since my plan is complete. *Annoy Naomi, mission accomplished.*"

Cami let out a little pout of protest, but I ignored it. She had trouble written all over with her outfit and lack of personal space. The minute I was around both sisters, it was very clear they couldn't be more different. Besides the basic facial structure, body type, hair, and eye color, there was nothing similar about them. I gave a tight smile to Cami before glancing at *not a date* Klutzy McGee and found her staring at me with hurt in her eyes.

Seeing that pain in someone else caused a protective instinct in me that I often thought of as Momma Bear. Gender wasn't hard lines, and the phrase *Poppa Bear* reminded me of a nursery rhyme. Momma Bears guarded those around them, and that's how I felt about Naomi. "See you at the game Friday, Fletcher? You bring the clipboards and bar charts, and I'll bring the charm?"

Her lips twitched just a half an inch up on one side before she nodded. "Leave the charm at home, please."

"Never."

With that, I lifted my hand in a wave before heading back to Freddie's table. Half of the Skittles were gone by the time I sat down. "You cheat on your very meticulous study plan?"

"I would never." His eyes flashed at me before he leaned back in the chair and jutted his chin toward Naomi and Cami. "How do you know the twins?"

Cami leaned over her forearms, her upbeat voice carrying across the library, but I couldn't stop watching Naomi. Her shoulders were slumped, and she looked at the table and *not* her sister.

"The twins? They have a name? A reputation? Oh, do tell." I tried not to look too eager, but if Freddie knew about them, that piqued my interest. He rarely got out and preferred playing videogames over socializing in person.

Freddie snorted. "Look at you getting all interested."

"Dude, no, not like *that*. They're the hockey coach's daughters. My mentor. I'd be an idiot to *think* about thinking about crossing that line." I ran a hand over the back of my neck and snuck a quick glance at them again.

"The pretty one is wild."

The surge of protectiveness hit me fast. Even without him expanding, I knew he was talking about Cami. Not Naomi. Didn't explain the tightening in my chest though. "They're twins. They're both pretty. Clarify more, Frederick," I said, a sharp edge to my voice.

"Cami. She's…a party girl. In a sorority, dances, parties."

"Okay, most college coeds go out a lot and don't eat Skittles in the library. Neither of those things make her *wild*."

Lines formed around Freddie's mouth. "It doesn't matter. I need to study." He put his airpods back into his ears.

My phone buzzed on the table, directing my attention to the name popping up on the screen. *COACH SIMPSON*.

It was the reminder I needed. My internship, my focus. I should under no circumstances be thinking about *his daughter* in any sort of way.

CHAPTER
FOUR

Naomi

Mona pursed her lips and tapped her pointer finger against her chin. "The rink is cold, yes?"

"Yes," I said, eyeing the mountain of clothing options on our living room floor. Helping me decide what to wear to the away game took the entire crew. We all knew I had the worst fashion sense—but best budgeting skills—so Kelly, Lilly, and Mona all pitched in to help me out.

"You obviously need warmth," Lilly said, picking up the orange long sleeve shirt that had a blue stripe on each arm and tossing it at me. "But to be *sporty* cute. You could wear that with a hat? And a blue vest?"

"And earrings. Hoop earrings are the quickest way to gain confidence," Kelly said, walking to stand next to Mona as she eyed the options on the floor.

Despite the nerves and roller-coaster of emotions I had about attending my first college hockey game, there was the lingering urge to look good that had everything to do with Michael Reiner. Never in my life had a guy dismissed Cami with a look and then eyed me.

He did that at the library, and I hadn't stopped thinking about it since.

"Why does she need confidence though? Our girl is fucking smart, cute, nice, and forgiving. If Cami were my sister, I would've punched her in the tit the second I saw her," Mona said, the fierce loyalty of her friendship reminding me that it was okay that Cami and I weren't close anymore.

I had these girls.

Lilly met my eyes and wiggled her eyebrows. "Because of the *other* sexy intern working with the team."

My face heated as all three pairs of eyes looked at me.

Mona tilted her head. "Excuse me?"

"Oh, she didn't tell you that this tatted up guy didn't even give Cami a glance?" Lilly said, coming up and smoothing my French braids before patting my cheeks. "Our girl here has the attention of Michael Reiner. Look him up online. Right now. He is… fine."

"I regret telling you this," I said, resting my forehead on Lilly's shoulder. She caught me at a weak moment, and I spilled everything. We didn't have many secrets between the four of us, but most stories of me flirting—or failing at flirting—were often withheld.

Mona and Kelly eyed her phone and gasped.

"What the fucking fuck? A hockey player?" Mona said, her face transforming into a scowl. "Girl, you know the rules there."

"Yeah, yeah, yeah," I muttered, not needing to analyze all the reasons why my semi-crush on Michael Reiner would remain just that. Thankfully, Kelly saved me.

"Look at his face. Just look at it. And his hair. Oh, and his tattoos. You're going to be sitting next to him at every game? Fletch, you're going to drool."

"I know! That's the problem!" I groaned into my fist as butterflies exploded in my stomach. It was foreign to *want* to be cute for someone else. Knowing that I wasn't attractive compared to my sister meant dressing was easy. I didn't put a lot of stock into my appearance because she would always be the prettier twin. But with Michael? He called me data girl and winked at me. "Ladies, nothing is going to happen. I might just be wanting to be a bit shallow? Is that… horrible?"

Lilly rolled her eyes. "There is nothing wrong with a little vanity. I know what you're wearing. Go put on your black jeans and come out here. We'd be breaking our roommate vow if we didn't sex you up from time to time. Now, chop-chop, Fletcher. Let mama take care of you."

My feet dragged on the pavement as I approached the bus loading area to the south of the rink. My mascara was the best it'd ever been, and my jeans and orange *fitted* sweatshirt looked good, yet nerves still fluttered around my gut.

The heat of the summer air lingered just a bit, but the wind was picking up as I neared the parking lot filled with lots of commotion. The equipment manager stood with a clipboard, eyeing all the gear, and players were everywhere, like little ants.

Some laughed. Some wore headphones. Others came out of the rink carrying their bags. One guy looked up as I neared and lifted his chin in a quick greeting before moving past me. I was used to that from hockey players. Polite indifference.

I pulled on the straps of my backpack tighter and tried to calm my heart rate. It wasn't being around athletes that had me nervous. My babysitters had been guys in hockey gear who grunted a lot. It was the fact I was doing this. Going to a game with the team *and* my dad. After spending most of my life avoiding the sport that drove my parents to divorce, now I was knee deep in it. *I can do this. I can be bold.*

I took a deep breath of the chilling fall air and jumped when a massive body appeared next to me.

"What up, Klutzy?" Reiner said, flashing me a smile that had no business making my toes curl into my shoes. What I wouldn't give to have his good looks and confidence. I'd rule the damn world.

"Reiner," I said, a little too breathy. It wasn't from his proximity or the fact he stared at me longer than a few minutes...or so I told myself. "You scared the shit out of me."

"Pay better attention then. You're about to get on a bus filled with hockey players. You gotta be prepared for anything," he said, his voice losing a bit of the playful edge. "So, stat lady, did you bring graph paper and bar charts for me?"

I rolled my eyes so hard I was surprised I didn't lose eyesight. "Oh my god, obviously. I carry them in my bag, always."

"Sarcasm suits you, Fletcher." Michael's eyes warmed for one brief second, and in that small moment of time, I wondered what it'd be like to always be on the receiving end of that look.

He was so large. Charismatic. Handsome. He didn't think twice about letting me be his fake girlfriend at the bar and had the ability to talk to anyone with an ease I never could. His dark blue eyes matched the Central hockey polo he wore, and his easy grins caused my stomach to flutter. Just looking at him made my breath lodge in my throat.

My mouth might've dropped open, but I wasn't sure because everything felt too hot. My skin. My neck. My body. I tore my gaze away from him and focused on the asphalt. "Sarcasm is the lowest form of wit."

"But the highest form of intelligence," Michael said, wiggling his dark brows. "I know that Oscar Wilde quote too. I should get a sticker."

I snorted. I couldn't help it. He laughed too, and the weird hold he had over me broke—which was good. I wasn't Cami and never would be. I liked Steve Kornaki type of guys, not athletes. I'd heard all the stories over the years. The debauchery. The stream of hook-ups. The heartbreaks. Hell, before Cami and I grew apart, I'd hear her cry through our thin wall at home.

I knew better than to entertain the idea of crushing on a

hockey bro. Throw in the fact he was working for my dad? It was a lose-lose-lose situation, and those were certainly odds I didn't want.

"Reiner, come with me," my dad said, his *coaching* voice on full blast. It was the same Dad voice he had at home but more authoritative. Like he added an extra syllable to each word to make people listen. Reiner stood straighter next to me and took a step toward him.

I wanted so badly to ask if I was just chopped liver but bit my tongue. "And me?"

"Oh, Naomi, hey. You should get on the bus. Sit in the front." He pointed to the one nearest us and put a hand on Reiner's shoulder. "I mean it. We'll be there in a second."

My chest tightened, and my skin felt too small for my entire body. I was just dismissed. Like that. No, *so glad you're here,* or *are you nervous,* or *do you have any questions?*

He had to realize this was so outside of my comfort zone. That my pulse worked too hard for the situation. But Dad was always about hockey. My mom knew it and left because of it. For one second, I thought about not doing this. Exiting the parking lot and going back to my apartment where things were easy. Comfortable. No smell of athletes or their drama.

Something rooted me to the spot though. Maybe it was grit or a sliver of competitiveness that I'd hidden for all these years. My professor advised me to work on an assignment that pushed my boundaries. To get creative with data. To my little nerd heart, that could mean a lot of things. It didn't require that I had to push my personal boundaries, but here I was. On the brink of walking away.

Time stilled at this seemingly huge moment that only I went through. No one gave a shit that I stood there, heart hammering and my palms sweating.

I'd follow through with it.

I'd never forgive myself if I walked away from this chance at *maybe* proving to my dad I wasn't so different from him. Plus, the small voice in the back of my head spoke up. *Be more like your sister.*

I hated the comparison, but it was true. She'd squeal at this opportunity to be around all the guys and our dad. But it was me, not her, and I'd decided I was staying. I was doing this thing.

Surviving my exhausting mental crisis, I got onto the bus like my dad said and waited. The ants—players—scrambled all over as the bus was loaded with all their gear for the evening game. It was a two-hour bus trip to the east, some Indiana team, and I'd brought enough snacks for the night.

Chips, carbonated water, and peanut butter were all I needed.

The bus smelled like socks that had been sitting out in the sun too long and a hint of mint. The lone air freshener hung near the dashboard, and I laughed. At least that worked.

Guys started boarding the bus, each guy glancing at me. Their reactions were the same. Brief recognition, like they knew me from class or something, then nothing. A part of me wondered if they thought I was Cami for a second but realized I wasn't and walked away. I wasn't sure why their reaction bothered me, but it did, so I focused on my phone. Being insecure about my appearance when there was a literal human who looked exactly like me was a weird thing to grapple with. My friends could boost me up and tell me over and over that I was crazy to think so low of myself, but it was hard to move past a decade of always being the less cute twin.

"Fletcher," a deep voice said, making me look up. It was a tall dude with the biggest eyes I had ever seen. "Pretty sick you're joining us."

My throat dried up. "Er, right. It'll be an experience."

The guy smiled before moving on. My face flamed at the attention. How did he know me? Did he confuse me with Cami? *He called me Fletcher.*

I chewed my lip as I overthought the entire three second

interaction when an enticing smell caught my attention. It was like outdoors and the air right after it rained combined into woodsy perfection. I took a deep breath just as Reiner's face came into view.

My heart thudded hard.

"I'm with you, Klutzy." He flashed a grin that went straight to my core and lifted a bag to put it overhead. The movement made his shirt drag up and his biceps bulge, and I slammed my eyes shut.

I needed to open a window.

"You eat enough today? You look a little pale," he said, sitting down next to me so our thighs touched like they did in the booth that night. It wasn't his fault, more his parents' fault. He was a tad too tall and his legs a tad too thick. *Oh my god. I'm thinking about his thick thighs with his delicious cologne surrounding me.* Plus, that sleeve of tattoos on his arm distracted me. The intricate designs were beautiful.

I fisted the strap of my backpack and swallowed. The gesture hurt, and I was pretty sure he could hear it. He watched me with the same intense eyes that distracted me at the bar, and I nodded. Right, he'd asked me a question. Answering him was the normal thing to do.

A line appeared between his eyebrows as he looked over the seat and down the aisle. "Any of the guys giving you shit? I know it can be overwhelming on a bus of hockey players, but *most* of the time, they're alright. Just rowdy."

"Fighting in college hockey isn't allowed," I said, almost shouting at him. Michael surely knew that already. I pressed my lips together as my face rivaled a furnace, and I scooted closer to the window.

"Oh, Little Miss Hockey knows a fun fact."

His sarcasm made me glare at him, but he just wore that easy smile with one dimple on the side. Steve Kornaki had dimples too, but those didn't have the same magnetic pull on me. Even though I tended to be logical and linear in thoughts,

Michael overwhelmed my senses and my brain. I needed space. Air. A moment to think. "Are you sure you have to sit with me?"

Michael's smile slipped, and he ran a hand through his unruly hair, the tattoos on his arm moving with the motion. The playful glint to his eyes dimmed, and my chest tightened. *Did I hurt his feelings?*

"I can leave you alone. No stress." He reached into his pocket and pulled out headphones before settling into a comfortable position. His thigh still pressed against mine, but I swore it lacked the warmth from before.

I didn't upset people. Going under the radar was my specialty, yet this larger-than-life guy seemed...bothered. My stomach soured, and sweat pooled on my forehead. I ran my arm over it and tried to think of what to do.

Linear.

He overwhelmed me.

I asked if he had to sit with me because I needed space. Not because... Oh. Did he take the comment personally? That I didn't want to sit with him? That'd be silly though. How would that hurt his feelings? He was so... extra in every way while I was average. I exhaled, unsure of how to fix this situation when my dad got on the bus with the assistant coach following him. Hank was skinny for a coach and wore dark glasses that made me blush because he was cute.

I might've had a crush on the assistant coach, but I kept that secret to myself.

"Has anyone seen Cal?" my dad asked, a dangerous lilt to his voice. I knew that tone. I'd heard it a few times when Cami or I were in huge trouble as kids. I didn't know a lot about Cal, but I felt bad for him already.

"No, sir," someone from the back said.

"Call him. This bus leaves in five minutes, with or without him." My dad stomped into the seat across from Michael and I, his attention not once landing on me. It was fine. He had to worry about Cal. This was normal behavior I was used to. I just didn't expect it to bother me. I hoped… or wrongfully assumed we'd talk on the bus or at least he'd acknowledge me being there. The indifference to my presence felt like a knife to the heart, and I wondered, again, if I should've said to hell with this.

My dad barked out Reiner's name, making my seatmate sit up straighter. He sat a row back and popped his head over the seat.

"You ever miss a road trip?"

"No, sir."

"Ever seen someone else miss it?"

"Yes, and it didn't end well for them," Michael said, running his hands along his thighs. He wore dark jeans that fit him well.

"What would you do?"

Michal's entire body tensed. His thigh grew harder against mine, and the muscles in his jaw flexed a few times. He ran his hand through his hair again, making it stand on end a bit before he blew out a breath. "Are you asking as an alt-captain or as your intern?"

"Either."

"This shit wouldn't fly. If I was captain of the team, I'd rip into this guy and give him two choices. Either be a part of the team or transfer." Michael looked down the aisle before continuing. "Helsing doesn't seem too upset. Your captain does though. Look at Erikson."

My dad hoisted himself up in the seat to stare down the bus. "Erikson, Helsing, get up here."

The bus filled with tension as the two leaders on the team approached the front. Everything fell silent. No chatter, no radio, no sounds of players shuffling things around. It was pins and needles.

Whoosh. The bus doors opened, and after two stomps, Cal was on the bus. Even though I didn't watch the team, I knew who Cal Holt was. The poster child for the Central Wolves hockey team.

The kid raised his brows and held up his hands. "I'm here, I'm here. We can leave now."

No one responded. The kid scoffed and rolled his eyes before passing our row and taking a seat further back in the bus. Once we were on the road, my dad, the two captains, Hank, and Michael had a long discussion.

I tried listening to music, but it didn't work. I was pulled into hearing how my dad talked about morals, leadership, teamwork. About how much he cared about shaping young men into good, decent, humans. The team was family for life, and that meant everyone.

My eyes got heavy, and I leaned my head against the window. I might have issues with my dad, but one thing was glaringly clear—he was a *good* coach. He never applied those same principals about family to his own though.

That was the part I couldn't understand. How could a man be so good at one thing but neglect the other?

CHAPTER
FIVE

Michael

Sitting outside the bench was weird. I'd been to one Central game since moving here a year ago, and I couldn't say I enjoyed it. I'd watch them on TV, but being this close to the ice and not playing felt like watching an ex fall in love with someone else and flaunt it.

My friends from back home, Patrick and Paxton, were in the NHL. My sister's boyfriend was about to play his senior year while I sat here, not even with the team, next to the coach's daughter—a woman who had walls higher than my sister's boyfriend.

Feeling sorry for myself again, hm? As I watched the team come back out for the second period, a deep longing had me in a funk. It happened from time to time. Grief did that to you. Ryann talked everything out and had Jonah to help her through those moments where she felt lost, just a vessel without a purpose. I used to have hockey. My chest tightened.

God, I missed my dad. Four years wasn't that long ago, and the urge to call him never went away. Advice on school, life, girls. He had all the answers. My mom would roll her eyes and poke fun at what he said, but his words always helped me.

Figure out what you want and go for it. Make a plan to get there. That's what he told me when I was eighteen and going to Moo U. I wanted to play hockey. That was it. That was my goal.

Once that chapter had ended, I needed to get the hell away from the memories. I achieved that. So, now...what was my goal?

"Oh, wow."

Naomi's eyes were wide, and she stared at the ice with her mouth slack. The chick had a cool-ass dad and was acting like she'd never been to a hockey game before. I deserved an award for not throwing her major shade. "You've seen a hockey game, right?"

"Of course," she said, giving me a side glance. "But it's been awhile."

"Define awhile."

"Years."

"Why? Your dad is the coach," I said, a little tense. Maybe I was feeling angry because I didn't have my dad and she did. "I bet you could go to every game forever."

"I could," she said, her teeth grazing her very full bottom lip. "But I don't."

"Why?"

Erikson passed to Helsing, the puck went back to Erikson, and then he took a shot and—missed. Cal was right there, looking furious, and anger coursed through me. We had a lot of shots on the goal without making a single one. We had more possession without a lead.

I leaned forward onto my knees and mumbled to myself, "They need to get rid of Cal."

"The *best* player on the team?" Naomi said, her voice going all high. "Aren't there like articles all around about his greatness?"

"Probably. I don't pay attention to shit like that. It's poison and just gets in your head. You should focus on yourself, your team, and the game." My knee bounced at Cal's pouting.

There would always be prima donnas in every sport. Despite the *there's no I in team* slogan, there would forever be an element of personal stats to contend with. However, the NHL scouts and teammates knew showboats. Cal had one season as a freshman to turn his shit attitude around or he wouldn't see playing time in the big league. I knew a part of me was bitter because I wasn't good enough to go pro. I could have all the tools when it came to character, but Cal had natural talent I never did.

To see him waste it on a shit attitude was absolute bullshit.

"You were a captain?" she asked, her voice smaller than before. I glanced at her for a moment. She wasn't watching the game. Naomi studied me with her large brown eyes fringed by long dark lashes. She had beautiful eyes, and they pulled me in like a damn magnetic field. Curiosity swirled behind the shades of golden brown, and my shoulders relaxed.

"Alt-captain." I leaned back into the seat and watched as Coach pointed at some of the guys on the bench and barked at them. They nodded and got ready to go in. Peters, Hansen, and Pollock were all second string, but we could afford to shake up our offense since we weren't scoring.

"You miss it."

"Playing was like breathing, and now I'm figuring out how to breathe again without it," I said, my muscles tightening at how much I shared with her. What the fuck? I just blurted those thoughts out to her? I normally kept my cards close, but damn… something about her made it just come out.

My ears burned, and I cleared my throat, but Naomi let out a little hum of understanding. The small sigh hit me right in the chest, and our gazes met.

She pushed her hair behind her ears and took a deep breath. "My parents divorced because my dad was too focused on his job, and I always felt... hockey was the reason our family broke up, so it's never been appealing to me."

"Fletcher is your mom's last name," I said, this little piece of information helping put together more of the Naomi puzzle in my mind. That made sense. Focusing on her and not my internal battle was way easier. "Okay, so answer this. If you hate hockey, why are you doing this project that requires you to attend games?"

"The same reason you're interning here, I guess," she said, her voice small and her attention moving toward the game. "To figure out what's next. To figure out how to breathe without hating my dad."

There was too much pressure in my chest, and I ran a hand over my heart, digging my nails in like that would relieve the tension. Two things struck me. The first—I was right about Naomi and I being similar. Our stories were different, but our wounds were fresh. The second observation was that every interaction I'd witnessed between her and her dad had felt awkward, but I couldn't place why. Now I knew.

"Also, hey," she said, her cheeks tingeing pink. She twisted her hands in her lap. "I was okay with you sitting with me. Earlier. When I said you didn't have to—I just...it's easier to push people away, you know?"

Boy did I ever. I smiled and fought the urge to put my arm around her in a hug. It wouldn't have meant a thing because I loved hugging people, but I didn't want to go too far with her. Instead, I clapped my hands. "Fletcher," I said, making my voice go a little softer.

"Hm?"

"We're more similar than you think."

She met my gaze, and I held it a beat, wanting her to understand that I could be her friend. The blush spread from her face to her neck, and she let out a little laugh. "We'll see."

Oh, I liked that challenge. I sat up a little straighter and found myself watching her more and more throughout the rest of the game. She took notes and scrunched her nose when she erased something. A few freckles on her neck peeked out every time she leaned forward.

The stupidest, briefest vision of dragging my tongue along those freckles had me adjusting my spot in the seat. I could think a friend was attractive and *not* imagine how good they would look naked. It had been done before.

It was easier to focus on her than the raging emotions about not playing. Hearing the skates on the ice, the sound when the stick hit the puck, the chatter between the guys where nothing else mattered but the team. That was my family. My home.

My phone buzzed in my pocket.

Ryann: Hey, I know tonight will be tough for you, but I'm proud of you.

Ryann: Jonah said, and I quote, 'he'd make a good coach,' which let's be honest, that's like a five star review from him.

Thank god for my sister. Her endless support meant the world, and I took a quick selfie to send back to her.

"If you're sexting, that was a horrible photo."

"Naomi," I said, letting out a loud cackle. "Please tell me you've never sexted if *that's* what your impression is. God, I can't even with you."

She let out a little giggle, and I liked how it sounded. Soft, gentle, cute. She didn't ask, but for some reason, I felt compelled to tell her about Ryann. "It's my sister, Ryann. She knew tonight would be hard for me."

"Does she live far?"

"Yeah. Back east. Thousands of miles away but we talk a lot. It was part of our deal when I came to grad school here." I smiled at the memory of the sit-down I'd made my sister have, where we wrote out our expectations. She wanted independence and to not have a hovering older brother, but I felt protective of her beyond just a brother. It was hard to explain, but her happiness and success was *mine* too, maybe it because it was just us in the world. Not talking to her wasn't a reality I could imagine. "She's my best friend."

"That's wonderful, Michael," she said, her voice soft. It was the first time she used my first name.

I liked how it sounded from her lips, more than I should've.

We didn't chat about anything serious for the rest of the second period and intermission. She excused herself, leaving me alone for a while. It made no sense, but I missed having her around. There was a comfort I'd found with her in a short span of time that I just recently reached with Freddie after living with him for a year.

With her gone though, I focused on the game for the final period and caught myself going through what I would've done if I were on the ice. Hanson needed to settle down. He was too fidgety and wasn't thinking before passing, like he forgot every drill he'd ever done.

Could be first game nerves, but it seemed like more.

Our goalie, Tyler Roland, had been having a hell of a game but was getting tired. He needed more drills to build stamina. To keep his movements sharp. I'd wager the other team would score by the end of the period based on how our defense was slowing down.

Fucking Cal though. The all-star wasn't engaging with the team. He was there, going through the motions, but it was clear his heart wasn't in the game. He was a stats chaser, wanting the most shots on goal. It wasn't unheard of to have a cocky eighteen-year-old, but someone had to deflate his ego a bit. And *not* the Coach.

The best discipline a player could have on a team was to instill a sense of pride and family for the leadership on the ice. They could police the team so the coach could worry about coach stuff—plays, stats, winning. Helsing was doing his job as alt-captain, but Erikson had to step up.

I wasn't sure if Coach Simpson was going to ask for my insights from the game, but I got out my phone and started typing all my ideas. What I would do at practice the next day. The specific workouts certain players needed.

As I did all this, my mind raced with ideas. It was an explosion of thoughts and plans and underneath it all, excitement. That small flame of excitement felt foreign in my body after a year of moping without direction, and fuck, I wanted it to last.

"Why the maniacal smile?" Naomi asked, sitting back down as her lemon scent surrounded me. Her lips quirked up on one side, and damn, I liked how her eyes softened when she grinned.

"I've never thought of myself as a coach before, but jotting down notes has been weirdly fulfilling."

"Is it common for hockey players to become coaches?"

"Can be, yeah. But it wasn't a path I really thought about. I always wanted to be on the ice, not two feet away from it." I cleared my throat. I wasn't sad about it anymore and had accepted the reality, but a part of me always wondered if I went to the gym more, drank more milk, and had done just a little bit extra as a kid if it would've made a difference. "I wasn't talented enough to go pro. I was decent, but I was more of a team player. I made others look better, and that was okay with me. I loved being that person."

"I can see how you bring out the best in others. You have this quality to you that is… enigmatic."

I raised my eyebrows as she blinked a few times, clearly embarrassed. Her words charmed me, and I gently nudged her arm with mine. "How thoughtful of you."

"Shut up." She crossed her arms, and I had a huge grin on my face the rest of the period. We won by one goal after the guys ran a play that put the puck in Erikson's hands. He had such excellent stick control that he maneuvered around their defense for a shot with less than three minutes left.

That play gave the rest of the team the momentum needed to finish the game strong. That was the thing about sports. It took one moment to change everything. To shift the tide, the attitude, the tiredness. My body came to life at hearing the cheers and how the guys on the bench jumped and pumped their fists. The team was good at winning together.

Would they be the same with losing?

"Wow, that was a fun game," Naomi said. Both of us stood and got ready to head to the bus area. It wasn't clear how much we were supposed to be in the locker room or not, and I wouldn't intrude without Coach telling me to get in there. The team moments were sacred, and I was an outsider.

What if I don't want to be an outsider though? I briefly thought about what it'd be like to coach a team one day, but the vision didn't take root. Not fully. I ran a hand over my face to regain my thoughts.

"Yeah, it was a great game. Lots to work on next week but a solid start. You get all your stats for your spreadsheet shit?"

"Don't knock the spreadsheet shit, okay? Data is very sexy."

"So is knowing the people on your team."

"You think stats are dumb," she said, taking a step back from me like I told her the earth was flat.

I held up a hand and lowered my voice. "No, I don't. I think they're a portion of the story. You need multiple data points to get a clear read on an athlete."

"I've been reading all about the NHL and how they use data for trades. You're saying it's not helpful?" She arched a brow and crossed her arms over her chest.

"Not at all. I'm saying, Fletcher, that sometimes the numbers don't tell the whole story. Look at Cal." I made my eyes go wide. "Great stats. Can skate faster than anyone on the team, right? On paper, he's the best. But do you see how the guys don't include him in a cheer? I bet if he scores a goal, no one will go up and jump on him. It'll be a lone celebration. He's not a good teammate. Nathan though? The quiet defender who stays in his lane? Great teammate. Average stats. I'd take a million Nathans over Cals if I were building a team. Show me the numbers to tell that story."

My breathing came out heavier than normal, and I realized how passionate I was about that. About stats. Maybe it was because of my personal journey, how my numbers were always *meh* but I had a coach who believed in what I brought to the team. I helped us win, but no data sheet would've told you that. I paused and ran a hand through my hair, leveling my gaze with Naomi. "Sorry to go off on a mini-rant there. I have feelings about this."

"Clearly." She grinned, lines appearing around her eyes and her lips curving up. "I can't wait to prove you wrong."

"Oh, a challenge, you say? You're going to show me data that accurately tells the whole story?"

"Yes, yes, I am." She took a step closer to me, and I looked down at her. She was a good ten inches shorter than me, and I wanted so badly to tip her chin up so I could see her full face.

It seemed that my new friend might be a bit competitive. "Bring it on then, Klutzy."

She licked her bottom lip, and a wave of lust coursed through me. Whoa. I took a step back and welcomed the cool air of the rink. That was weird. One flash of her tongue and my body got all tight? No. No thank you. Coach's daughter. Coach's daughter who *hated* hockey and her dad. A major no-no. I held out my hand and waited. She placed her palm against mine, and I ignored the zing that shot up my arm.

It was just a soft hand that felt nice. Nothing more.

She puffed out her chest and spoke in the strongest tone I'd heard from her yet. "You're on, Michael Reiner. I'm gonna knock you on your ass, hockey boy."

This was going to be fun.

CHAPTER
SIX

Naomi

The bus pulled into Central's campus around midnight, and regret weighed me down. Why the hell did I walk to the stadium? That meant I had a fifteen-minute trek back at midnight. Sure, our campus was safe, but it wasn't the best choice I'd made in a while. Honestly, I wasn't positive when the last time I made a great decision was.

Two years ago? When I chose to sit by Mona in the dining hall? Yeah—that was my best choice without a doubt. Those girls were my ride or dies, my friends for life.

"I want pancakes."

I grinned before I could stop myself. "At midnight?"

"Yes." Michael wiggled his eyebrows at me, the faint streetlights causing shadows to dance across his face. The sight of him in his Central Wolves sweatshirt made me want to curl up next to him and listen to his deep voice. He reminded me of chilly fall nights and warm cider. Somehow, the guy got past all my walls after a few hours together and now I was thinking about cuddling him.

"Um, I think there's a twenty-four hour place a few blocks

from here." I yawned, and my shoulders sagged once the bus stopped in the lot. I wasn't ready to say goodbye to Michael, which made zero sense. We barely knew each other, and I'd see him again at the next game.

"Reiner," my dad said, interrupting my attempt to figure out if Michael was inviting me to get food with him or if it was just a statement.

"Yes, sir."

"Tomorrow morning, eight a.m. My office. I want your analysis. Naomi, when will you have a report for us?"

"When would you need it?"

"Would 9 a.m. be too soon?"

Seeing how it was midnight and already the next day? I kept my mouth shut and nodded. "Nope. I can have it to you by then."

"Email it to Michael when you can."

Send my report to Michael? Not to my dad who was the reason I wanted this internship in the first place? I said none of those things as his flippant response made my eyes sting. Just another example on an already long list of ways my dad tossed me to the side.

My dad stood and gave a quick motivational speech to the players—which I ignored— and put Cal on bus clean-up duty. The guys cheered after the assignment, and I didn't stare at Michael as he got our bags out from the overhead compartment.

I yawned again and put my backpack on, looking up at the midnight sky. It was so dark with a sprinkling of stars, and it was pretty. Calm. Michael stood off to the side, talking to Erikson about something as they both laughed. It would've been weird to go ask him about the pancakes, so I took a deep breath and started heading toward my place.

"Naomi, hey," my dad said, my muscles tightening at the sound of his voice. *Is he going to change his mind about the report?* "Did you walk here?"

"Yes, but it's fine. I can walk back."

"No, no. Of course you're not." He frowned and nodded at a player who walked by. "I'll drive you."

The offer was appreciated, but it was a gamble on when he could actually leave. Memories of waiting hours for him flashed in my mind—the hurt, the frustration, the glaring fact that hockey always came first. The missed chess games, spelling bees, band concerts because of *hockey*, yet he never forgot about one of Cami's dance recitals or half-time shows. I gripped my bag tighter and met his gaze before taking a step back. "No, it's okay. I won't keep you from coaching stuff."

"It'll only be a few minutes. Just gotta drop the equipment off and send a write up to the media. Ten minutes, max."

"Don't worry. Take your time. I'm uh, getting some food with Michael anyway."

"Oh, are you? Good. You won't be alone then. Can't have my daughter heading back by herself." He smiled, but it looked off and forced. Someone called his name, and I could see his attention shifting beyond me, where we both were more comfortable.

My stomach somersaulted with nerves because the reality was that after this year, I wasn't sure if there was any chance of a relationship. He'd still be here, but I'd be a senior and then I'd leave. We'd do the call on birthdays or a holiday, and that was about it. I had about two seconds before I'd completely lose his attention.

"You're a good coach," I said, my face burning and my weight shifting back and forth on my feet like an awkward dance. "It was cool seeing you in action today."

His face lit up like I told him he hung the moon. He beamed at me, a look I hadn't seen before. "Thank you, Naomi."

He stared at me for a few seconds more, indecision on his wrinkled face, but then he put his hands in his pockets. "I'll see you next game, right?"

"Yup."

"Be safe."

I nodded, and the weight on my chest returned. He turned his attention to Hank, and I was forgotten. I didn't compliment him with the expectation he'd say something nice back, but he didn't ask how it went for me or what I thought. If I got the data I needed.

I was background noise in his world of hockey. The ball in the back of my throat grew, and I adjusted the straps on my bag to begin the route back home. The girls and I had a system if we ever had to walk alone, and I sent them my location. I didn't get more than ten feet before Michael's voice stopped me.

"Uh, hello? Are we getting pancakes or not? I'm starving, and you never offered to share your snacks once. I saw them in your bag, Fletcher, and honestly, I'm kind of offended."

I snorted, and butterflies inhabited my stomach. Michael stood there in his hoodie with the sparkling eyes and the easy smile. Teasing me. The weird Fletcher-Simpson twin. "Are we at the food sharing stage of our friendship?"

"I sure fucking hope so. If not, tell me what to do to get there," he said.

He grinned real wide and jutted his chin toward the sidewalk to campus. "Lead the way to the diner, please, and see if you can manage without falling over."

"I'm not that—" I said, losing my balance on a lone rock set out to get me. I righted myself as Michael looked smug as hell. Damn it. I laughed, amused at the situation too. "Shut up. Not a word."

"1-0."

"What?"

"Your current tripping score is 1-0. This is golf though. You don't want points."

"Is everything a competition to you?"

"No, but I do like winning. Let it be a stat competition, who trips less, or a quick game of putt-putt. The high of winning can last a few days."

Winning wasn't something I did often, but whenever I solved an advanced formula or a string of code I was stuck on, that *oomph* of figuring it out sure hung around. It had to be just like that. "So, are you always a midnight snack eater, or is today special?"

"Since I stopped playing I've been giving myself more room to indulge. I still work out and monitor my food intake, but there's no guilt of a late-night pancake run anymore." He patted his stomach, and my fingers twitched.

I wanted to touch him so badly to see how strong he was, how tight those muscles were. I made a fist at my side to prevent myself and started walking toward the diner. Movement was good. Michael caught up in a few steps and hummed to himself. This attraction to him was going to be a problem for a plethora of reasons, mainly because he wasn't my type and I wasn't his.

Then there was the interning together thing.

Oh, and he was trying to be a hockey coach like my dad.

Okay, so three reasons why my attraction to him was bad. An *if then* statement formed in my mind. *If* I'm attracted to him, *then* I needed to find reasons not to be. That would solve my problem.

My biggest turn-off list. My roommates and I got drunk on rum last year and giggled the entire time we came up with the grand list of biggest turn-offs in our partner—no matter how they identified. The top scoring ones were:

Messy eater (at the table, not in bed)

Rude to waitstaff

Talked to hear their own voice

Selfish in bed (must provide Os)

Serial daters (heartbreaker is their middle name)

Maybe Michael would chew with his mouth open and be a dick to the waiter. One could certainly hope.

"Do you need help processing any of the stats to have that report ready tomorrow? That's a quick turnaround," he asked as we headed onto Green Street where the diner sat a block away.

"Offering to help to get insider information for our bet?"

"The bet we still don't know the stakes for," he said, a hint of flirtation in his voice. He whistled a fight song and gave no indication that he'd solved what he wanted for the end of the bet.

We got to the diner, and the smell of grease and fries hit me before we even opened the door. Michael rushed forward to hold it and gestured for me to go inside.

Shit. Good manners so far.

"Table or booth?" the hostess said, her eyes widening once she saw Michael. I couldn't blame her. He grinned at her, making her blush, and answered for us.

"Booth, please. Thank you so much."

She led us to a seat for two in the back corner, and Michael's eyes were saucers as he eyed the posters of ice cream sundaes on the wall. He leaned back into the booth, stretching his long arms over the red vinyl, and sighed. "I'm getting it all."

"I'm not splitting the bill with you then."

"Wouldn't expect you to, Fletcher," he said, his intense gaze staying on my face. I'd dated before and even had a serious boyfriend my sophomore year before he moved abroad, but none of my past guys possessed the level of fierceness that Michael had. Like everyone else in the place disappeared and it was just us.

I pulled on the collar of my shirt to get some airflow going. I was sweating. "How are you doing?"

"Me?" He frowned. "I'm excited AF. Look at the photos." He pointed to the wall behind me which had massive framed photos of desserts. Brownies, ice cream, sundaes.

"Damn."

"Is it weird the desserts seem sexy to me?" he asked, making me cackle.

"Actually, no." My face burned, but I carried on. "What I

meant was about the game. It sounds like this was your first one that close to the rink without playing."

He closed his eyes, and every muscle in my unathletic body tensed, ready to fight his demons for him. A heavy sadness radiated from him, but it was brief. Just a moment. He wiped his hand over his face, and any trace of sadness disappeared. It baffled me how he could just do that. I'd cut off an arm to have the ability.

"Nah, it was alright."

"How do you do that?" I fired back at him, leaning closer across the table.

"Do what, exactly?" An adorable line appeared between his brows.

"Just brush off what you really wanted to say. I saw your face." I pointed at him, much like a toddler jabbing at a plane in the sky. "You seemed sad."

He narrowed his eyes and tilted his head to the side as he eyed me. I was entranced by him and what he was going to say, but our waiter showed up.

"Hey y'all I'm Billy. What can I get started for y'all?"

"Pancake breakfast, bacon, and one of those ice cream things on the photo, please," Michael said, collecting my menu along with his and handing it back to the waiter. "Fletcher?"

"Oh, uh, a small chocolate shake. Thanks."

The waiter left, and the air felt heavier, enclosing us in our lone booth surrounded by sounds of middle-of-the-night laughter. Michael sighed before letting out a stiff laugh. "I have low moments. They can last hours or seconds. It's not depression—I've seen a therapist, and if I feel like I'm having more down days than normal I'll call her, but moving here from back east? To get away from my life? Sometimes I don't know if it was worth it."

"You miss home."

"Hockey wouldn't be waiting for me there, and I don't have a house to go back to." He sat straighter and picked up a straw wrapper. He ripped it into a million pieces, creating a pile of confetti. He was someone I would call an emotional powerhouse. I could almost feel the anger and regret coming off him in waves, and I was about to reach across the table to squeeze his hand. Because I too knew how that felt. To not have a legit house to go back to. My childhood home belonged to someone else now, and empty apartments and take-out were how I thought about my teenaged years.

My hand stretched in the hair, inches away from touching his when he said, "Hey, isn't that your sister?"

He might as well have thrown an entire bucket of ice on me. My spine snapped into a steel rod, and my stomach dropped. Of *course* Cami would be here. I turned to the right, and she laughed loudly, looking perfect in her cut-off sweatshirt and ripped jeans that hugged her toned body.

But it wasn't her style that got me. It was Gage on her arm. Their arms were looped together in a *we're dating* sort of way, and my teeth ground together. If I was a cartoon, smoke would've blasted out of my ears.

Cami wondered why we grew apart and why I never wanted to hang out with her. It was more than my envy of her and my dad's relationship. It was this. The fact she had stolen three guys who I'd been dating.

Three.

"Wait, hold up, is that...the dude from the bar?" Michael was smart. He blinked twice and arched one brow. "So, your sister is dating someone you were seeing?"

"Yup."

"I feel like… that's not cool?"

"Nope." I was a pot of water boiling over. My face was too hot, and my eyes stung like I got sunscreen in them. I had the urge to run, cry, and punch something. Each emotion fought for dominance, but none won, and I was an emotional mess, spiraling on the inside.

"Shit, they're coming over. Need a pretend boyfriend again?"

"I'm not sure."

"Hey, I got your back, Fletcher." Michael reached over and squeezed my hand for one second. The heat of his palm resting on top of mine, the roughness of his skin...it was easy to feel protected. I met his gaze, and his entire face softened. "I'm on your team."

CHAPTER
SEVEN

Michael

I prided myself on thinking quick on my feet. Years on the ice made me intuitive, able to see the play before it happened. This was a blindside, and I chewed my lip before deciding the plan. Sibling betrayal struck a chord with me, and judging by the tremor in Naomi's hand, this wounded her.

"Hey, you two!" Cami said, all charm and cheer. She either had to be the best actress within a three-hour radius or she just didn't care that her sister was upset? Anger had my head pounding.

I'd rather die than hurt Ryann. If I upset her...I'd do whatever I could to mend that bond. Everyone was different, and maybe life circumstances made it tougher for the twins, but I had no warm feelings toward Cami. None.

Naomi didn't answer, and my heart hurt for her. I'd gotten used to the wit and sarcasm, and seeing her sit there, upset and quiet, made the pressure grow in my chest. *Momma Bear is coming back.*

"Hey," I said, narrowing my eyes at Gage. "You look familiar."

"Oh, you probably know Gage. He's just one of those guys who is friends with everyone," Cami said, nudging his side with her elbow. Gage paled, and his mouth was pressed in a firm line as he stared at Naomi.

What a bastard.

"Yeah, he was bothering Naomi last week."

Cami frowned, her cute face scrunching. "What do you mean?"

"Babe, come on, let's leave them alone. They're on a date or something." Gage tried pulling her away, but Cami looked back and forth between me and Naomi.

"What do you mean?" Cami said, her voice stronger than before. This time, she spoke directly to Naomi. "Why did he just say that? Was Gage upsetting you?"

"Cami, ignore this shit," Gage said, making me want to punch him in the jaw. I wasn't sure if it would ruin my internship or not or get me in trouble with the school, but it would've been worth it.

The dick totally knew what he did and didn't care. It was unclear if Cami did though. Her frown deepened, and she took a step closer to Naomi. "Nana, is this true?"

Naomi froze. There was no other way to describe it. Her eyes went wide, her mouth wouldn't move, and all the color in her face washed away. "Uh, well," she stuttered, blinking at the table instead of her sister.

"Here's your food, y'all!" The waiter came around the service station with a large tray, and Gage's relief was visible. He smiled, the asshat. He pulled Cami back from the booth and led her toward their table.

"It all seem good?" Billy asked.

"Sure does, thanks," I said, smiling to rid the moment of the horrible tension. The waiter didn't give us a second glance before greeting someone else at the door, and I waited until

Naomi looked at me. "Hey." I lightly tapped my foot against hers. She didn't react, so I kept it there with our legs touching. "Want a bite of my pancake?"

"You're not going to… talk about what just happened?"

"Nope. I'm going to eat this sexy pile of sugar carbs and offer some to you." It was tough *not* saying what was on my mind, but the topic of conversation wasn't my choice. If Naomi brought it up, I'd talk with her, but she needed to lead the way.

She snorted, and just like that, she was back. "I'm not a fan of sharing food."

"Whoa, excuse me." I feigned shock. "Then we can't be friends."

"I bet you eat at buffets too."

"Are you trying to insult me? Of course I eat at buffets. It's where I can make some gains. Ten dollars for all you can stuff in your face? Yes, I'm devouring everything in there."

She picked up a spoon and took a bite of her shake, her gaze sliding toward the entrance for a second before landing on me. "You must think I'm pathetic."

"Why the fuck would I think that?"

"Because I couldn't call out what my sister did." Her cheeks pinkened, and she sucked her bottom lip into her mouth. "This isn't the first time, either."

Gut punch. I blew out a long breath and chewed my extra-large bite of pancakes, tapping my fingers on the table. Multiple times? That was so shitty. I swore I saw confusion on Cami's face, like maybe she had no idea what Gage did, but if this wasn't the first instance? There was no way. "Okay, question."

"Answer," she said, her eyes flashing with humor for a beat.

"Are you not a fan of confrontation? Is it the drama that makes you nervous? What do you have to lose by having a conversation with your sister?"

"That was three questions. You only said question, as in singular."

"Ah, nice catch, Fletcher. But your wit will not help you

avoid my questionsssss." I made the s last really long, getting her to smile a bit.

Score.

"Just thinking about speaking my mind makes me terrified. I was sure I was going to throw up. I could've caused a scene with all these people watching me," she paused, swallowed, and cracked her knuckles. "Plus, what if I'm wrong? What if she likes me even less? Our family is broken, and I just...these excuses sound so lame, don't they?"

"Don't downplay your reactions. It's not helpful at all." I cut my pancake in half and set the piece on a napkin. "You should take a bite. It's recommended to help with situations like this."

She stared at it with an arched brow. "Germs."

"I'm a healthy, safe guy. Just minor cooties."

She shook her head and let out something that sounded like a laugh, but it could've been a cough. Wasn't sure. Still, she took a bite of my food and rolled her eyes. "Oh, wow."

We ate in silence for a few seconds, and I didn't tell her that Cami and Gage were in an animated discussion across the diner. Didn't feel right. Once Naomi drank her shake and I devoured every crumb of sweetness on my side, I leaned back into the booth and smiled. "Today was a good one."

"Uh, maybe for you."

"No, in general." I leaned onto my forearms and stared at her soft brown eyes. They weren't pure dark brown. There were flecks of golden hues, maybe even a little green if the light hit them right. "The days aren't all good or bad. It's the little moments that add up. Today was overwhelmingly positive. Besides the thing with your sister, was there more bad or good between you two?"

"Good."

"Then you can't let one bad moment determine your whole day."

Naomi's gaze softened. "Why are you so good at this?"

"All the counseling," I said, also thinking about Ryann and

how we *had* to learn to communicate. Also, my previous coach, the team. "It's easy to focus on the negative, and it's human to feel shitty, but it's a choice to let it dominate your life."

I stood up, hoping she'd let the conversation go because while I tried to stay positive, the wound about not playing hockey and losing my parents was still fresh. "Come on, Fletcher. I'll escort you home."

I held out my arm, and she walked into it. She held her head up high and her button nose stuck in the air. She adjusted her ponytail and kept her face blank as we went to the counter.

"My treat," I said.

"No, no way," she said, trying to pull out her card. I swatted it away.

"You get next time, how about that?" I handed some cash over and winked at her. "If we're going to have multiple late night food runs, we'll take turns. I think that's fair."

She narrowed her eyes. "You're assuming we'll do this again."

"Uh, yes. The season can be long, and I'm enjoying my retirement by eating carbs." I rolled my eyes. "Duh."

Naomi let out a snort in an oddly adorable way, and I led her out of the diner. The air had chilled immensely, and I was glad I had a sweatshirt.

"Lead the way," I said, shoving my hands into the hoodie pocket. A part of me wanted to keep my arm around her and hold her close to me, but that had to cross some line.

"I'm ten minutes west of here," she said but then stopped and gave me an odd look. "Can I ask you something?"

Warning bells went off, and I quickly said, "Yes, I am charming all the time. Thank you for asking."

She laughed. "No, I mean, yeah, you are. It's annoying. But that wasn't my question."

My throat tightened just a bit because I knew what was coming. I could sense these things. But before she could even ask, I said, "I'll tell you about it all someday, but not right now.

I'm sure you want to ask about why I had counseling, and I just… not tonight."

"Okay."

She didn't sound put-off or sad, but I could also be a dumbass. If a girl told me she was fine, I believed her. I mean, why wouldn't you just say *I'm upset?* It was the reason dating was a no-no for me when I'd played. Too much drama when hook-ups were so much easier.

I'm not playing anymore though. Did that mean I should try dating? My gaze slid to Naomi, and for a few seconds, I stared at her pursed lips. Her cute nose and soft eyes. Her birthmarks and sexy neck. She smelled so good and was easy to talk to. She was also the first person I'd felt comfortable with in years. But, but, but her *dad*. My internship. Even thinking about dating her made me deserve some time in the penalty box.

God, my mind was all over the place.

She shivered, and without thinking, I put my arm around her and tucked her tight against me. "You should wear more clothes."

"Next time I'll prepare for midnight food runs better."

"Damn straight," I said, enjoying her body pressed along mine. Her long sleeve shirt wasn't enough, and she trembled. I ran my hand up and down her arm a few times and stopped. "Here."

"Wait, what are you doing?"

"Giving you my sweatshirt. I'm chivalrous, obviously." I took it off and placed it over her head, despite her protests. The chilled air sent goosebumps all over my body, but if I walked back fast, I'd be fine. Plus, I'd grown up back east. I could handle some cold temps.

"But what about you!"

"I'm meatier."

She shoved her arms through the sleeves, and it was four times too big. She looked ridiculous, and I smiled at her.

"What?" she said, her tongue wetting her bottom lip as she stared at me. "It goes to my knees."

"I know. It's adorable."

I'm not thinking about what you'd look like in just my clothes. Not even a little bit. Nope.

"That's me. The adorable little nerd." Her gaze warmed, and we continued back on our walk. She tried putting her arm around me this time, in the process stumbling over her feet and falling into me.

I was forced to put my hands on her hips to catch her. "Naomi, Jesus. You okay?"

"Uh, yeah. Just my dignity took a hit." Her hips were full, and suddenly, I wasn't cold anymore. Not when her chest pressed against mine and my hands were still on her.

Take them off. Stop touching her.

"Score is 2-0," I said, looking down at her. Our mouths were inches apart. Maybe six inches. Her chocolatey breath hit my face, and she wet her lip, sending a bolt of lust through me. How easy would it be to lose myself with Naomi for a night? Hear what sounds she made when I kissed her and see how she reacted?

"Michael," she said, her voice deep and throaty. My stomach tightened with need when her gaze moved to my mouth.

"Hm?"

My mind buzzed, and I lowered my head to hers, just a bit. She sucked in a breath, and just as our noses touched, a car drove by, blaring their horn. The intrusive *loud* noise had me jumping back, letting go of her. She breathed a little heavier, as did I, but this was for the best.

Her dad was my boss for the entire season, and it was just game one. *Get it together, Reiner.*

"Be careful with those two left feet," I said, my voice a little husky. I cleared my throat and glanced down the road. Bricked buildings lined either side of the street with lots of trees that had been here for years. It was generally student or professor housing in this area, and I admired the ivy on the walls.

It was better than thinking about how I almost kissed her.

"This is me," she said, sounding a little dazed. I totally understood. "This unit."

"You live on the ground floor?"

"Yes, with three other roommates," she fired back. I held up my hands in surrender, and she gave me a small smile. "I'm sick of all the *oh no you shouldn't do that as a woman* stuff."

"Then I will keep my dumbass mouth shut."

"Appreciated." She pulled her keys out of her bag and gave me a long look, one I couldn't decipher. "Oh, here."

She started taking off my sweatshirt, and in the process, her shirt rose, exposing her midriff and a very sparkly gem right in the center of her stomach. She had a bellybutton piercing.

God, why was that so hot? I wasn't a teenage boy, and I'd certainly seen piercings before on nipples, stomachs, you name it. But seeing the blue diamond on Naomi's body sent a wave of heat through me because it was a secret part of her.

"You need it for your walk back." She shoved it at me, and I didn't think twice before putting it back on.

Fuck. It smelled too much like her. Lemon and cookies.

"Thank you for letting me borrow it," Naomi said, running a hand over her hair as she leaned against the doorway. She had a great pose. One leg propped up, one arm hanging down. She looked incredibly kissable like that, but maybe it was the moonlight hitting her face.

"You're welcome," I said, my feet weighing me down like two cement blocks. I needed to go. It'd be smart to leave and walk home to see Freddie. But I didn't want to. That was the problem. Being around Naomi was…refreshing. "I should—"

"I'll see you next game, right?" she said at the same time, interrupting me.

"Sure will."

"Good night, Michael."

"Yeah, good night, Fletcher." I lifted my hand in an awkward wave and forced myself to walk down the sidewalk. The cold air could knock some sense into me, making me push all those inappropriate thoughts of Coach's daughter out of my head.

The *last* person I should be thinking about kissing was my boss's daughter who *hated* the sport I loved.

CHAPTER
EIGHT

Naomi

My roommates Mona and Kellie took their trivia *seriously.* They reminded me of Michael and his constant state of competitiveness. My face flushed. Five days since our *almost* kiss and he crossed my mind no less than a million times. That was a statistical fact too.

"Are you paying attention to the rules? Come on, Fletch," Mona said, elbowing me as the trivia master asked the question at Triv Tavern, the hipster bar on the west side of campus. Old-school video games covered the walls, and cassette tapes were passed around like candy. The question was something about movies, and Kellie was our movie guru. Her photographic memory almost felt like cheating, but it felt really good when we got matching t-shirts and a hundred dollar gift card to come back.

"It's *While You Were Sleeping.* Trust me. My mom is obsessed," she said, whispering as she yanked the pencil out of Mona's hands. Our fourth roommate, Lilly, met my eyes and smirked.

Our team, the KLMNs due to our alphabetized names, was

ahead by ten points, but our rivals, Quiz in my Pants, were intent on beating us. We'd attended Wednesday night trivia every week at Triv Tavern, minus holidays since last year. It was our tradition and something I'd miss after we all graduated and grew up.

"I fucking knew it!" Mona shouted after the question master said the answer. One of the Quiz in my Pants guys flipped her off, and soon enough, it was the next round.

We weren't allowed phones during the question part because it'd be so easy to cheat, but that didn't mean the missed calls from my sister weren't weighing on my chest. She'd called four times since the diner. She thought we should talk. To meet up. To discuss Gage.

I wasn't sure I wanted to. It'd change everything, and that unknown held me back. Now, I at least knew not to trust her. Opening the drama up? Having feelings all out in the open? Confronting her and acknowledging the pain she'd caused? I understood what that added up to, and no thanks. It'd hurt.

"Dude, you should know this one. If you flip a fair coin four times, what is the probability that it'll have at least one head?" Mona said to me, her authoritative voice making me sit up straighter.

I went through the mental math. "15/16."

"Sweet. Thanks, brain."

"You're welcome, heart," I said, repeating our constant joke. Lilly was the hormones, I was the brain, Mona was the heart, and Kellie was the stomach. That girl could *cook.* Together, we were the perfect human.

We finished the first round when the doors chimed. Out of habit, I looked up, and my breath caught in my throat at the sight of Michael Reiner and a guy who looked very much like Clark Kent. Memories of that *almost* kiss flashed through me—the way his lips were just a hair apart from mine, the weight of his hands on my hips. His soft breath tickling my face at how close we were. I swore my body remembered the heat radiating off him, and I clenched my legs together. Mm. I liked it way more than I should.

Michael looked around the bar, his face lighting up with amusement when his gaze landed on me. He widened his eyes and flashed me the biggest smile before he winked.

"Um, hi, what the fuck is going on?" Mona asked, leaning closer to me and eyeing Michael. She waved at him, making my face flush, and he waved back. "Why is he winking at us?"

"Me. He's winking at me." Wow, that felt weird to say.

Mona blinked a few times and bent toward me. So close, her mouth almost touched my face. She had issues with boundaries. "Why? I want one."

Clark Kent guided Michael to another table on the other side of the bar where two other guys sat with their backs to us. Michael positioned himself so I got a full view of him, and boy, he looked smug.

And happy to see me. My heart sped up seeing joy on his face, all because of me.

Which was also weird.

"If you don't explain what's happening, I'm going to throw a fit. A full, embarrassing fit," Mona said, pointing to Michael across the room. I swatted her hand down as my face burned. "We saw how hot he was, but here he is flirting with you. A hockey player."

"Mona, my god. We're friends."

"Friends don't wink at each other, girl."

"Yes they do. We should all do that more," I said, winking at Kellie, Lilly, then Mona. Kellie ate it up and tried returning the gesture, but it looked like she had something in her eye. "Okay, I take it back."

"I don't care that he's a hockey dude," Kellie said, her eyes dimming a bit. She knew my aversion to athletes, especially hockey players. "If a man looked at me that way, I'd do just about anything."

"He's not a hockey dude… He's interning. I think he wants

to be a coach," I said, my face hot enough to melt butter. Michael kept glancing over here, and each time, my stomach swooped.

"Interesting," Kellie said. "That is definitely one of your rules. *NEVER DATE A HOCKEY COACH.*"

"I'm aware," I said, hating the way my body clenched with regret.

"Wait, did he break any of the cardinal no-nos?" she asked, hope laced in her voice.

"I mean, we haven't even kissed, so rule three is unclear." The orgasm rule. "He was nice to waitstaff and doesn't talk too much, but he could be a serial dater. I honestly don't know. Ladies, look," I said, taking a deep breath and hating how red my face got. "We're friends, and while I'm attracted to him, I know better than to go down this route. I'll end up getting hurt, and it'd be safer to just remain friends."

"Maybe friends with benefits, hm?" Kellie said, turning over her shoulder to ogle him.

Of course, Michael stared right back, amused as hell. *How can I explain this to him?*

"I can't… do that," I said, my face getting even redder. At this point, I might as well burst into flames. I adjusted the denim shirt I wore to let some air in, but it didn't help. Not that it mattered, but I looked cute tonight. Fun headband with a knot right on the top, my favorite denim shirt, and my black jeans that made me feel confident.

If I were to run into Michael, I'd want to wear this. But as I said, it didn't matter.

"Okay, nerds, we're starting round two. The theme is sports."

A collective groan went through the place from everyone but Michael. He let out a whoop, and Clark Kent patted him on the back. This would happen because he showed up. The karma gods were at work for Michael, and I found myself grinning when he met my eyes and mouthed *'Game on.'*

Maybe I was more competitive than I thought.

"First question: What is Canada's national sport?"

Lacrosse. I knew that one. Everyone assumed it was hockey, but it wasn't. "Hey, give me the pen."

I wrote it down and winked at Michael. I bet he put hockey.

"Question two: Scottie Pippen has a word tattooed on his forearm. What does it say?"

"Who the fuck would know this?" Mona said, growling as she scanned each of our faces. "Should I know this name?"

"Chicago Bulls. Early 90s. Come on," Lilly said, taking the pencil. "My dad is legit obsessed with that team. We have posters all over our basement, and he rewatches the games every time he can. His tattoo says Pip."

"And you know this because…" Kellie asked the question I was thinking.

"Because I've stared at that poster in our basement for twenty years."

She jotted the answer down.

"Question three: Who was the last NHL player to leave the league without having used a helmet?"

"Fletcher, this one is you!"

I squeezed my eyes shut, unable to summon a single name that could be the answer. I was really letting my middle name legacy down. I shrugged, my stomach tightening with defeat. "I'm sorry, I'm not sure."

"Ugh, your boy sure does."

He wasn't my boy, but her meaning was clear. Michael grinned and wrote the answer for his team, somehow looking hot and annoying at the same time.

"Question four: This basketball move was banned from the years 1967 to 1976. What was it?"

"Lilly, you're the resident basketball guru now," Mona said. "What was the move? A dribble? Fuck. I don't even know why people play basketball." Mona shoved the pencil toward Kellie.

"Shit, I don't know." She frowned and scrubbed her hands over her face. "Slam dunk?"

"I'm writing it. I hate not even guessing," Mona said, drawing attention from the table next to us. I shushed my friend.

The last four questions were about soccer—a sport none of us had ties to, and we turned in our card with all our hopes crushed. If Michael got all of them and gambled with the double-double, earning twice the points, they could tie with us.

That wouldn't do.

At least we could count on our rivals not knowing anything about sports. They were self-proclaimed nerds.

"Five minute break before round three, people. Get drinks, use the pisser, and hustle back!" the game host said.

I jumped out of my chair at the same time Michael did, and we met somewhere in the middle. He wore fitted jeans, a long-sleeve blue shirt that said CENTRAL on the front, and a backwards hat. His hair escaped from the hat on the sides, and his blue eyes sparkled at me, making my tongue feel two sizes too big for my mouth.

All from eye contact.

I was in TROUBLE.

"That last round make you sweat?" he asked, his gaze moving from my face to my shirt and legs. It was a quick perusal, but I swear my skin prickled from his attention.

"Yes, it did."

"I knew you were competitive. Hm, dare I say we make another wager?"

"At this point, I've lost track of how many we have going on." My voice came out all flirty and deep, and I stared at the curve of his mouth. *We almost kissed.*

"Three, if we count tonight. The data versus knowing people debacle, which I'll win. Then, the tripping count, which you're already losing big time, and then this one." He laughed and tugged on the end of my ponytail. "I want you to take a photo with the school mascot at the next game if I win."

"Hell no," I fired back. "When *we* win, you have to do a PowerPoint presentation on your favorite number."

"Easy. Sixty nine." He replied so fast I snorted. He caught my eye, and we shared a laugh for a good thirty seconds before he stepped closer to me. "So, your friends were looking at me like I was your show and tell."

"Right. Ignore them. It'd be easier," I said, my shoulders sagging. "They were just…it's not often I'm friendly with guys like you."

"Like me." He frowned and picked his hat up off his head before running his fingers through his hair. God, it was so thick. I wanted to touch it, feel how soft it was.

I cleared my throat, my stomach sinking at his expression. "Hockey player, sorry. Not… not that there's anything wrong with you. You're perfect. Perfectly fine." Sweet mother, I was embarrassing myself. "I just don't associate with hockey guys. Ever."

He narrowed his eyes just a bit. "Because of your dad."

"Yes."

"And you think I'm perfect."

"Shut up." I swatted at his arm, and my touch lingered for just a moment, but we both noticed. I dropped my hand like he caught fire and stepped back. "I meant that you're just… ugh."

"I'm teasing you. Fletcher. It's so easy." He grinned at me again, the absolute joy radiating from him like a sun while I was a measly planet. My heart thudded against my ribcage just as the game host announced a one-minute warning. "Get ready to lose," he said, the tone right between flirty and competitive. I chose to assume he just wanted to win because my brain would catch fire if I thought about him flirting with me.

"You get ready," I said, sounding like a total idiot. "Game on, Reiner."

Our team got third place. The next round was all geography which was another weakness. Quiz in our Pants won the gift card this week, and Michael's team, Let's Get Quizzical got second. We groaned at the point totals, but if I were honest with myself, seeing Michael's face was worth it. He looked gleeful as both our tables finished our drinks and started walking out of the trivia bar. Mona stayed right next to my side, and the second Michael was in reach, she held out her hand.

"Hey there, I'm Mona, this one's best friend."

"Hi, Mona," Michael said, his smile slipping into the charming guy I saw that first night. "You made a great choice in friends."

"I really did. I appreciate you acknowledging it." Mona introduced Kellie and Lilly as I stood there, watching my two worlds collide. It wasn't as catastrophic as I imagined it'd be.

A jock and some nerds. Proud nerds, at that.

"This is Freddie the Fourth and his brother, Camden, and cousin, Kyle." Michael put a hand on Freddie's shoulder. "This big guy is my roommate and brought me here. I'm glad he did though. Say, I can't wait to cash in on our bet."

"Oh, what bet?" Kellie asked, her already too-wide eyes growing by the second.

"She has to take a photo with the school mascot at the home game Friday and do the pose I tell her."

"Hey, that wasn't part of the deal," I said, already imagining him making me do some dumb hand gesture.

"Shouldn't have lost then." His eyes flashed with amusement, and I stuck my tongue out at him.

He laughed. "See you Friday, Fletcher."

It was a simple statement, but my entire body warmed like it was a personal invitation. I met his gaze and said back, "You sure will."

He left with his friends, and right as they turned the corner, my roommates lost it in a flurry of giggles.

"Oh my god, he's so hot."

"Did I see tattoos?"

"I'd sit on his face any day of the week."

I laughed with them, but it was Kellie's comment that stuck with me throughout the night.

"He looked at you like you were a snack. You don't stand a chance, Naomi. Might as well accept you'll bang him soon."

CHAPTER
NINE

Michael

It was a little humbling to learn how much went on behind the scenes with coaching college hockey. My dumb ass assumed it was a fun gig, making plays and motivating players. It was laughably more.

Coach Simpson got into the office early every day at seven a.m. after already working out. Then, he'd spend all morning preparing for practice or, in today's instance, the game. He'd watch films of the opponent, confer with his assistant, and check stats. Then he'd come up with a few plans of attacks. First string, second, and back-up goalies.

Then it was working with high schools all around the country and beyond for recruiting. Central State didn't just *find* all-stars. Simpson busted his ass to make connections and build a program that was inviting.

Then he had office work, forms for traveling, and collaborating with the trainer to make sure the guys were healthy. It was endless. That was just on the logistics end too.

Dealing with twenty guys was the hardest part. In the week I'd been shadowing him, there had been ten instances of drama.

Four of them involved Cal, starting with the guy showing up late for the bus time.

Coach had me in the locker room before game time tonight just to observe. His assignment said to *study the players.* Super clear instructions.

I was a visual learner, so I took in the blues and oranges all around the walls. Their jerseys hung on hangers with their gear shoved onto top shelves. Pictures of girlfriends, families, and their heroes covered the individual lockers. When I played, I had one photo of me, Ryann, and our parents, and a bright red puck I got at my first pro game as a kid. I didn't need more reminders than that. Back then, I had people who loved me and a sport I was passionate about.

The recovery room was to the right. Erikson was in there with a trainer as she taped up his right ankle from a brief twist.

He'd be fine.

Coach went into his office and engaged in an animated conversation with the assistant, Hank Wade. My stomach filled with nerves. This felt like home with the smells and sights, but I was a stranger. No Jonah giving me intense looks, no twins making me laugh, and certainly no inside jokes I was privy to. The twins had a new life and were so busy that a text here and there were all I had with them.

One of the players, Jay Mullens, held out a fist to me. "Hey, read about your team back east."

"Yeah?" I fist-bumped him back. "All lies, I'm sure."

"The twins went pro. You didn't."

"Wasn't for me." I eyed the team, my left eye twitching. It was a harsh reality to know that your chances of getting drafted went down once you hit twenty. NHL teams preferred you young, then wanted to watch you grow and get better in college. That meant fifteen of these guys had already missed their chance. Not that I'd say it.

Dream crushing wasn't my thing.

"I want to so bad after this year, but I'm not standing out.

Not with the forwards we have." He sighed and leaned in closer. "Any advice, old-timer?"

I scoffed but wasn't mad. If anything, the kid amused me. "There are two types of players that matter to scouts. The all-stars and the ones who pass them the puck. Keep being a good teammate and leave everything on the ice. If it happens, it's well deserved, but if it doesn't, you gave your soul to the sport. No regrets."

He nodded, his dark eyes making him look older. I had to check my notes, but I was pretty sure the kid was here on scholarship. Still, he didn't have the same swagger or talent as Cal.

I hadn't seen the prodigal son yet, but it didn't take long. He pushed himself up, shirtless, taking a selfie and ignoring the equipment manager. The poor kid stood next to him holding out a towel and clean jersey, but Cal laughed and kept taking pictures of himself.

The red-headed kid couldn't be more than eighteen and was nothing but skin and bones and freckles. *David.* Cal faced him, and I wasn't sure what he said, but *fuck off* carried over the room, and David's face turned bright red. Fire engine red.

My blood boiled.

"Holt," I yelled, making some of the guys next to me jump. My voice had an *oomph* that Ryann always bitched about because it apparently carried throughout the house. Right now, I used it. The kid looked up and smirked.

My god, if I was alt-captain, I'd be furious. Both Erikson and Helsing glanced up from the bench wearing equal expressions of confusion. I marched over to Holt and was glad to see I had a good three inches on him. "Any particular reason you enjoy being a dick to the equipment manager?"

"What are you talking about? The guy was in my space."

"Yeah, with your jersey." I picked it up from where it was neatly folded and tossed it at his chest. "You don't deserve to wear this. Being part of a team is a privilege," I said, my voice now low. This wasn't for show. I knew I should've kept my mouth shut, but David's crushed face flashed in my mind.

If Coach Simpson thought I overstepped, I'd handle it.

"Yeah, okay. I'm here on a full ride. Thanks for the advice though." The kid went back to his phone, and my hand literally twitched. I wasn't violent. Never had been despite playing hockey, but fuck. I wanted to punch this kid.

"Scouts ask questions, Holt. They interview coaches, staff, and teammates. Just think about that the next time you're an asshole. No NHL team would take a chance on you."

With that, I pointed at Erikson and Helsing and barked, "Be fucking leaders."

Coach Simpson leaned against his office doorway, his expression tight and his lips pressed together. It was hard to tell if it was annoyance, disappointment, or anger. Probably a combination of all three and I held up a hand. "I'll be in the stands."

"Come here after the game."

"You got it, sir. Good luck." I ducked my head, my adrenaline pumping harder than it had since I was on the ice. I paced the hallway that led to the stands and took a few minutes to settle my breathing.

Why did Coach and the captains let Cal act like that? Was there something I didn't know? I pinched the bridge of my nose and forced myself to go calm down. Patrick and Paxton would've handled that with me in a heartbeat. No excuses for being a piece of prima donna shit. God, I missed home. The team, the food, the way things fit together easier there.

My muscles throbbed from tensing so damn much that I sighed in relief at seeing Naomi sitting behind the team bench. She styled her hair in two braids, and two large hoops hung from her ears. Her hat had the team logo on it, and she even wore a Central State jersey.

I was a sucker for women in hockey jerseys. The fantasies were endless; wearing just the jersey, the long legs, *fuck*. I now pictured Naomi that way and shook my head hard, like it would fling the image out of my mind.

I'd already pissed her dad off once today. Twice in a night was out of the question. I didn't have to fake my smile though as I approached her. "Hey, Fletcher. Ready for your selfie?"

"Of course, a bet's a bet," she said, grinning at me. Her pink lips pulled up, and she leaned in closer once I sat down. "Here's the thing though… I went ahead and already did it."

"Excuse me?" I took the phone from her hands and zoomed in on the photo in question. She definitely stood next to the bird. "We didn't agree on *what* you'd do in the photo."

"That's not my fault. You said take a picture at the game, and I followed through. The devil is in the details, Reiner."

"You think you're slick, don't you?" I studied the image more and found my mood improving. She wore four bead necklaces in the photo and looked like a huge hockey fan. I refrained from making a comment about *how* she got those beads. "Well played, Naomi."

"Thank you. I lose gracefully." She took her phone back and sat up straight so her shoulder wasn't touching mine. "What did my dad think of the data report?"

My stomach sank. I showed him the report last Saturday, but he just tossed it on his desk. He didn't even *glance* at it. He wanted me to summarize the contents, so I did. But she looked up at me with so much hope that I couldn't be that crass. This mattered to her.

"Not sure it hit the mark." I winced. "Look, I'm no expert at data and I was a decent player but not an all-star, so maybe my advice is helpful, maybe it's not. But," I said, pausing to read her reaction.

The only indication she could've been upset was a little line between her eyebrows. She tilted her head to the side, like she was interested in what I was going to say. "Your dad has a bunch of guys who do stats for him. I'm not sure why your dad wanted you to partner up with me. His motives are unclear, now that I think about it. He runs a great club, but there's a lot I don't understand."

"Try living with him as a kid," she mumbled, easing any tension I had.

I smiled. "Think *differently*. I know you're all data and numbers and blah, blah, blah, but he probably has that information already. Think outside the box, or in this case, rink." I showed all my teeth in a cringe, gauging her reaction. "Sorry? Was that too lame?"

"No, it's good advice." She brushed off my stupid comment. "There's an internship I want this summer for a big data warehousing company. They receive thousands of applicants. Our professor told us to be original when we apply. Everyone chose social media data or a political engagement online as topics. Stats in hockey isn't a new angle by any means, but it felt natural. A way to be unique against my peers."

"Then stand out. Make the numbers jump off the chart."

She rolled her eyes. "I appreciate the insight. Gives me something to think about."

"Right on." I leaned back into the seat and propped my elbows on my thighs, the adrenaline from earlier still trying to find an outlet. My knees bounced, and my neck burned. Did I go too far? Would Coach stop my internship? I'd end up confused and without a goal, again. The team warmed up on the ice doing laps, and Cal didn't seem any different.

Did I fuck things up without making a change at all?

"Hey, you alright? Your left leg is shaking a whole lot."

"I might've done something stupid." I glanced at her, and she had that line between her brows, no judgement, just curiosity on her pretty face. "Like, mess up my internship stupid."

Her pretty eyes widened. "Shit, what did you do?"

"I overstepped. I saw something going on with a player, and I addressed it. Might've cussed. Definitely yelled. It just… wasn't cool how he treated another person." I ran a hand through my hair and pulled the ends a little bit. My shoulders sagged with regret, and my stomach twisted as I replayed the moment. It wasn't my call. It wasn't my team.

"Hm," Naomi said, clicking her tongue a few times. "You might've overstepped, but did you feel like it was the right thing to do?"

"Yes."

"What was he doing?"

"I don't want to blast any player. Locker room stuff is sacred, and I'm sorry if that sounds shitty, but I believe it. Teammates have moments in there, good and bad, and part of the strength of the team is keeping those private." I ran a hand over my face now, tensing when Coach Simpson looked up and met my gaze from the bench.

His dark bushy eyebrows were set in a firm line, and he narrowed his eyes. My stomach about bottomed out, but I nodded at him. Naomi lifted a hand in a wave which he didn't return.

"Oof, he looks pissed."

"Yeah. Yeah, he does," I said.

"Should we say our goodbyes now? I don't want to drag it out, but I feel like a quick hug would be okay? You're definitely gone after today," she said, teasing me.

I couldn't help it. I laughed. I nudged my arms against hers, making her laugh in response, and just like that, the nervous ball of *oh shit* dissipated. "Well done. I needed that."

"My dad is a reasonable guy. If you called out shitty behavior, then shame on him for not doing it himself. I don't think you'll be fired from a job where you earn no money, but not many people stand up to him. He's an intimidating human and very few cross him. There are pros and cons to that."

"For sure, but what I'm having a hard time with is the fact he has to see this shit is going on, yet he's not dealing with it." My knee bounced again. "He's been a coach forever. He knows his stuff and has his methods, but instead of trusting them, I took matters into my own hands. That's not being a good teammate."

"Talk to him. He'll listen."

"Are you sure? No offense, Fletcher, but I'm sensing you have some unresolved issues there that you haven't brought up with him either."

Naomi groaned, and the lightness in her eyes disappeared. Great. Now I pissed her off. I was just going through the Fletcher-Simpson family tree, making them all angry. Was Cami around so I could annoy her next? At the reminder of her sister, I made a fist.

"Hey, hold up," I said, turning to her so my thigh pressed all the way against hers. "Real talk, did you ever speak with your sister? I wanted to ask you all week but couldn't get ahold of you. I did search for you online, but there are like four Naomi Fletchers on social media, and two of them were a picture of a goat."

Her lips twitched, and she ran her teeth over her bottom lip. "Maybe one of those is mine."

"Okay, then I need an explanation why your picture is a goat. They were both very cute and pretty. Gorgeous goats."

She swatted my arm just as the horn blasted to announce the starting line-ups. We paused conversation as we stood for the anthem. The rival team, the Woodhens, didn't have an empty seat in the house, and I took a small step closer to Naomi to get away from a very large man to my right.

The movement had our hands touching, and I didn't pull away. That contact of her small hands against mine sent a zing of electricity up my arm, all the way to my chest. Huh.

I was suddenly reminded how long it'd been since I hooked up with someone. At least a month. A long time for me. I used my other hand to adjust the hem of my hoodie and held my breath when Naomi perched on her tiptoes.

"Oh my gosh, look at their goalie," she whispered, her lips

almost touching my ear. "He's picking his nose during the anthem."

"How un-American," I said, my tight voice surely giving away my reaction to her proximity. She smelled like fresh spring and lemons, and she even gripped my bicep for support as she stood. I swallowed hard. "I think guys forget we can see them all."

She snorted and went back to her normal height, moving her mouth away from my neck. My entire body was on high alert from the locker room incident, and after adding in this insane awareness of Naomi, it was going to be a long night.

The best distraction for all of my problems? Hockey. I focused on Coach Simpson, how he watched the guys with his signature intense stare. Was he looking for signs of weakness or lack of focus? Or did he notice how Cal stood just a bit too far away from the other four on the ice?

Did he see Helsing and Erikson have an angry discussion while they warmed up? A part of me felt like it was about Cal, about what I said in the locker room, and my face heated, *again*.

We sat back down, and I angled myself closer to Naomi, and she did the same. There was a group of older women to her left who clearly had some drinks, and it was like slow motion when the woman waved her hand in the air, the very full beer sloshing around, and *splat*.

"Shit!" Naomi gasped. Beer covered her hat, face, and sweatshirt. Annoyance prickled down my spine.

"Oh my god, I'm so sorry." The woman paled and wobbled a bit. "You're covered in beer. It's shitty beer too. I didn't want to pay for the good stuff."

Naomi stared at her hands, her eyes wide as beer dripped off her face onto her shoulders. "Am I in a movie?"

"Here. Here. Take this!" The woman shoved a hundred dollar bill at Naomi. "I never thought I'd be this sloppy, but Marge and Linda insisted on the shots. The shots! What am I? In college again? No. I'm old now. Go buy a new sweatshirt and clean up, hon. Have that handsome man of yours help you."

"Bud Light?" Naomi said after an awkward silence.

"Yes."

"It tastes horrible."

"I know." The woman laughed. "Please, go clean up. I can't look at you without feeling shame."

"Come on, Fletcher." I held out my hand, and she stared at it a beat before she took it. "Let the handsome guy help you out."

CHAPTER
TEN

Naomi

Michael led us up the stairs toward the main area. He held my hand tight as we navigated through the crowd. I wasn't a damsel in distress or anything, but the gross smell of beer made me feel a little woozy, and I was grateful to not have to worry about where I was walking.

He made a beeline for a family sized restroom and pushed the door open. "Are you alright? You didn't seem too upset, but damn, I can't believe that woman did that!"

I chewed my beer-stained lip and walked toward the sink as he locked the door...with him on the inside. He got paper towels and wetted them before handing them to me with a dark look on his face.

"Um, thanks?"

"Here, you have it all over your face." He frowned as he took one of the towels and brushed it over my forehead. This wasn't sensual by any means, but I closed my eyes and took in the moment: his body heat so close to mine, the concern on his face, and his clean scent overpowering the beer smell. I felt taken care of, even for a moment. Like I meant something to him. It was… wonderful.

"You're going to be sticky," he said, pulling me back to reality.

"Yeah, well, shocking no one, I once tripped at a frat party and wore beer for like six hours." I scrunched my nose. "Mona won a beer pong tournament, and I couldn't leave her there."

One side of his mouth curved up as he tossed the napkins into the trash and got more. "Let's see the damage on the jersey."

I winced. I forgot I wore the jersey my dad got both Cam and I ten years ago. They were nice. "I think I have to get this dry-cleaned."

"All the more reason to be mad."

"It was an accident. Better her than an opposing fan who wants to fist fight, right?" I joked, trying to decipher why Michael wasn't in his usual teasing mood. Could he be worried about what happened in the locker room? Or maybe…

"I hate that this happened to you," he said, his voice just above a whisper as he took a step closer. My breath caught in my throat when he lifted the hem of the jersey. "Arms up, Fletch. Let's see the damage."

Out of all the ways I pictured Michael taking my clothes off, it wasn't in a family-sized bathroom at an away college hockey game. Most of those thoughts involved my bedroom. Either way, my face burned red as he helped remove the jersey.

"I'm going to run some cold water on it to see if we can get the smell out." His nostrils flared a few times as he glanced at my chest for point two seconds. Nothing more than a look. His jaw muscles tightened, and he turned the water on too hard.

My breathing was a little too fast for the situation, and he would be able to tell if I didn't settle down, but why did he give me that look? Why did he seem pissed?

I wore a dark navy Under Armour shirt under the jersey because a) it was warm, and b) the jersey was itchy on its own so I liked to cover all my skin before wearing it. I moved to the right to see myself in the mirror when I saw it. Or rather, them. My nipples.

The skin-tight fabric didn't leave a thing to the imagination at my perky small boobs. I mean, I was freezing cold and wet, so it made sense they were at a level ten, but was that why Michael seemed mad? He had a thing against nipples?

"I think I got the worst of it." His voice was off. Strained. "We should buy you a sweatshirt for the rest of the night and put this in a bag."

"Yeah, thanks."

He turned around from the sink, and his gaze dropped again to my chest for a little longer. His breathing got louder, and he ran a hand over his jaw, his sharp blue eyes warming. God, did the bathroom get smaller? Were the walls shrinking in as we stood there eyeing each other?

"Did you get all the beer off?" he asked in the same deep voice that I really, really liked.

"Most of it. It's in my hair which is gross." I picked up one end of my braid and shrugged. "Thanks for the help."

"Sure."

I shivered. Not just from the chill in the air but also from the intense way he stared at me like he thought I mattered. In the least sexy setting ever, my body hummed with how much I wanted to touch him.

"Damn, you're cold. Here." He started taking off his sweatshirt and exposing his stomach, and ugh, it was *perfect*.

Toned and hard. The two lines on either side made my intelligent brain go *oh me likey*. I admired the way he had a little trail of hair that went from his belly button to the waistline of his jeans, and *oof*. Warm, Michael-scented cloth landed on my face.

"Damn it, Naomi, I thought you saw me toss it."

"Right, yeah, I did. I just caught it with my face."

He laughed, that low timbre heating me up inside out, and I

scrambled to put the sweatshirt on. To dive into Michael's clothes again. It was the same one I wore before, and it hung off me in awkward angles.

"You look adorable."

"Yes, adorable was what I was hoping for in your behemoth-sized hoodie."

"Well done then," he said, smiling back at me as he took a step closer.

"It'll probably smell like beer when you get it back."

"Ah, well, thank god I have a washer."

"Yeah, that's good news." I gulped when the tips of his toes almost touched mine. Was this his quirk? Did he always stand this close to people or was it a *me* thing? I wanted it to be a me thing very much. He wore just a t-shirt that clung to his impressive chest, and he too, was chilled. His nipples strained against the fabric.

"Um, aren't you cold?"

"I'm alright."

"Your nipples seem to differ."

"Checking out my boobs, Fletcher?" he asked, grinning. He ran his hands over his pecs a few times.

"They were right there. I couldn't help it."

"That, I understand." He cleared his throat and lifted a hand to my face, his fingers pushing some of my wet hair behind my ear. My knees wobbled at how soft his touch was. I *loved* feeling his hands on me.

"This is probably my fault, by the way," he said, his voice quiet.

"What is?"

"The beer getting spilled on you." He removed his hand and took a step back, and I wanted to stomp my feet and pout about it.

"Wait, how is this your fault?"

"The way you looked in the jersey. I had some inappropriate—"

"*Anyone in there?*" A loud fist boomed on the door, making me jump a foot in the air. Michael tensed too and unlocked the door, ushering us both out as a mom with three young kids entered.

"Seriously? Can't you wait to hook up later? Some people who actually have kids need this bathroom!" she said, making me feel as small as an ant.

"We weren't hooking up! I got beer—"

"She doesn't care. Just let her be," Michael said, his mouth right next to my ear. He put a hand on my shoulder and pointed to our left. "Gift shop. I'll let you lead, but be careful."

"Yes, sir."

I wove through people, but my mind was on what he was about to say before that mom interrupted us. He had some inappropriate… what? Thoughts about the way I looked? Did that mean he liked how I looked?

Did I care?

Oh, my god, this was exhausting.

After a full minute of dodging people, we arrived at the gift shop. It smelled like new clothing and popcorn, which was welcome after being in a bathroom. I glanced around the store and stopped when I found nice thick sweatshirts. That was what I wanted.

I pulled a bright orange one off the hanger and held it up. "Got it."

"You don't wanna splurge on a jersey?" He pointed to the wall of them. "You got a hundred bucks. Go wild."

"I'm good. That jersey is my favorite one, plus I'm freezing and want something snuggly."

"Snuggly it is." He rocked back on his heels, and his face lit up as another large guy approached us. "Sam, dude."

"Reiner!" The guys did a prolonged bro hug with a lot of back patting. Sam hit Michael in the arm like three times. "What the fuck are you doing here? How is this possible?"

"Small world." Michael smiled real wide and pointed over his shoulder. "I'm with Central."

I loved seeing Michael like this, energized and happy. It was clear seeing an old friend pleased him, and my insides got all tingly.

"Wait, you're playing for them? No fucking way! That's sick."

"No, not playing." He ran a hand over his hair. "Interning with the coach."

"Bro, that is so you." Sam hit his chest again. "I called it. I swear."

"What do you mean?"

"You being a coach. It makes perfect sense." An older woman said Sam's name from behind him, and he sighed. "I'm helping my mom get holiday gifts for everyone. In October."

"Never can be too early," Michael said, laughing. "Are you just visiting, or do you go here?"

"I go here, yeah. Working on my masters." Sam's face reddened just a bit. "Got injured two years ago and never really returned back to normal. I miss it but not as much as I thought."

"It was good seeing you, man. Stay in touch." Michael pulled him back into a hug.

"For sure. Let me know when you get a coaching gig. I'll harass you online obviously."

Watching Michael light up caused a sticky warm feeling around my heart. The clear joy on his face and his former teammate's was a testament to who he was. He brought people happiness, and I wanted to hug him, hard.

"Same old Sam." Michael's smile remained once Sam joined his mom, and after a few seconds, he looked at me. "Shit, was that rude? I should've introduced you."

"Oh no, don't worry." We moved up a few spaces in line to buy the sweatshirt. "You didn't have long to talk. I'm guessing an old hockey buddy?"

"Yeah, we played with each other like… eight years ago.

When I was in high school. He lived back east for a year then his dad got reassigned." His eyes were unfocused, and he kept tapping his fingers at his sides. "You hear what he said?"

"About you being a coach? Yeah, I did." I smiled and reached over to squeeze his forearm. His fidgeting was kinda cute. "Is that what has you all worked up?"

"A bit. I just… why did he say that?"

"Because he means it? You have a natural charisma, Michael. It's very obvious, and I know you said you couldn't share *what* happened, but you calling out behavior in the locker room even though it's not your role? That's what leaders do. They aren't afraid to rock the boat if it's the right thing. You keeping it secret despite the fact they aren't your team? That's leadership. Maybe it's weird for you to be watching the game instead of playing it, but in the short time I've known you, it's clear hockey is always going to be in your life."

"I could kiss you right now." He closed his eyes and took a deep breath. When he met my gaze again, my stomach flip-flopped with the warmth and trust swirling in his blue eyes.

He could kiss me. He said that. To me. With his mouth. My mind got fuzzy, like when I stayed up too late and woke up early the next morning. Was he thinking about our *almost* kiss as well?

"Next!" a woman screeched from behind the counter. We didn't move though. He stared at me like he was about to kiss me but then the woman yelled again. "You two, let's go."

Shit. That was us. Holding up the line thinking about a kiss. *Get it together, Fletcher.*

I bought the sweatshirt and put the dirty one in the new bag. We left the shop and found a small cut out where people wouldn't run into us. "You can have your sweatshirt back."

"Thanks." He took it from me and put it on in one smooth motion. "I was being a real hero, but damn, I was cold."

"Such a nice guy," I said, teasing him. His smile fell a little bit, and it was like a rock formed in my gut. Did I do something?

"I'm really glad we're friends, Fletcher," he said, his voice as serious as his expression. It might've been my imagination, but he said the word *friends* with more oomph.

"Right, yeah. Me too." I forced a smile, hating how it felt like a rejection. I liked his company, and I was pretty sure he liked mine too. But he just said he could kiss me...did friends say that to each other?

Maybe I had the wrong friends then.

"Here's the real question though." He wiggled his eyebrows with his typical playful smile. "What are you going to buy with the extra cash?"

"Are you thinking what I'm thinking?" I jutted my chin toward the warm pretzel booth, then the ice cream station. "We could have several rounds of treats?"

"God, this is the best night." Michael held out his arm. "Come on, Klutzy, let's stuff our faces with your hard-earned money."

I wrapped my arm around his waist and breathed him in, accepting the fact that we were just friends. He was a touchy-feely guy, and I'd just have to be okay with the fact I was lusting after a friend, hard.

Plus, I knew better than to fall for a guy who was going to be a hockey coach. Hello! It ruined my dad's marriage and his relationship with me. I should be running far away from Michael Reiner, yet I squeezed him a little tighter as we waited in line to get pretzels.

When our fingers brushed not once, but twice as we waited in line, I repeated the word friend over and over in my mind.

That was all it ever could be.

CHAPTER
ELEVEN

Michael

I wanted to kiss her. It was simple. Easy math. The way her tits pressed against the tight shirt in that small bathroom, shit, I wanted to yank her against me. Even the anxiety about talking to Coach after the game wasn't enough to pull me from my attraction to Naomi. She sat next to me now, the third period starting, and my skin felt too small for my body.

"Helsing is having an off night," I said, unsure if I needed to distract myself or Naomi. "He's not making clean passes, and he's unfocused."

"Oh, I couldn't tell." She jotted something on her clipboard and furrowed her eyebrows. The gesture made my lips twitch because she had so many facial expressions. It was hard to keep up with them all, but I liked studying her.

Whenever she watched the game, her eyes narrowed and she leaned forward, like sitting closer would make it easier to study. I bet she sat like that in classes too.

"This might shock you, but I don't watch a lot of hockey. I know the rules and understand the game, sure. I couldn't tell you if a player was having an off night though." She tapped her pen on the metal part of the board and frowned at me. "That's bad, huh?"

"Bad? No."

Me thinking about her mouth and what's under her jersey is bad. I picked a nonexistent piece of lint of my jeans. "I'm surprised you're agreeing to do this as your project. Don't get me wrong, I love hanging out with you. But with the stuff with your sister and dad, it seems like the sport leaves a gross taste in your mouth."

Yes, distract yourself with her problems. Way to go, man.

I shook my head, hoping to clear my thoughts.

She stilled, and my stomach tightened with regret. I was being a jerk because I couldn't get my attraction to chill out. "Don't answer that," I said, too quickly. "If you don't want to."

"No, you're right. My roommates would appreciate you calling me on my shit," she said, a hint of a smile on her face. "Also, way to ask about the situation with Cami in a very smooth manner."

"I did ask earlier but then there was a beer fiasco, a shopping trip, and the game." I waved my hand in the air and cheered when Erikson scored. I stood up with my fist in the air, the only person to do in our section of the bleachers. I spun around, cheering louder, and smiled at the pointed glares from the home fans.

Tie game.

"I haven't talked to her yet," she said, her voice small and lacking what I now referred to as the *Naomi energy. N-energy, if you will.* Her posture went slack, and she scrunched her nose. "Tell me I'm being a chicken."

"I'd flap my arms and bock like a chicken if I thought it'd be helpful, but it's not." The same surge of protectiveness I got around her the last time had me leaning back and putting my arm on the back of her chair. I wasn't touching her per se, but it felt right. Like what a good friend would do to support. "Being afraid to have a hard conversation with someone you love isn't being a chicken."

The opposing team amped up their offense and were playing *hard*. Our goalie was on guard, and it felt like ten years before we cleared the puck. No one was stepping up on the ice. Not even Cal. I never thought I'd be able to watch a game *and* have a conversation with someone since hockey seemed to push everything else out of my mind.

It was nice being able to do both.

Naomi brought her knees up to her chest and wrapped her arms around them, holding the clipboard with her fingers and letting it dangle in front of her. "She's my sister, so obviously I love her. I just… don't like her. This makes me sound bitter, so please don't judge me."

"Hey, this is a judgement free zone." I put a hand on her shoulder for one second and squeezed. She let out a little moan, and I had to let go because I started thinking about that damn sound and how sexy it was.

"She has it all, okay? The looks, the dance team, the guys. During the divorce, she and our dad had all these rituals and *their things* together, and while I understood we all dealt with it differently, I just," she paused, and a little red colored her cheeks. "She has no reason to intentionally hurt me, but she does over and over and then expects me to want to see her? It's bullshit. And my dad will say things like, if you could find time in your schedule to see your sister, she's on the dance team and is way busier."

"Ah," I said, hating how my chest tightened at her confession. A flash of annoyance at her dad—my temporary boss—had me clenching a fist against my leg. While her specific situation didn't apply to me, the feeling of abandonment was familiar. "I'm sorry."

"It's not your fault," she said, her *N-energy* back in full force. "I know I need to talk to her, but it's hard."

"For sure it is."

We got possession back, fucking finally. Cal had the puck, and Erikson was wide open on the left. Defenders came at Cal, forcing him to pass, but he didn't. He maneuvered around them, took a shot, and *missed*. Erikson's face was hidden by the helmet, but I could feel the annoyance radiating off him.

He shook his head and skated hard at Cal, swinging his arm up to point at his chest. Oh, words were exchanged. Cal shouted back. I couldn't even fathom what I'd do if a freshmen punk yelled at a captain on the ice. Hot damn.

"This isn't good, nope," I said, putting my hand on her shoulder again. "I swear I'm listening and we're going to analyze this sister thing to death, but this is bad."

"We don't have to analyze it, Michael," she said, a little pouty edge to her voice. I moved my hand from her shoulder to her knee, my motives not really clear. To reassure her? To touch her? I patted her a few times and lingered too long before I let go.

She remained silent.

Coach barked orders to the guys on the ice, and when Cal and Erikson skated toward the bench, Coach pointed at Cal's chest. If I had to guess, Cal was getting an ass ripping. Guys like him always wanted to be a hero.

I swore Cal looked up and met my gaze with a hint of red evil in his eyes. Okay, not like a real cartoon character, but a little bit. I waved back and winked. If the punk was going to blame me for his shitty attitude, this was going to be fun as hell.

The smug feeling left when Coach followed Cal's stare. He flexed the muscles in his jaw and glared at me for two seconds before going back to the game. My stomach sank, and worry ate me inside out. I'd disappointed adults before. I was a wild teenager who was popular and played hockey. I'd been an idiot, but letting Coach down wasn't something I wanted to do.

Especially since I was in a weird transition phase of not quite knowing what my life looked like after school. It was always hockey, then taking care of Ryann, and school. Ryann was on her own, I didn't play hockey anymore, and it was my final year of school.

My neck burned as my mind went to the worst-case scenario. Maybe I'd be dismissed. Which, I wasn't sure that could happen because the contract we signed explained what grounds for dismissal were, and it wasn't over calling out bad behavior.

Okay, so if I wasn't let go, I could've broken his trust. I did overstep. I ran a palm over my face, and a small, delicate hand touched my forearm.

"Hey," she said, pulling me from the mental gymnastics routine where I tried to reassure myself I wasn't fired.

"Hm?"

"It'll be fine."

"You don't know that." My knee bounced again. The final minute played out, and we won by one goal. It was a sloppy win, but I'd take that over a tie any day. Naomi wrote some stuff on her paper, and I stood, ready to face whatever came my way.

That was one lesson my parents taught me before they left this earth. Being a man was about owning up to your mistakes, not just celebrating the wins.

My entire body buzzed with dread, like I knew I was about to fail a test but went to class anyway because I had to. Everyone loaded the equipment on the bus, and Naomi leaned against the window. I had two options. Wait for him to talk to me or approach him first.

He laughed at something the assistant coach said as he walked up the bus stairs, but his smile faded as he looked at me.

I cleared my throat and stood. "Coach, could we have a word?"

"Sure thing." He scooted over in the seat, his face neutral. No frowning, no pinch of annoyance between his eyes.

"Congrats on the win," I said, wiping my sweaty palms on my thighs. "Sloppy, but a win is a win."

"We were sloppy."

"Look, I want to apologize for overstepping before the game. I understand how sacred it is between teammates in the locker room. Now, I won't apologize for calling out bad behavior, but I'm working here under your advisement, and I was out of line."

Coach stared at me with the same unreadable expression. Not a hint of a smile, nor a frown. He blinked, ran a hand over his face, and nodded. "Lesson for you, kid. What would you do to shift the culture right now? We won, but half the guys are still pissed."

"Mandatory team get together. Clean up trash on a road or volunteer at a school. Retirement home. I've found that if you can count on a teammate in a situation that has nothing to do with hockey, you trust them more on the ice." I smiled at a memory from years ago where we spent an entire day reading to preschoolers.

I had marker written on every part of my shirt, but I'd chatted with a senior that day while I was a freshman, and our friendship started because of the volunteer time. "Forgive my question, Coach, but why are your captains letting Cal act like that?"

"That's one of six reasons I don't sleep at night."

"The other five?"

"Each daughter, the ending of Lost from a decade ago, my goddamn back, and my endless to-do list."

"Oh yeah, those are solid reasons."

Coach smiled for a second before lowering his voice. "I've dealt with guys who think they're hot shit. I know the drill. Cal is no different than Frankie G who played one year then went to the Coyotes. I've been doing this a long time, yet Cal... he plays at another level. He could be one of the greats."

"Yeah, true, he's good." The same, nauseous feeling

returned at disagreeing with him. "But I'd take six average players who played as a unit over Cal any day."

"Okay, go on." He leaned against the window and crossed his arms, studying me with narrowed eyes. "Tell me why."

"Because...hockey isn't an individual sport. It's not like baseball or football where you have your pitcher or quarterback who can make or break a game. Like, they win as a team and lose as a team, but everyone knows if a pitcher has an off day, that contributes to a loss. With hockey, it's not one person. Every part of the game relies on another teammate. If the goalie misses a block, where were the defenders? They're a unit. A brotherhood. And one person thinking they're too good for the team? That's a cancer."

"I think you found your coaching philosophy," he said, smiling wide and putting a hand on my shoulder.

"Never thought about it like that," I said, feeling my face burn hot at the way he looked at me. Like he was proud of me. Like what I said was right. *Does Naomi ever feel this way with him?*

"It's a good outlook to have. Finding your philosophy is hard, and it can take you a while to figure out, but yours is solid. That takes character, Reiner. Your parents would be proud."

Sucker punch to the gut. A ton of different emotions hit from both sides. "I hope so," my voice cracked, and I cleared my throat. "If you want me to apologize to the captains, I will."

His brows disappeared into his hairline. "Not Cal?"

"No. I would've said the same thing to anyone I saw behaving that way. Like a piece of shit. So, no, I'm not apologizing to him."

"I had a feeling about you." He laughed to himself, and I wanted in on the joke. "It's your call if you want to, but I don't care either way."

"Why not?"

"Because my philosophy is about cultivating leaders. Being

good men on and off the ice. You need to do what feels right to you, but tell me you didn't notice how Erikson and Helsing played differently tonight. They're rattled. They know there's an issue on the team, but they don't know how to fix it yet."

"So, you let them figure it out. What about play-offs? The record?"

"We're winning, Reiner. It's messy, and yeah, I'm anxious as fuck, but watching those guys learn how to lead a team is how I manage any sleep at all."

I nodded, letting his words settle over me. I pushed myself up from the seat. "Thank you, Coach."

"Tomorrow, nine am. Meet me and Hank at the diner to talk post-game."

"And the stats from Naomi?"

He blinked, his gaze moving to the back of the seat, and for a moment, he looked sad. "Get the report and give me your thoughts."

"You sure you don't want her to join? She might have some good insight."

"Sure, yeah." He pressed his lips together tight and nodded. "Yeah, have her come along too."

"I think that's a great idea, Coach." I grinned, waiting for him to nod before going back to my seat. Naomi had headphones in and her eyes closed, looking peaceful and cute all at once.

She bobbed her head back and forth, and her lips moved, like she was singing the lyrics to whatever song she had playing. Around her, my soul relaxed. I wasn't worried about *life* and what was next. I could just be.

"Hey," I said, pulling out an earphone and putting it in my ear. The string was short, so I moved my head closer to her, so close her breath hit my face. "Ah, punk music. My favorite high school genre."

"Shut up," she said, yanking the earbud back. "How'd it go?"

"You didn't listen?"

"No, it was private. I didn't think it'd be cool of me to eavesdrop on you," she said, her voice small. "It went well? You're smiling."

"It did, and guess what?"

She narrowed her eyes, her expression looking so much like her dad's it was a harsh reminder that any lusty thoughts of mine should be chucked out the bus window. "Hm?"

"You're joining us tomorrow at the diner for our post-game chat. Bring those data sets, you cute little nerd. You're officially invited to the jock table."

CHAPTER
TWELVE

Naomi

I paced our small kitchen, and Mona snickered. I barely got any sleep the night before while putting together my potential idea.

Player Profiles. Like interactive hockey cards.

Areas of strength. Areas that needed work. Areas where they made the team stats better.

Qualitative and quantitative *dynamic* data for players. It took hours to compile one for Helsing. Hours. But it was the first flicker of an idea that got me excited. It came to me after all the bullshit with Cal. How could a guy like him—all stats and talent—be worse for a team? How could we prove that?

Dashboards for player profiles? I was sure they'd been done before, but ones created *for* the end user to manipulate as the season went on? I saw the benefit—full profiles and adjusting game plans based on the results. It could work… or my dad could shoot it down. Just thinking about him dismissing the idea was enough to have me bite my nail for the third time.

"You're adorable right now, all nervous like you're trying

out for Mathletes," Mona said, adjusted her hair as she stared at me.

"First off, I was a Mathlete and won a thousand bucks for a competition," I said, holding up a finger. "Secondly, I am nervous. I finally feel like this project has legs. I'm *excited* about it."

She nodded, her face softening in understanding. "Okay, then I won't tease you about how you definitely put an extra layer of mascara on and that probably has nothing to do with that sexy-as-hell baby hockey coach."

"Michael," I said, my face heating at how transparent I was. God, all the casual touching we did felt scandalous. Just thinking about how close we were to kissing in that bathroom...I swallowed, hard. "It's not, I'm not…"

"Girl, you look good."

I eyed my favorite ripped jeans, bright orange chucks, and long-sleeved CENTRAL t-shirt. It wasn't my favorite outfit, but it bolstered my confidence. "We almost kissed," I said, already preparing myself for Mona to squee.

She didn't though. I arched a brow and stared at her like she grew two heads. "Wait, you're not reacting."

"I'm thinking."

"You're never this quiet."

"Shh," she said, narrowing her eyes at me. "He's a hockey dude, working for your dad. He goes against all your rules. Sure, he's hot, and y'all had chemistry, but Fletcher, he'd break your heart."

"You don't know that," I said right back, even though it was statistically the truth. Hockey would always come first to him, and I knew how that story ended.

"True, and he might be a great guy. But he'll be a hockey coach." She chewed the side of her mouth and slumped her shoulders. "You know what it did to your family."

I didn't need a reminder. My stomach soured, and the butterflies I had earlier when I thought about Michael migrated away, leaving me feeling cold and empty. Offering her a tight smile, I grabbed my bag and keys and walked toward the door. "Wish me luck."

"Hey, I'm not trying to upset you. Just, I've watched you try to piece together your family for years. I want you to be happy and to have fun, but remember where his life is heading."

My muscles tightened as I left our apartment and made my way to the diner. Mona always gave it to me straight. We were all friends, but Mona never held back. The issues with my dad, the fact my mom was so focused on her new family that I felt left behind, and the situation with Cami. She knew the good and bad about me, and her heart was in the right place.

Falling for Michael Reiner wouldn't end well for me. It didn't matter how much I enjoyed his company or the way I was so connected to him. Or how he stood up for what he felt was right, even if it pissed my dad off.

"Naomi?" a familiar voice knocked me out of my mind. My sister wore a full face of make-up, jeans, and a crop top that showed her toned stomach.

Even early in the morning on what I assumed was her walk back from wherever she spent the night, she was beautiful. "Hey," I said, my insides twisting.

"You never texted me back. I've been trying to call you." She ran a hand over her perfectly tousled hair and glanced at the ground. "Are you heading somewhere? Could I walk with you?"

"I'm meeting...someone, yeah. I can't be late." My face flushed. I was lying to my sister about seeing our dad, but I knew if I mentioned him, she'd tag along, and the conversation would be all about her and dancing. Not the idea I'd come up with.

My throat felt tight, like I swallowed six pairs of socks as she stared at me. Her eyes, so similar to mine, seemed sad. What did she have to be sad about?

"Gage told me he wanted to ask you a question at the bar

and you were rude. Is that what Michael meant when he said Gage was bothering you?"

Even with that question, she loaded it like *I* did something wrong. Like I was horrible to Gage because he'd spoken to me. "Cami, I can't… stop the bullshit. Please. It's me."

"What are you talking about?" she asked, her mouth forming a perfect oh. She looked pretty when she was confused, angry, or hell, even when she cried. Not me. Never me.

"You got Dad. You have the dance team. Why… why do you always have to go after guys I'm dating?" My voice came out just above a whisper, but I might as well have shouted. Cami blinked and tilted her head.

"*What?*"

"Brandon from sophomore year. Tyler from senior year. Gage. All three of them I dated. I went out with them. Then, weeks later, you're with them. I don't get it. Do you hate me?" My words were shaky, and my eyes stung.

This was horrible. Everything I'd avoided the past week or so because I knew. I knew whatever I said would cement the fact we weren't those sisters who called each other every week. Once we graduated, we'd see each other at holidays and that was it—same as the rest of my family.

I sniffed as my entire body pounded from the confrontation. The greens of the trees seemed brighter, the smell of fall clogging my nose, and my tongue was too big for my mouth.

"You think I hate you?" she asked, her voice hollow.

"Why else would you do that to me?"

She stared at me, her jaw tightening as her grip around her phone turned white. My sister paled and the red lipstick made her look like a vampire. "You dated those guys...before me."

"Cami. Please. The clueless act works for Dad but not on me. You're better than this." I wiped under my eyes, regretting wearing mascara because I rivaled a raccoon with school spirit. "I need to go."

I looked down and walked by her, refusing to glance back at

my twin. The divorce sucked for a lot of reasons, but the biggest one was how it changed us. It'd been six years, but the hurt only got worse. I'd experienced one big break up before and cried for a week until I realized I would be okay.

A sister break up was worse—especially my twin. This person was created at the same time as me, shared DNA with me, yet...we couldn't be more different. The girl who used to share her sleeping bag with me, brushed my hair, and helped me paint my nails was gone.

I stumbled on the sidewalk, righting myself after my feet flirted with the crack in the ground, and I held both hands out in the air like a surfer. I didn't fall, thank god, but it was a close one.

"Add another point to the tally, Fletcher."

Michael. I wiped under my eyes again, annoyed at Cami for making me cry. I didn't have time to clean myself up, so I put on my best smile before facing him. He wore a backwards hat and short sleeves, the dark ink of his tattoos covering his whole arm. My god, my tongue felt too large again but for different reasons. Lusty, wanting to lick him reasons. "Hello."

Hello?

Could I be any cooler?

"Hello to you too. I'm going with my gut on this one and saying that's four. Four to zero." He neared me, but once he got closer, his smile dropped. "Hey, what's going on?"

"It's nothing. Sorry. Ignore me, please. Especially the racoon eyes."

He reached over and wiped a tear off my face with his thumb. My stomach swooped at the tender way he touched me, and his frown deepened. "You're a pretty raccoon, if that helps."

I snorted and swatted his hand away. "Shut up."

"Seriously, the prettiest raccoon I've ever seen."

"You're not helping," I said, even though my lips curved up and I was already letting go of the tension.

"Yes, I am." He narrowed his eyes as his gaze dropped to my mouth for a full second. My breath lodged in my throat, and my lips tingled from his attention. But then he put his hands in his pockets and sighed. "Please tell me you're not sad because of data and hockey."

"No, that's not it." I took a shaky breath just as the sun hit his face, amplifying the strong jawline, the wavy brown hair, and the slight crookedness to his nose. His blue eyes had flecks of brown in them, and his lashes were longer than I expected. He was honestly the most attractive guy I'd ever been around.

No wonder my stomach squirmed and my pulse raced in my neck. I placed a hand over the evidence so he couldn't see how I reacted. "I ran into Cami just now."

"Shit, really?" He looked over my shoulder, his brows drawing together in concern. His attention shifted back to me, and he put his arm around my shoulders. "Something no one tells you is how hard it is to have a sibling. Sure, it's fun when you're growing up and you have a built-in friend, but as an adult, it's not as easy."

I'd never heard anyone say that before. He was so right. So damn right. He squeezed my shoulder and let go, taking his clean scent and warmth with him.

"My sister and I get into fights sometimes. They aren't fun, but those tough conversations help trust grow."

"But your sister didn't do things to intentionally upset you."

He tensed and let out a little laugh. "Not true. She dated this guy on my hockey team which was a total no-no. It worked out, but we yelled. We cussed. Love the guy now, but that's not the point. Fighting is normal. It means the love is there. You're hurting because you love your sister."

"Huh. Interesting way to take it." Was that why my chest felt stuffed with balloons? Because I loved Cami? I mean, of course I did, but we'd grown apart. We weren't really friends. I rubbed a hand over my heart. "She acted like she had no idea about dating the guys I did. She puts on this act, and it makes me so mad I just..." My voice shook, and Michael's face softened.

"When your reactions aren't as fresh, I'd try to talk to her."

"Why? I'm not sure this is something we can just get past." I knew I sounded pouty and whiny, but I didn't care. "I have friends I love, closer than sisters, really, so why make the effort when she just hurts me? Sometimes it feels like it wouldn't be that much of a loss."

Wow, the truth came out, and a disgusting, icky feeling flowed through me.

Lines appeared around his eyes, and he flexed his jaw, almost like I'd annoyed him. Guilt squeezed my stomach, like I did something wrong in saying that, and I blinked.

"Right?" I asked, needing him to understand that this hurt was years deep. Not just right now.

He ran a hand over his face, looking older and sad, and my heart flipped over. That sadness. I recognized it, but it looked so out of place on him. This charming, gorgeous hockey guy was all smiles and jokes, but with the slumped shoulders, the tense lines on his face...what had I done to upset him?

"Only you can answer that question, Naomi. Come on, let's go meet your dad." He motioned with his hand for me to go first, and I did, but I couldn't shake the feeling I'd done something wrong.

I snuck glances at him as we walked toward the diner, the chilly morning air hitting my face, and Michael kept his attention forward. I replayed my words, and yes, they'd sounded harsh, but Cami had hurt me over and over while I kept letting her. The loss of our connection was already there but voicing it out loud like that was weird.

Mr. Chatty didn't speak a word, and after a few minutes of silence, I reached out with my hand to stop him. Silence from him felt different. Heavier. I hated it. It was like an internal itch I couldn't scratch, and I needed to find the root of it.

He walked into my hand, his toned stomach pressing

against my wrist for two seconds before I pulled it back, like his sheer strength electrocuted my entire arm. Like a million ants crawled from where my fingers briefly dug into his stomach, all the way up my forearm and to my shoulder.

"Hey," I said, swallowing the nervous ball that made my voice come out deeper than intended. "I feel like I upset you, and I don't enjoy this feeling."

"You didn't upset me," he said, no warmth to his tone. He might as well have been talking about the weather or taxes. *It's supposed to rain. Did you do your W-9?*

"Michael, please," I said, something in the lilt of my voice making him look at me. Pain swirled around his eyes, numbing my own issues.

What had him looking so sad? We stared at each other in an impasse of sorts, neither of us saying a word but I knew in my soul we were having a moment.

I didn't know if it was a good or bad one, but when his tongue wet his bottom lip, I felt the motion low in my gut. "I'm sorry for whatever I did."

He bit down on his lip as he let out a groan of frustration, and he rolled his shoulders back. "It's really not you, I promise. I just…"

His face pinched together, and without thinking, I grabbed his forearm, like that touch would urge him to share his thoughts. I didn't want him to hide from me. I already shared too much, and it would even the scales.

He studied my hand on his forearm, and he released a long breath that tickled my face. He cracked his neck side to side, his jaw set in determination. "My sister and I are the only ones still alive in my family. We lost our parents in a car accident a few years ago, so I have a different perspective when it comes to family. I don't… don't talk about it often, and I'm sorry my internal reactions came out. I didn't intend for them to."

My brain worked fast. It put the pieces together quickly, and I didn't like the end picture.

"You've been listening to me complain about petty shit with my sister and dad when you lost your parents," I said, absolutely hating myself. It felt like a gut punch. He had to think I was the worst. What a privileged life I led, bitching about my sister dating guys and my dad having insides jokes with her. They were alive.

My eyes stung for the second time that morning, and I wanted to throw up. "Oh my god," I said, more to myself than Michael. "I'm so, so sorry."

"What? No. No," he said, stepping closer to me and putting a hand on my shoulder. His thumb touched my neck, and he grazed the skin there once, then twice. My body lit up from his touch. "I didn't tell you to make you feel bad."

"How can I not? My problems are so trivial compared to yours."

"Stop." He was pissed now. Flared nostrils, harsh tone. "This isn't a competition of who deserves to be sad or upset. Life doesn't work that way."

"You must think I'm awful for saying that then."

He didn't respond right away, and my gut twisted. This entire time, I thought Cami was the villain in our story, taking our dad and intentionally upsetting me. But his few seconds of silence made me wonder if I was to blame too.

"I don't believe you're awful, Naomi. Not at all." His thumb brushed my cheek again, and he dropped his hand. His deep voice felt like a comforting hug, and half his mouth lifted with a grin. "Not even a little bit. I think family is complicated and that pain is a moveable scale."

"I had no idea of your past, Michael," I said, my nose getting stuffy and my head fuzzy. "I can't even process it."

"You don't need to." He smiled again, no more sorrow in his eyes. "I'm not giving you advice because you didn't ask for it, but if I may suggest something…" he paused, arched a brow, and I nodded a little too fast.

He could suggest just about anything and I'd agree to it just to get the horrible pang out of my chest.

"Yes, of course, yes," I said.

"Take whatever time you need to, but," he said, pausing, a small twitch in his left eye. "You have an opportunity to change things. You're on campus with her. Life goes fast, and I can only share my experience, but I miss the hell out of my sister. We'd get weekly lunches where I'd annoy her, or my teammates would pick on her. You're going to graduate soon and move, and it'll get harder to communicate, see her, and figure out the conflict between you."

My entire body pounded at his words. He was right, but I wanted to stomp my foot and disagree. He didn't know how much she hurt me, how much I'd wanted a sister the last few years. But I chewed the inside of my cheek and nodded.

"I can literally feel smoke coming out of your ears, Fletcher." He flashed a quick grin and jutted his chin toward the diner. "I'm happy to talk to you about this anytime you want." He shrugged and ran a hand through his hair, giving me another sinful glance at his biceps. I sighed, pushing out all the negative thoughts about Cami.

This wonderful guy suffered through losing his parents and still found ways to laugh *and* talk to me about my petty shit. I could fix this with Cami. I had to. I'd never forgive myself if something happened to her and we never resolved…this issue between us.

Michael had helped me see that. A different kind of warmth spread from my chest to my fingers, more than lust or kinship. Trust, a longing for him. The morning sun hit his face perfectly, showcasing his dark hair and gorgeous blue eyes. There really was something magnetic about him.

He held the door for me, wiggling his eyebrows as he said, "Let's go, nerd."

I walked past him, taking in his clean scent, and it hit me. I felt some sort of way for Michael Reiner.

I was screwed.

CHAPTER
THIRTEEN

Michael

Michael: Facetime later
Ryann: Wow, not even an ask. That was a demand.
Michael: Today's a day I hate not being at Moo U.
Ryann: I want to give you shit for going thousands of miles away, but I won't. Yeah, we can Facetime. Miss you.

I scratched a hand over my chest a few times, feeling Naomi's watchful gaze at the diner. People at Central didn't know my tragic past. It was easy to dodge questions about my family by saying they were out east. It wasn't a lie. My family—meaning Ryann—was out east. One major reason I'd left home was because everyone knew my story there. Here, no one did.

Sharing that with Naomi felt like I checked off a box I didn't mean to. She had *that* look. The narrowed eyes, the sympathy etched on her face. The urge to confide everything in her kept growing, and I didn't want that. I avoided her gaze and focused on Coach instead.

"I can't decide between the hash browns, toast, or eggs," he said, flipping the menu over and squinting at the back.

"What're you eating? Wait, don't answer that. You're young and in shape."

"Can't go wrong with fruit, sir," I said, adding just a bit of humor to my voice. He eyed me before setting the menu down and shoving it to the side.

"Naomi, order whatever you want. It's on me today."

"Thanks, Dad," she said, her tone a little softer than normal. I wondered if she was thinking about the news I shared, how I lost my parents. Was she realizing how lucky she was to have her sister and dad here? Or would she let her grievances get in the way?

"So, post-game analysis. I've had some time to think about last night's game and how we can make adjustments before our home opener in two weeks. But, future-hockey-coach, I want to hear from you. If they were your team, what would you say to them when we meet this afternoon?"

My gut reaction would be to not talk about the game at all and do an activity that required teamwork but suggesting as much felt risky. I'd already crossed a line by saying something to Cal last night. I scratched my jaw and took a breath, hoping to buy myself some time. "Well, I'd ask the captains what they thought."

"Good start. What else?"

"I'd want to point out what could be improved but also what went well."

"Okay. Then?" he asked, a little bit of spark in his eyes. I had the feeling he enjoyed this banter, this give and take between us. He leaned forward onto his elbows just as a waiter approached us. We paused conversation and ordered food. I got a breakfast burrito, Naomi, a pancake breakfast, her dad, eggs, and the assistant coach, French toast.

Not seconds after the waiter left, Coach narrowed his eyes at me. Despite having two other people at the table with us, the conversation felt like a challenge just for me. "You're holding back, Reiner. I can tell. The team is yours in this scenario, so what would you do?"

I tapped my fingers on the surface of the tabletop and snuck a quick glance at Naomi. She watched me with her lips slightly parted, and god, her lips were so full. Like pillows. Soft and pink and *focus*. I cleared my throat. "I'd make them do something that forces them to need each other. Shows their vulnerability."

"Dad, if I may," Naomi interrupted, drawing all three of our gazes to her. Her dad sat up straighter, like he wasn't used to her speaking up this way.

Interesting.

I shifted in my seat, and in the process, my leg brushed against hers. It was a total accident, but then Naomi hit her knee against mine in a playful, flirty form of knee-footsie, and goddamn it, I fought a grin.

She was standing up to her dad and flirting with my knee. Today was a strange one.

"What is it?" Coach asked, tilting his head as he stared at his daughter. When he did that, the resemblance between them was right there in the eye shape and the way their noses fit their face.

Maybe I shouldn't be getting excited about our knees. I moved over to the right so we weren't touching and gave Naomi all my attention. Her cheeks had red patches on them, and she pulled on the hem of her shirt a couple of times before she opened the folder. "I created a player profile filled with stats and observations. I've only had time to do one so far, but I want to add an element to it."

"Okay, I'm listening," her dad said, his eyes moving toward the paper with a picture of Helsing on it.

"There are motivation profile tests that cost around fifty bucks. I want the guys to take them. If I consolidate the data and combine the findings with the stats, I'll be able to provide an in-depth analysis for each player. What pushes them. What motivates them to be a good teammate, or in some cases, to be a bad teammate. This would help address the lack of team unity that is apparent."

"Profiles," he said, slowly and purposefully. He clicked his tongue and stared at me, then his assistant coach, then back to Naomi. I swore I could feel her anxiety growing as the silence went on.

"This is a badass idea," I said, needing to reassure her. I'd use that shit in a heartbeat. "I can't imagine all the correlations you could find there."

"Right? What if we have a way to connect that Helsing is motivated by collaboration and team wins and the fact he has the most assists? Or the opposite? There would be targeted interventions in place to help the team," she spoke too fast and too loud, and it was cute as hell.

Her nerves disappeared, and instead, she was a ball of excited energy. I loved it.

"It'd be cool to track opposing teams too, to see what the best match ups are."

"Oh yes, once we get something in place, the sky's the limit, really." She flipped over the sheet of paper and grabbed a pen from her bag. "The survey results compared to last year's stats and the ongoing ones from this year, plus observations… we could come up with a set of questions that are consistent by player."

"What do you mean?" I asked, trying to read her scribbles on the paper.

"Like, a Likert scale. 1-4. *Likely to take a shot himself or pass the puck. Likely to score. Likely to block.* Again, just spitballing here. We'd have to agree on these questions so we could apply them to every player."

"Wait. This would help the players… how?" her dad asked, his voice a little gruff. With that one question, Naomi deflated.

Her shoulders slumped, and her eyes lost that little glint she had seconds ago. Being an outsider to their family, I could see *exactly* how she took that question. He was assertive, and without the innate assumption that his intentions were good, she'd shut down.

But I learned a bit about her dad since I'd come to campus. He was direct, and when it came to hockey, he was intense. So, his question was to gain understanding, not belittle her idea, and it seemed I was the only one to understand that.

I needed to help, now. "Coach, what's confusing to you? What the players would have to do? Or how we could get the information to them?"

"They fight me on study tables and tutoring, so getting them to complete this quiz would be hard. Does it take long?"

"No, not at all, Twenty minutes," Naomi said. "We could buy however many we want and give them codes with a deadline before next game. That's all they would need to do."

"Hm," he said, nodding to us and elbowing his assistant coach in the side. "What you think, Hank?"

"Sure. I want to see what little Fletcher comes up with." He smiled at Naomi, and she grinned right back.

My muscles tensed at that grin. She never smiled at me like that. How old was Hank anyway? Thirty? I thought he had a wife or something. I frowned at him, but Coach spoke again. "Send me the details, Naomi, and we'll do it."

"Great." She beamed and scrunched her little nose. She put the paper back into the folder and slid it between herself and the wall. Her happiness radiated off of her, and I decided I liked her being this smug. This happy.

Naomi Gordie Fletcher deserved to be proud and happy, and it felt *good* knowing I helped her navigate that miscommunication. Because wasn't most conflict just that? Misconceptions or misunderstood messages?

"Dude, he was kinda into my idea. I wasn't sure at first, but I think it'll be great," Naomi said, an hour later as we strolled across campus. Neither one of us said where we were heading, and I wasn't going to ruin the moment by asking what we were doing.

It was nice just being with her and chatting with someone I enjoyed spending time with. Nothing more, nothing less. There was no reason to overcomplicate the feelings going on in my mind and think it was more than that. I couldn't afford to think it was more. "I'm excited for you."

"Thanks, by the way," she said, her gait slowing. She reached over and gripped my forearm. "I know what you did."

"And what is that, besides being wonderfully charming?"

She rolled her eyes and scrunched her nose again. Goddamn it. The motion shouldn't be that cute, but it was, and my own lips curved up as I stepped toward her. Her grip tightened, and she said, "Clearing up the confusion."

"Ah, well, it was easy as a third party. Also, let me ask you this. Hank."

"Hm? There wasn't a question in that statement." She let go of my arm and giggled. "Are you insinuating something?"

"This is a judgement free zone, obviously, but I picked up on some vibes there."

She snorted and waved a hand in the air, but it didn't hide the slight blush creeping up her neck. "There isn't anything to pick up."

"Liar," I said, unsure if I was teasing her to get a real answer out of her or because it annoyed me. She was off-limits. Coach's daughter. The biggest hell no of all and yet...if his assistant coach was into her, then maybe it wasn't horrible to think about kissing her every time she smiled?

"It's nothing."

"Oh, Naomi Fletcher has a crush on Hank." I elbowed her side softly, and she did it right back, except in true Fletcher fashion, she tripped.

One of her feet got stuck on the other, and in slow motion, she fell into my side. *Oomph*. All her weight landed on me, and I caught her before we both hit the cement. I wrapped my arms around her, holding her against my chest as she regained her balance, and *fuck*.

She tilted her face up and stared at me with her large brown eyes framed by dark lashes. The same heat I felt in my gut reflected back at me. Her pouty, smart mouth was right there, and she wet her bottom lip with her tongue.

My skin prickled with want and desire as her lemon scent clouded me. I ran my hand up and down her back, almost groaning at how she arched against my hand. It wasn't even intentional. It just happened. "Uh, are you, okay?" I asked, my scratchy voice a dead giveaway to the storm brewing inside.

"Hm, yes," she said, breathless and needy. She made no moves to let go, nor did I. We just stood there, wrapped in each other's arms with my heart trying to see how many times it could beat a minute. I would win first place, for sure.

"Naomi," I said, pleading with her for *something*. For her to kiss me, for her to understand why I couldn't kiss her. It was all very confusing, and when she tightened her grip into my shirt, I swallowed so hard we both heard it.

High pitched laughter caused me to jerk back, jumping away from Naomi like I'd gotten caught smoking pot in high school. A woman walked by, talking way too loud on her phone, and my face heated. I'd been about to kiss her. There was no question.

I rubbed the back of my neck and frowned as Naomi glanced at the ground. I should say sorry, *anything*, but my voice stopped working. It was like my mind knew I had to say something, but my mouth disobeyed every order. Who was running my body anyway? It certainly wasn't my brain because I knew I should be leaving her alone.

"Um, hey, do you have plans tonight?" she asked, looking

back up at me. The sun hit her face just right, and her eyes seemed more hazel.

"Nope." I'd probably work out and annoy Freddie.

Wow, my life had changed in a year. As an undergraduate, I partied and always had something to do with the guys on the team. Here though, I didn't have a circle. A familiar wave of sadness clouded over me as memories of the team hit me. The hockey house. The festivals. The pranks. The endless list of people to call if I wanted to work out or grab a drink. Here… I had two people. Freddie and Naomi.

Because you keep people out. I told my mind to shut the hell up. I hadn't gone to therapy since I moved out to Illinois, and I knew I should. Ryann and Jonah brought it up every other time we talked, but it just seemed like another thing to do. Plus, I knew *why* I was this way.

It was so when they left, it wouldn't hurt as bad. I understood that. It was hard enough just having Ryann and Jonah in my circle. The twins were too busy with their lives and new teams, and it was tough seeing them fulfill their dream of playing in the NHL. Once it got closer for them to go, it was easier to back off. Cutting people out was easier if you did it to them first.

Letting more people in? God, they'd be able to gut me. I shook my head to clear my thoughts and forced a smile. "Why? You got some fun plans going on?"

"Well, kinda." She shrugged one shoulder and scrunched her damn nose again. "Our building has themed open-house nights once a month. It's this ridiculous social outreach to bridge the gap between our neighbors which sounds dumb. But we love it."

"A house party," I said, grinning. "With shitty beer?"

"Pretty much. The theme is 90s grunge."

"Oh, will we be listening to Nirvana and wearing oversized flannel shirts?" I asked, a spark of excitement hitting me at being able to go all out. I loved that shit at Moo U and hadn't found a way to get involved here yet. Schoolwork took most of my time, and I'd die for a distraction to keep me from feeling lost. This felt like the old me. The fun Michael.

"Absolutely. Here, give me your number. I'll text you the address."

"Smooth. If you wanted my number, all you had to do was ask," I teased, finding comfort in our familiar, lust-free zone we did so well in.

She rolled her eyes. "Such a player."

"Used to be," I said, too quickly. I wanted her to know that, and her gaze lingered on my mouth for a few seconds. "Anyway, can I bring my roommate? I'll get a permission slip signed if needed."

She snorted. "For sure. I'll see you later then?"

"Sure will. Don't trip on your walk back. I'm still keeping score."

She smiled, and for the first time in a while, I was excited to put myself out there. I was doing this college thing away from home, without hockey to fall back on, and it was equally terrifying and exhilarating. Now, my only problem was my growing attraction to Naomi.

It was becoming a real fucking issue.

CHAPTER
FOURTEEN

Naomi

Mona, Kellie, Lilly, and I each chose extra baggy ripped jeans and tight tank tops, and we wore plaid shirts tied around our waist. I even put on extra eyeliner after studying 90s grunge online. Fashion was more of Cami's thing, but I swore some of these trends had come back. Just thinking about my sister had me feeling uneasy. I hadn't reached out or texted, and I wasn't sure I wanted to yet —even with Michael's words flashing through my mind.

Michael. My stomach swooped. He was coming over to party with us. It felt big. I chewed on the side of my lip as I poured myself a drink. Vodka and fruit punch. A drink before he got here would help settle my nerves. Probably.

"I found this dope ass 90s grunge playlist. They were so angsty. I love it. I would've killed it if I grew up in the 90s," Mona said, lying on the couch as she tossed a tennis ball up into the air. Our apartment had a cut-out from the kitchen to the living room, so it was easy to talk while I prepared the drinks. "The movies, the music. Ugh, it was made for me."

"In typical Mona fashion, she's being dramatic," Kellie said, putting a choker necklace on and then applying dark lipstick in the hallway mirror. "They started the music upstairs. Should we head up or wait for Clark Kent and Hockey Hottie to arrive?"

"I'm impressed with you for inviting them," Mona said, a playful smile on her face. Her dark eyes and smirk were filled with questions, but I pretended to ignore them.

"I'm an impressive person," I said, bringing the cup to my mouth and sipping. It was perfectly sweet.

"Uh huh, sure, yeah." She rolled her eyes and joined me in the kitchen. She prepared her own drink and leaned one hip against the counter. "You like him."

"Um, like?" I said, sounding like a preteen. My muscles tightened, and I might've started sweating too. I liked dessert and crime podcasts. Michael? It was definitely more than that. "Sure. We're friends."

"Aren't you friends with Weston from class? Why not invite him?"

"I see the point you're trying to make, but Michael's different. He...he's new, and I don't know, I thought we'd have fun." My face was as red as the Solo cup, and I took another sip.

"I'm all for having fun, but you're an intelligent woman. One of the smartest I know. I just want you to be careful because I haven't seen you this nervous since you liked that guy in your computer science class freshmen year."

"I'm not nervous," I said, my hand hitting the cup and knocking it over. Red liquid spilled onto the counter, and I quickly yanked some paper towels off the roll and wiped the mess up. "Much."

Mona snorted and poured me another drink but didn't say anything else on the matter. It was weird to have her warn me twice about Michael. Nothing even happened. We were friends, people. Friends! Friends who almost kissed once!

Music blasted from upstairs, and without a text from Michael, I could feel my roommates' annoyance. Kellie sighed a lot, Lilly kept looking at the ceiling, and Mona arched one pretty brow at me.

"Okay, let's head there," I said.

They jumped up and were all smiles. Disappointment hit me like a pound of flour. Michael was either really late or not coming. Was this what Mona meant about being careful? My feelings were already too involved if I got this upset over him not coming.

I took a large sip of the drink and put on my happy face as we headed to the apartment hop. The first unit showed *10 Things I Hate About You*, and people were already doing shots.

Mona and Lilly walked right up to the counter to join a drinking game, and Kellie yanked me toward beer pong in the walkway. The setup was right there in the open, outside, and someone had hung twinkle lights on the ceiling. It was kinda cute.

"We're next in line, please!" Lilly shouted as someone from the unit across from ours wrote down our names. The cool thing about these parties was the fact we knew our neighbors. It was so much better than the dorms with the awkward shared bathrooms. It was a mini-community here, and I pushed out all the negative thoughts about Michael not showing up. I was being bolder. More like my sister.

Maybe there was a reason he wasn't here though. It wasn't like he owed me anything. As Lilly and I played a game of beer pong and the drinks flowed, my worries went away. I didn't care if Michael was here or not to have fun.

Psh. I didn't need him.

I had my girls and friends, and *shit!* I tried gripping the edge of the beer pong table to catch my balance, but I missed and fell onto the ground. My ass stung from the contact, and a very large person appeared in front of my face.

"Typical Fletcher," the voice said, the deep timbre causing a waterfall of excitement through me.

"Michael," I said, looking up and smiling at him. The lights reflected off his face and eyes, and god, he was handsome. I became limp when he pulled me up and ran his hands over my arms, like he was dusting me off.

"You showed up."

"Yeah, sorry if I was late. My damn sister was an hour late to our Facetime call." He smiled and looked around the unit. "This is sick."

"I'm happy you're here," I said, ignoring how soft my voice went and how my mood improved by a thousand percent. My calculations were correct. One thousand percent increase.

"Me too," he said, laugh lines appearing around his eyes. He pointed his thumb toward the Clark Kent look-a-like. "Freddie, this is Naomi."

"Ah, yes. The girl from the trivia bar who has a sister."

"Hi, Freddie," I said, not really paying attention to him. Michael scooted closer to me and put his hand on my lower back, making my senses go haywire. His fingers slightly dug into me, and his touch was so warm. Strong fingers, thick. How would they feel *inside* me?

I gulped at how *dirty* my thoughts went from just a simple touch.

"What's a guy gotta do to get a drink?" Michael asked, his breath tickling my ear, and I shivered.

"Uh, Freddie, would you fill in for me?" I pointed to Lilly who watched with a small smirk. "I can go make you both a drink."

"Sure." Freddie shrugged and stood next to Lilly at the table. He towered over her the same way Michael did with me, and my friend eyed him up and down.

Watch out, Freddie. If Lilly wants you, she'll do what it takes. I giggled as I headed down the stairs to our place.

"That was a cute sound, Fletcher. Why the laughter?"

"My roommate. Your roommate. I hope Freddie can take care of himself." I opened our door and tossed the keys onto the counter with a clink. Michael followed, and when the door clicked shut, I was suddenly very aware that it was just the two of us.

In my apartment.

Alone.

I took a steadying breath and kept my back to him as I walked toward the kitchen. He gently grabbed my hand and spun me around. "I want to see what 90s Naomi would look like."

My hand tingled from his touch, and goosebumps broke out head to toe as he took his time checking me out. A slow smile formed on his gorgeous mouth, and he nodded. "Yup, I dig it."

An awkward sound came from my throat. Not a laugh or a cough. Like a snort and he raised his brows.

"Uh, sorry. You look 90s-ish too."

"I already had this windbreaker for reasons I'm not exactly sure of," he said, laughing and rocking back on his heels. His matching blue track pants made a swish sound when he walked, and he reminded me of an elementary school gym teacher.

He was so at ease right now, it wasn't fair. Was his heart racing and were his palms sweating at just thinking about the two of us alone? God, I wanted to rip that windbreaker off his broad shoulders. I wanted to feel his hard chest and examine every one of the tattoos on his arm.

Shit. He asked me something, and I wasn't paying attention. "Hm, what now?"

"Are you okay?" He frowned, and those dark brows came together. "You seem a bit...distracted?"

"Oh." I was. Very distracted.

Distracted by my attraction to him, how upset I'd been when he wasn't there, and how elated I'd become when he showed up. Constantly thinking about how he'd kiss. Then Mona's warnings slammed in. The whole hockey issue. There was a lot going on in my mind. I needed to keep busy and do something with my hands before I touched him. "Vodka? Rum? Warm beer? What would you like to drink?"

His frown deepened, but he followed me into the kitchen. He smelled so good, like freshly cleaned clothes and sandalwood. I opened the cabinet to grab a glass, but we'd used all the ones on the bottom shelf. "Shit."

"Let me be a gentleman and help," he said, moving behind me and placing one hand on my shoulder. With the other, he grabbed the glass on the highest shelf, but in the process, he pressed his chest to my back. I froze and didn't move a single muscle.

"Th-thanks," I said, my entire body on fire. How could he not tell? My face had to be redder than a tomato at this point. All from lust. "I'll pour it for you."

"No, no need. I couldn't have you spill it accidentally, hm?" He got ice, poured the fruit punch and rum into a glass, and held it up. "I feel like we should toast. Do you need me to make you one?"

"Mine's around here." My chest heaved, and I found my leftover drink from before we headed upstairs. I clinked my glass to Michael's. "Cheers, Michael Reiner."

"Sure thing, Naomi Fletcher."

We held eye contact as we each took a sip, and my god, I'd never been this attracted to a guy before. I wanted to jump on him, and instead of being polite and taking a small sip, I downed the rest of my drink.

"I'm officially tipsy," I said out loud instead of in my mind. "Oops, I didn't mean to announce it to you. But I did. So now you know."

"I appreciate how open you are." He laughed. "I'll keep you updated on my status too."

"Please and thank you."

He laughed again, harder this time, and he leaned his very sexy hip against my counter. "So Officially Tipsy, what does one of these parties look like?"

"It's so fun. We bounce from unit to unit. This month's is on the floor above us, so we didn't have to prepare our unit. But there's a 90s movie going on in each one and games and you saw the outfits."

"This is kinda cool. Our building would never do anything like this." He took a long swig of the drink, and I watched, transfixed as his throat moved with his swallow.

Tipsy Naomi had no reservations about being into Michael. Tipsy Naomi was seconds away from kissing the hell out of him and saying fuck the consequences. I took a step near him and ran my tongue over my bottom lip, my skin already tingling from anticipation.

As I got closer to him, his nostrils flared, and he jutted his chin toward the door. "Should we bring libations to Freddie and play some games? You know I love a good competition."

His blues eyes sparkled, and I could think of nothing I'd rather do than play a game with him. I'd lose, most likely, but it'd be fun.

That was what my tipsy mind agreed on with Michael—falling for him, kissing him, sleeping with him—it'd be fun. My life didn't have a lot of *fun,* and that was my new plan. Have a good time with him and leave the feelings out of it.

"You're on, Reiner."

His eyes flashed with heat, and his gaze dropped to my mouth for one second before he moved out the door. I admired his ass the entire time, but he didn't catch me. Tipsy Naomi was sneaky and horny. Who would've thought?

CHAPTER
FIFTEEN

Michael

In my twenty-four years, I'd done some dumb shit. I once did a beer-bong before a test. I jumped off a roof into a pool. I'd even eaten a large moth for ten bucks. But all of that was small compared to right now. Agreeing to come to Naomi's place after she had a few drinks hit the top of that list. I needed space and air to escape her tantalizing lemon scent that made me want to rip off that tight tank top and explore her body with my mouth.

She usually wore loose clothing that hid her curves and that chest. Fuck. I ground my teeth together when she lifted her arms over her head, exposing a little bit of her stomach. Naomi was beautiful. Intelligent, funny, and beautiful.

My attraction to her was a collection of things. Like the way she smiled and how she scrunched her nose. It was how goddamn clumsy she was and how she always smelled good. It was how she wanted to fix her family so badly but didn't know how. It was also the confident way she nerded out about what she liked. I watched as she tripped on her own feet when we left her small kitchen and made our way toward the door.

"Jesus, how have you not broken every bone in your body?"

My tone came out harsher than I meant, but her tripping made me uneasy. Plus, I reached out to steady her. It was the polite thing to do, and I only let my fingers linger for an extra second. Okay, more like ten seconds.

"I'm a graceful faller."

"No you're not."

She took another long drink, and a little spilled down her lip. She stuck out her tongue to lick it at the same time I moved my thumb to wipe it up.

She licked my finger in the process, and my stomach tightened with an aggressive need. "Naomi," I said, neither one of us moving. My thumb remained on her jaw, caressing her smooth face on its own accord.

She sucked in a breath, and all that mattered was kissing her. Not the sounds of the party going on around us, not the fact her dad held my future in his hands, or the fact we were most definitely wrong for each other. I moved my hand to the back of her head, digging my fingers into her hair, and yanked her toward me.

I'd kissed a lot of women, but not once did my skin tingle with anticipation as I closed the distance. Not once did my heart fucking skip a beat before pressing my lips against someone else's. Her little intake of breath made me pull her closer. Then, I finally kissed her.

Her lips were soft and full, and she opened her mouth to let me in, and *my god,* I wanted this woman. I slid my tongue into her mouth, devouring the sweet taste of her. It was all tongue and teeth, and I couldn't kiss her hard enough.

"Naomi," I murmured into her mouth, needing her to know how much I fucking loved this.

The way she tasted like vodka. The way my heart raced from her aggressive touches and how nothing made sense any more except kissing her. I sucked her tongue and tilted her head back, deepening the kiss as I trailed my hand down her smooth neck. She moaned, and an aggressive urge rolled through me to kiss her even harder.

She gripped the edge of my windbreaker and kissed me with so much energy I tripped backward. Gravity played tricks on me as I stumbled to catch my balance. I wrapped my arm around her and cradled her against me as I righted myself, and she looked up at me with a goofy grin.

"Damn," I said, my lips swollen and wet from our kiss.

"My kissing made you trip," she said, her smug smile doing crazy things to my heart and mind. She wasn't wrong.

I narrowed my eyes and bent down to kiss her again because that was addictive. But then someone shouted my name from behind. The voice had a familiar ring to it. My arms were still wrapped around Naomi and the sweetness from her drink still in my mouth as I turned and saw Erikson lifting his hand in greeting.

Fuck. Naomi might as well have hit me with a taser. That was how fast I jumped off her and stepped back, regret weighing me down. Did he see us? Me? Her?

What if he told Coach?

"Dude, what are you doing here?" I asked, wiping my mouth with the back of my hand, afraid that evidence of the kiss would be right there.

Like, *hey yeah, I just made out with the coach's daughter. How shitty am I?*

"For the party, man. You're cool that I'm here, right?" he asked. He frowned and winced when his gaze landed on Naomi. "Shit. Coach's daughter. Not the fun one either."

"I'm oodles of fun, you behemoth! Oodles," she shouted before marching past me and disappearing into the crowd. If I wasn't so worried about getting caught, I'd laugh at tipsy Naomi yelling at Erikson.

Erikson raised his brows. "Okay then."

My jaw tensed, and I shifted my weight from one foot to the other. My brain was still slow since that dynamite kiss, and I thought about his words. Not the fun one? Freddie said something similar at the library, and I didn't like the insinuation. "Naomi's cool. she won't give a shit you're here. Just don't act like a dumbass and we'll be fine."

"Fair enough." He nodded and smiled at a group of girls giggling at him. "See ya, Reiner."

"Yeah, you too." I waited until he was distracted with the girls before running a hand over my face. The universe had a funny way of telling me to knock it off. Seconds after I got a small taste of Naomi, Erikson showed up. If that wasn't a sign I shouldn't be thinking about her like that, I didn't know what was. My mouth still tingled from her nipping my lip, and I needed to find her. Now.

Shit. I ran a hand through my hair and scanned the crowd. So much plaid and dark colors everywhere. Oasis played in the background, and I only knew that band because my high school coach was obsessed and made us listen to them when we pissed him off. But that didn't matter. Finding Naomi and talking to her did.

Someone in a tight tank and plaid shirt walked by, but nope, it wasn't her. Fuck, were all the girls here wearing the same thing? Okay, okay, think. We kissed, and I ditched her the second a hockey guy showed up.

Naomi already had mixed feelings about hockey, so this didn't help. She was probably embarrassed, or mad, or upset, or any combination thereof, and I needed to fix it. I went from unit to unit, searching for any face I recognized, but they all blurred together. I returned to her apartment, but no one was there. I thought about texting her, but what would I say? Sorry for kissing you and then acting like I wasn't?

This was why shit got messy when you hooked up with people you saw all the time. Flings were easier. No feelings. No attachments. No wondering if the coach would figure out what you did and kick your ass. I groaned just as I heard a familiar laugh.

My stomach swooped like I was on the downward arch of a rollercoaster, and I scanned the crowd until I found her. She had another drink in her hand, half of it already gone, and she looped her arm around her friend's waist. A blush painted her cheeks, and she tensed when her gaze landed on me.

I considered myself emotionally intelligent, but I couldn't pinpoint what was swirling in her brown eyes. Hurt? Lust? My shoulders tensed, and I reached up to massage the part where my neck met my shoulder. It throbbed with tension. Guilt weighed on me more with each step closer to her, the brief yet explosive kiss replaying in my mind on a constant loop. The way she tasted, the warmth of her mouth, her little moan of pleasure when our lips finally touched.

I fisted my hand at my side and forced myself to focus on what was next, already preparing for the conversation to be horrible. How did one exactly apologize for a kiss they enjoyed and planned to never do again? "Naomi, could I speak to you for a moment?" I asked, my voice taking on a real weird formality that made me wince.

I wasn't a damn waiter asking if she needed a refill of water. I was just the guy who kissed her and ditched her. She worried the side of her lip before slowly unlooping her arm from her friend's.

She glanced at the ground and shrugged. "Sure, yeah, okay."

Sure. Yeah. Okay. Not a great start. I put a hand on her lower back and guided her toward a cut-out on the balcony. We were *alone* without being alone. It was secluded enough for this conversation, but public enough that I wouldn't be tempted to apologize by way of kissing. Again. Even though it wasn't a terrible idea…

"What is it, Michael?" she asked, her tone missing that *N-energy*. She gripped the railing with both hands and sighed as she narrowed her eyes. I followed her gaze to the landscape, taking in the bricked buildings and the hint of campus you could see from here.

"I'm sorry," I said, feeling it in every cell of my body. She'd been hurt enough from her dad, sister, hockey, life. She didn't need me confusing things by kissing her when it couldn't lead anywhere. Not really.

"For what, exactly?"

"All of it." I swallowed, the movement causing an uncomfortable lump in my throat. Her coldness toward me hurt more than I anticipated. She wouldn't look at me, and her voice...it was distant. "Naomi, please," I said, unsure what I was pleading for. Her to forgive me? For her to look at me like she liked me again?

"What?" She faced me, red covering her cheeks and neck. Her eyes narrowed with impatience. She crossed her arms and tilted her head to the side. "I don't appreciate being kissed then dismissed."

"I know." I ran a hand through my hair as all the muscles in my face tightened. "Fuck, I know. I regretted it the second I did it."

She recoiled like I'd hit her. It took me a second to replay my words, and I reached out to gently touch her shoulder. "No, *no*. Not kissing you. I don't regret that one bit. I meant... reacting like that when Erikson said my name."

She looked at the ground and nodded, avoiding my gaze. "It's fine," she said to the floor. I squeezed her shoulder and waited for her to look up. When she finally did, it felt like someone pulled the cement floor from under me.

Sadness. The same kind of sadness I carried around in my soul reflected back at me. I moved my hand from her shoulder to her neck, wishing I could take her pain and keep it as my own. I was better equipped to handle it. But I wasn't done, and whatever I said next could make her continue looking at me like that. "I don't regret kissing you, but it shouldn't happen again."

"Okay."

Just okay? No why? No questions? I frowned. "It's not you, I swear. You're gorgeous, and any guy would be lucky to have you."

"It's alright," she said, forcing a tight smile. "I swear, I'm not just placating you. I get it. It's better that we're not involved anyway."

"Because of…" I said, really needing her to fill in the missing gaps here because her blatant acceptance threw me off. What did I want? For her to beg? For her to demand an explanation? Why was I being a tool about it?

"Hockey," she finished. The way she said the word sounded cursed.

"Right," I said, somehow needing to fill the awkward silence. It was more than hockey, but none of those reasons came to mind. Instead, I dropped my hand from her and took a step back. "I don't have a lot of friends here, Naomi, and I want to keep you as one."

"Yeah, we can remain friends, for sure." She smiled, but the movement didn't reach her eyes.

"Okay, cool." I exhaled, hating the rock in my stomach. It wasn't pebble-sized either. It was more like a boulder, growing by the second as Naomi pulled away from me.

"I should get back to my friends," she said, pointing her thumb over her shoulder in the wrong direction. My lips twitched even though the mood was off.

"Right, sure." I shoved my hands in my pockets and forced a smile as she walked away. But then she stopped, turned around, and frowned so hard lines appeared all over her forehead.

"I invited you here. It'd be rude if I ditched you."

"Nah, don't worry. You're allowed to be rude after what I did." I sighed. "I'll probably head out anyway."

She pressed her lips tight together before saying, "Are you sure?"

"Yeah. Yeah, I'm tired and have a lot of studying tomorrow." I channeled the same talent I honed after our parents died—the ability to seem unfazed and smile when my insides felt the opposite. "Don't even worry about it. Have fun. Don't trip again, or I'll know."

"You won't know."

"I'll sense it," I teased, enjoying how her real smile showed signs of poking through. "Goodnight, Fletcher."

"Yeah, you too, Reiner."

I lifted my hand in a wave even though I was five feet from her. When I walked by, I held my breath so as not to take in her citrus scent. I kept up the act as I said goodbye to Freddie and winked at Naomi's friends. It wasn't until I was a block away from the apartments that the weight of everything hit me. Pretending to be okay all the time was exhausting, but it kept people from asking questions.

However, tonight it was the fucking worst.

I was alone. Even if I was back home, Ryann had Jonah. I'd be the third wheel of our family. If being friends with Naomi was the only way I got to keep her, then that's what I'd do. But my heart hurt as I walked toward an empty apartment.

I was back to being by myself, again, and even though it was the right thing to do...it sucked.

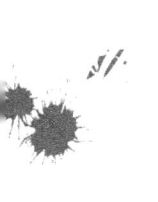

CHAPTER
SIXTEEN

Naomi

I'd never been to a game with overtime, and man, I was tired. It had been a long week, emotionally and mentally, and the thought of riding back in the bus with a bunch of rowdy hockey players sounded as appetizing as ten day old pizza. Yes, I was happy we won—I wasn't a monster. But I wanted to put on my favorite pajamas and go to sleep.

The guys did whatever they did in the locker room where Michael shadowed my dad, so that left me waiting until they headed outside. It was fine. I could just lean against the wall and close my eyes. Even as I did that, the urge to sleep grew stronger. My skin prickled, and *shit*. My weight shifted as I slipped, sending a flurry of alarm bells through my limbs. My heart tried to jump out of my chest, and I took a few deep breaths to settle myself.

"Wow, Fletcher, what's the score now? Five to one?" Michael said, making my lips curve up despite how tired my face was.

Yes, things were still a tad awkward between us, but distance since the weekend helped. I hadn't thought about the kiss more than six times. *Okay, more like a million.* Despite how much I liked it and him, I knew staying friends was the right thing to do. The safe option. Keeping him in the *friend* category would protect my heart.

Hockey would come first for him, and I refused to come second to the sport that broke our family apart. But his casual use of *five to one* made my stomach swoop because that *one* was when he fell over from our kiss.

It was great for my ego for a second but then I shrugged.

"I didn't trip, exactly," I said, yawning.

"It seemed pretty close to it." He raised his brows and grinned down at me with that half-smile I thought about far too often. It should've worried me how addicted I was to him. To his smile, his laugh, his jokes. I missed him this past week even though I shouldn't. However, my sleepy brain didn't have the strength to put up walls tonight.

"My eyelids feel like a million pounds."

He frowned, and if I wasn't mistaken, his fingers twitched at his side. "You need to sleep, Naomi. Overworking yourself isn't going to help anything."

"Yes, sir."

His lips flattened into a straight line as he put a hand on my shoulder and guided me out of the visiting school rink. I told myself it was to make sure I didn't fall because let's face it, I was a hazard to myself when I had a full night's sleep. But he kept his hand there the entire walk to the bus. It was warm and nice, protective. Friendly.

A friendly touch.

That was becoming my least favorite F word.

Yes, we shouldn't be together, but that didn't stop me from thinking about all the what-ifs. That was why distance was good. It limited the sexual fantasies I had about Michael Reiner.

He had large hands, and *mm,* I bet he knew how to use them. He sure knew how to kiss. *Oh god, settle down.* I gulped down a breath of cold air, stifling the growing fire between my legs.

School always came first, then my friends. Ever since my breakup freshman year with Theo, I never had a crazy attraction to anyone. Not like this. But even then, I was sad for a week after six months together. Theo and I had even slept together, but the attraction wasn't anything like how I felt for Michael.

Never like this.

Just one kiss and all my reasons for *not* doing this flew out the janky bus window.

We got into our usual seat on the right side of the bus, and he put our bags up top while I squished myself against the cool window. We'd done road trips together two other times, yet this felt different. More charged. More...feelings.

I couldn't help but wonder if he thought about last weekend as much as I did. Did he regret kissing me or maybe regret not doing it again? Would he move on to another girl, and god, would I have to see it?

Just thinking about him touching someone else had my stomach twisting into pretzel knots, and I slammed my head back on the seat with a groan.

"The bus is the worst for a nap. You can use me as a pillow if it'll help. I've been told I'm quite comfortable," he said, patting his shoulder while he teased me with his dimple. He wore the same hoodie I'd fallen in love with, and I tried not to overthink my actions.

Was he this way with all his *friends?* Offering up his sexy shoulder with the seductive promise of being a pillow?

What else did *I've been told* even mean?. By who? Certainly not his teammates. A surge of jealousy had my stomach tightening. God, what would it feel like to be one of those women? My throat dried up, and my voice came out like sandpaper. "Uh, thanks. Yeah."

He tilted his head to the side, the overhead bus lights only providing me a glimpse of his strong nose. My face burned, and I figured it'd be easier to deal with these thoughts while not staring at him. I put my head on his shoulder and tensed when he picked up his arm to place it around me.

His hand rested on my hips. His large and warm fingers drifted toward my thigh, and holy shit. I sweated even though it was forty degrees outside. He smelled like fresh laundry, outside, and *him*. He was so toasty and comfortable, and I snuggled deeper into his neck.

The kiss from last weekend replayed in my mind, how he gripped my head and pulled my body tight against his. My tongue felt too large for my mouth, and I swallowed, hard.

I closed my eyes but could still hear every inhale he took. His chest moved up and down as his fingers tapped on my thigh to the music on the radio. There was no way I could sleep now. Not with my body pressed against his and his breath hitting the top of my head.

"Stop thinking," he said, his grip on me firming. "I can literally hear your mind making grinding sounds like a machine."

"No you can't."

"Maybe not sounds but I can feel your tension. Relax, Naomi. I got you."

He did. He really had me, and those words made my eyes get a little watery. Maybe allergy season was later than normal this year and the pollen in the air got to me. Yeah, that was why my eyes filled with moisture.

Or, I don't know, perhaps it was exhaustion. Or maybe cramps. Not sleeping and getting hit with PMS was the worst combination. Throwing in a fantastic kiss to be followed by a *just friends* conversation didn't help the matter either.

My fingers dug into his stomach as I got closer to him, and he moved his hand from my thigh to my lower back and rubbed small circles there.

Oh my god.

He kept doing the motion while everyone got on the bus. He didn't stop once we were on the road and the chatter died down for the rest of the two hour ride back. He put light pressure over my sweatshirt, and *oh*. He slid his fingers under my sweatshirt so his rough finger pads were on my bare back, and goosebumps exploded from head to toe.

I was pretty sure I panted at this point. From a little back rub.

He kneaded the area just above my waistline, and a groan escaped me. He stilled, his entire body turning as hard as a wooden plank, and my stomach dropped out of my body from mortification. Was it too sexual of a groan? I wasn't sure. All I knew was that he heard me, stopped, and now things were awkward. It was my fault. We'd agreed to be friends. I agreed enthusiastically with him after that kiss, but now I ruined the moment, and I wanted to pout about it.

"Did that feel alright?" he asked, just above a whisper. His voice was scratchy, like maybe, he felt a little like I did. Like friends was a stupid idea when we clearly had chemistry.

I didn't care that Mona was right—that after our kiss, he chose hockey over me. With his talented fingers on my skin, my resolve got a little blurry.

Hope bloomed in my chest. "Yes, that felt good."

"Good." Something light touched the top of my head, and he continued the motion again. "I want you to relax."

"Mmkay," I said, my brain trying to figure out what that touch was. Did he hit my head with his chin? Or… did he kiss me? No, that would be weird. We were friends.

Did friends rub each other's backs and cuddle on a bus? Probably not. But then again, what did I know? I inhaled his fresh scent, and after a few minutes, my body settled down. My breathing grew deeper, and my mind cleared. Sleep. It was so close, and I needed it.

Falling asleep was one of the best parts of the day, where everything faded into the background and my body shut down. My overactive brain would get a break. I wasn't sure how long I slept, but I woke up with my entire body overheating.

My hand rested on Michael's stomach, just inches from his belt. His muscles were tight and strained against my fingers, and I dug my nails into his sweatshirt just a little.

He shifted his weight but kept a firm grip on my waist. My head had dropped from his shoulder to his chest, and his heartbeat thudded against the side of my face. I wasn't sure what his resting heart rate was, being as in shape as he was and a former athlete, but there was no way his should be beating this fast.

Boom-boom, boom-boom, boom-boom. It was persistent and as fast as mine. Two things struck me as we remained like that, his arm around me and my head on his chest.

The first—we flirted with the line of being more than friends. The second...he practically threw himself down the stairs to get away from me when Erikson called his name, so why the hell was he letting me sleep on him while on the bus?

Those two actions didn't add up, and math always made sense to me. I wanted so badly to ask, but fear of ruining the moment kept me silent. It would change the air between us, and for once, I just wanted to enjoy what it felt like to lay against Michael.

After ten minutes of listening to his heartbeat and the chatter of the coaches in the seats ahead of us, a crick formed in my neck, so I adjusted my position on his firm chest. I tensed, waiting for the second he knew I was awake and would demand I get up, but it never came.

If anything, he relaxed more and moved his hand from my lower back toward my thigh again, gently pushing me closer to him. My pussy throbbed with want and need, and I almost cried when the bus eventually arrived on campus. It was after midnight, and I was so stupid tired and honestly a bit horny that I fought tears as we unloaded our stuff.

It was weird to miss someone who wasn't mine. I blamed staying up way too late working on the results from the motivation tests the players took in a lame attempt to impress my dad. Add in the hormones and the fact I thought about Michael all too much...it was a crock pot of emotions, and I was a horrible chef.

"Hold on, Fletcher, I'll walk you back," Michael said, putting that damn hand on my shoulder for a quick squeeze. When did that gesture become downright sinful? A shoulder touch had no business making me lock my knees together and stifle a moan.

"Sure, right." I swayed on my feet and said to hell with it. I plopped down on the curb and rested my chin on my hands, my elbows on my knees. I might've overdone it this week. I realized that now, and my bed seemed so far away. Miles and miles.

"Hey, Naomi, do you want to get some dinner tomorrow?"

I looked up and squinted at... *my dad*. He stood with his hands in his pockets and an unfamiliar expression on his face. He rocked back on his heels, and it struck me that he seemed nervous. Which was silly.

It was my tired mind playing tricks on me. First, a sexy shoulder squeeze from Michael and now my dad asking me to dinner? Was the universe going to rain Skittles to make this lucid dream even weirder?

"To talk about the data? I'm not sure I'll have it ready. I'm sorry," I said, the lump forming in my throat again. "I'm extremely tired, but I could probably try to have it done on Sunday."

He frowned and shook his head. "No, no data. I mean, yes, I'm looking forward to seeing it, but that's not why I asked about dinner."

"Oh, then what's it for?"

I swore my dad blushed. He ran a hand over his face, and my dad sighed. "To eat."

"Should I prepare anything?" I asked, still very confused as to why this invitation was happening. I hadn't had a meal with just my dad in... years. "Oh, is it a family thing?"

"No, just us."

"Um," I said, my nerves growing like weeds after a summer rain. "Sure. Yes."

"Great." He smiled for a second before the same hard look I was used to replaced it. Firm eyebrows, lines around his mouth. "Do you have a favorite place to go on campus?"

Wow, what a weird question. I did, but I always went where *he* requested the past few years. "Shirley's Sinner," I said, the dive bar that had the best club sandwiches.

"Six work for you?"

"Yeah, yeah it does."

"See you then, Naomi," he said, giving me a long look before heading back toward the guys.

My dad just asked me to dinner.

Me. Not Cami.

What the fuck! This was amazing. I smiled at the realization this could mean things were changing for us. Good things, I hoped.

"You still with the conscious?" Michael said, his large body coming into view from my right. I wasn't sure what he was doing or if he heard the conversation with my dad, but I grinned up at him.

"Yes. But not for long." I pushed myself up, but a soft grip came around my arm, and he practically lifted me. It'd be easy to just fall against Michael and let him put that wicked arm around my shoulders for the walk home.

But being out in the open with the fresh, chilled air around us, some of the magic from our little seat on the bus was lost. I cleared my throat once I stood and flashed my best grin at him. "I won't trip once on the walk home."

"Love the confidence, Fletcher, but the bags under your eyes aren't really giving me reassurance. Come on, lean on me if you need to."

We started our walk toward my apartment complex, and every once in a while, our hands brushed together. Just our knuckles. Like a quick whisper of wind over my skin and I yanked my hand back. I'd gotten my cuddles and Michael fix for the week, and I needed to regain my strength for next Friday.

Thank the stars we had two home games in a row. No more bus rides. No more excuses to sleep against him.

"I've been thinking—"

"My dad asked me to dinner," I blurted out, wussing out of whatever he was going to say.

He frowned for a second, the line appearing between his strong brows before a slow smile spread across his face. "Hey, that's great. You excited?"

"Yeah, I think so. It's weird. He's never done this, and the more I think about it, I'm wondering why now."

"Maybe he wants to repair the damage he did. Maybe he wants to talk to you. The motivation might not matter. It's the fact he asked that counts."

"Yeah, you're right," I said, that pang in my chest flaring up just thinking about how Michael didn't have parents anymore. God, there weren't any words to convey how sorry I was for him.

To make it worse, I thought about his comment from last weekend. That he didn't have a lot of friends here and he wanted to keep me as one. If I pulled away or let my lusty thoughts take over, it'd ruin the friendship he needed. Damn, this sucked.

I wanted to kiss his entire body while also hugging him and promising I'd be there for him. That he didn't have to lose me too when his life was so full of loss already. My eyes stung again, and I sniffed.

He snapped his gaze to mine and stopped walking, a frown stretching across his handsome face. "Hey, whoa, are you okay?"

"I'm fine," I said, my voice cracking as my eyes stung. "Hormones, I swear."

"Ah," he said, nodding and looking off into the distance. "I get it." He held up his hands in the air and let out a sheepish smile.

I sniffed. "Do you? Do you *really*?"

"Not personally, which I assumed you knew that," he said, his eyes narrowing a little bit. "My sister was very vocal about all that fun lady bullshit—her words, not mine. She'd cry into a bowl of ice cream before watching a war movie. I never asked questions, just stayed clear of her."

"Wise man." My mood improved just a little bit. "I feel like my life is out of control right now with all these emotions, and this fun lady bullshit amplifies it."

"I can relate to the out of control feeling," he said, softer this time. "That was me at twenty. Playing on a hockey team that won a lot. I got a ton of attention on campus, but being back home was a dark cloud. Dealing with the funerals, with my younger sister who needed to finish high school. The house. The belongings. The only thing that kept me sane were my teammates and the game. That spinning never really stopped, to be honest. It just lessened. Even now, I don't know what I'm doing half the time or why I'm doing it."

"I thought you wanted to be a coach?"

"Sure, probably. I chose sports management because it made sense. I came here to get away from the memories and the stifling feeling that I couldn't escape my past. Talking about it pisses me off because am I really away from it when it's still on my mind?"

"Michael." This time I reached over and wrapped my arm around his trim waist. I squeezed him, hoping to offer some comfort any way I could. "There's a difference between escaping your past and healing from it. It sounds like you might be confusing the two."

"Wow, pot meet kettle."

His words stung. If he wanted to push me away, it worked. I dropped my arm from him and hugged myself. We continued toward my place, and I shivered, unsure if the air got colder or the mood between us did. His face was tight, and his jaw flexed every other second, so I focused on the sidewalk and not tripping.

I successfully made it to my unit when he shoved his hands in his pockets and offered a small smile.

"Thanks for walking me home," I said.

"Sure thing."

He stared at me with the same intensity he did that first night at the bar, and it would've been easy to get lost in those sky-blue eyes. To run a hand over his jawline and kiss him again.

Instead, I waved. It was better this way. My emotions were a mess, and 'just friends' was our safe zone. "See you around then."

"Goodnight."

He waited there as I got out my keys from my bag and let myself into our place. After the door was shut and locked, I peeked out the window to see him staring at the door with longing on his face.

It caught me off guard, and my breath hitched. I had to be misreading that look, the lowering of his eyelids and tight jaw. He was pissed. That had to be it. I shook the image of Michael standing there alone out of my mind and didn't even brush my teeth before diving headfirst into my bed.

I could overanalyze it all tomorrow. Sleep came first.

CHAPTER
SEVENTEEN

Michael

Cinnamon bagels and coffee could most likely fix anything. If the world leaders sat down with these warm pastries and a fresh brew of hazelnut roast, I think they'd all be in better moods. I wasn't sure how I went so long without enjoying carbs, but baby, I missed them.

I carried the pastry box and a large to-go box of coffee as I walked toward Naomi's place. Not only did I owe her an apology, but I had this driving urge to see her today. To make sure she was feeling okay, to see if she needed a friend before seeing her dad tonight. Or maybe to see if she wanted help with the data profiles for the project.

I could lie to myself and to her, but the truth settled deep down that I liked being around her. She made me feel less alone. Now, I just had to get her to answer the door. There were no sounds on the other side after I knocked, and it was after ten. She would probably be up already.

Frowning, I took one more shot at knocking before coming to the realization that she was allowed to not be home.

Michael: Hey, I'm leaving some 'I'm sorry' breakfast gifts outside your door.

Naomi: Gifts? Breakfast? Sorry?

Michael: Yes, those are words. Good job, LOL. Are you home?

Naomi: In ten seconds.

What? I scanned the building and didn't see anyone walking up or even a car approaching. Soft footsteps came from the other side of the door, and with a small click of metal, the front door slid open. Naomi squinted up at me, and it took all my effort to not drag my gaze down her body.

She wore shorts and a tight navy t-shirt with a math formula on it and looked like she'd just woken up.

"Shit, were you sleeping?"

"No. I hadn't gotten out of bed yet, but I was awake. Show me these treats, please. I can smell them, and my mouth is watering. It's sad, really." She ushered me in, and just-woke-up-Naomi was cute. Her face had soft sleep lines on it, and her hair was in two braids, but they were messy and had strands going every direction.

She didn't wear a speck of make-up and . Once she lifted the lid of the box, she licked her lips. "Oh god, I want to be alone with them."

I snorted. "Should I leave?"

"Would you? I want to do obscene things with them."

Obscene things. My mind flashed to all the thoughts I'd had about her lately. How I wanted to lick every part of her body, tease her perky tits with my mouth. I wanted to hear her moan over and over. All the things I wanted to do to her despite the fact we'd agreed to remain friends. *Sure, Michael, friends. Okay, bro.*

I cleared my throat. "I really came here to apologize to you."

"Oh." Her lips parted, and she looked up at me through her lashes. A small line appeared between her eyebrows. I wanted to touch it, to smooth it down. Which would be weird.

I didn't often think about caressing women's faces. "You

said something last night that I needed to hear about my past, and I snapped at you. That wasn't cool at all, and I'm sorry for reacting that way. You didn't deserve it."

She chewed on the side of her mouth and held my gaze, her large brown eyes so damn expressive. I could study her movements for a year and still not know all of them. My spine prickled with worry as the silence went on, but I didn't break it.

I said my piece, so now it was her turn. She could accept my apology or not, and I'd have to deal with it. I just didn't want to leave yet.

"Thanks. Do you always bring pastries to people you've wronged?" She reached in and took a large bite of the cinnamon sweetness. She crossed her eyes and let out a long moan.

A sexy moan.

I swallowed hard as she chewed and got some of the cinnamon on her face right above her lip. My body tightened, and it was like we were back at the party, her lips inches away from mine. I wanted to taste her again. Suck her tongue. Kiss her until she forgot all about data. *Focus.* She asked me a question. I should answer it. "Ah, no. I don't bring them for everyone."

"Just me then."

"Yes, just you."

Her eyes warmed, and my heart did an odd thing where it seemed to skip a beat or two. *Just you make me want to touch your face, kiss you, say to hell with all the reasons why kissing the coach's daughter is wrong.* I said none of the thoughts going through my mind though and offered what hopefully was a smile.

She blinked and pushed the lid open more. "Did you already have one on the way, or do you want to come in and enjoy them with me?"

"What if my answer is yes to both questions?" I teased, the weight that appeared on my shoulders since last night vanishing just like that. She laughed and walked toward the kitchen counter where there were two barstools. I dropped my gaze to her legs and noticed how her shorts barely covered her ass. Her skin looked smooth, and those goddamn shorts left nothing to the imagination. I wanted to *grip* her ass and hoist her onto the counter. *Fuck.*

I slammed my teeth together and worked my jaw muscles, as if that would help the growing attraction to Naomi.

Attraction wasn't foreign to me. At all. I'd been intrigued and drawn to lots of women. Being a hockey player meant easy access. But, and only recently, I'd discovered that random hookups didn't help the ache in my chest.

Nothing really did but being around Naomi. Which was more than lust. I just wasn't sure what yet. She stood on her tiptoes, showcasing her calf muscles, and grabbed two mugs and the box of coffee from me before moving toward the living room. The kitchen felt safer, for me at least. But she didn't look back.

She curled up onto her couch and tucked her feet under her butt before patting the cushion next to her. "Come on. I'm watching Law and Order."

She didn't wait before handing me a cinnamon treat and pushing play. I fought a smile because despite the attraction and confusing thoughts I had around her, she had moments that reminded me of my sister. Like now. Focused on food and TV. God, Ryann would get a kick out of her.

Wait. Would Ryann ever meet her? Probably not. Unless…

Unless what? I scolded myself and took a bite of the buttery carb goodness. My taste buds exploded with the flavors, and I leaned back onto the couch. Something like *guhn* escaped my lips, and Naomi snorted.

"It's so good, I can't help it."

"Mouth orgasms are real," she said, taking another bite and crossing her eyes. "If you could apologize to me with these more often, I wouldn't say no."

My brain was stuck on the word *orgasm* coming from her mouth and refused to move away from it. I bet she'd blush, and her large brown eyes would be filled with passion. She'd moan and her hair would go everywhere once I ran my fingers through it. She'd be loud too. Not holding anything back.

I'd want to get her off with just my mouth at first. See how wild I could make her before sliding into her. *Fuck.* Not again.

My dick swelled at the picture in my mind. It didn't help when Naomi shifted in her seat, making her legs rub against mine. Her legs were so fucking soft, and the sweets combined with her citrus scent...this was a terrible idea coming over here. I trailed my gaze from her head, down her neck, and to her legs again. Even in her large shirt, hints of her curves teased me.

Dude. I literally asked to be friends. FRIENDS.

She's Coach's daughter.

"I love this show, and it's been on forever. Decades. It's so cool to have that legacy, don't you think?" She glanced over at me, and her eyes widened.

I couldn't imagine how I looked. I'd been told I was intense on the ice, ready to do what it took to win. My blood pumped the same as it did during a game, and she sucked in a breath.

"I can't stop thinking about kissing you," I said, going with honesty. It tended to be the best option even if it made shit awkward. "Again," I said, my voice going lower.

Naomi's chest heaved, and she bit down on her bottom lip as spots of red covered her neck. Her gaze dropped to my mouth for one second, then another, and I tensed, ready for whatever she threw my way. She could tell me to piss off, and I'd listen.

"It's crossed my mind a few times too."

"Yeah?" Hope exploded in my chest. I scooted an inch closer to her. "What are you thinking about, exactly?"

"Michael," she said in her husky voice that made me breathe faster. The air was tense, and every sound seemed amplified. The dialogue on the TV, the way she panted, the click of her throat as she swallowed.

"I want to kiss you." She leaned forward and pulled her

knees up to her chest. "So badly. God, being around you makes me forget everything else."

"I can relate to that." I rubbed my free hand on the thigh of my jeans and focused on the TV. "Even though it's a bad idea."

"The worst."

"Okay, so we both think kissing each other is a bad idea yet we can't stop thinking about it?" I asked, almost on the verge of laughing. "We're a pair, aren't we?"

She laughed, deep and warm, and I wanted to keep that sound. Her joy helped fill the emptiness in my chest. She leaned against the back of the couch and took a sip of the coffee as she eyed me over the mug. Her face changed with her thoughts. It was adorable and confusing to see her eyebrows move, her nose scrunch, and her gaze shift toward the hallway and back to me a few times. "I have a solution, sorta."

"I'm listening." If it involved pulling her onto my lap, then I was in. I was so in.

She blushed and wet her bottom lip twice before she lowered her voice to a whisper. "Friends with benefits."

Oh god. I wanted that *so* badly. But that seemed more my style, not hers. I had to make sure. "Naomi," I said, my voice coming out desperate and grave. "Wait, hold on. What are you suggesting *exactly*? Spell it out for me."

"Look, we can never date. That would *never* happen," she said. She made her eyes go wide, and I didn't appreciate her confidence in that word.

"Never?" I repeated, but it didn't come out like a question. She nodded and took my response like I agreed with her.

"For obvious reasons. Plus, we see each other all the time, and the season is long. It'd suck to have to be near you and all that, but friends with benefits." She wiggled her eyebrows. "We have chemistry, *but* our friendship is important to me."

"It's important to me too." I scratched my chest right over my heart. "But...I'd be lying if I said I hadn't thought about you naked a million times."

She giggled and covered her hand with her mouth. "This is so bizarre. Talking about it like this. Right now. My skin is on fire, and I kinda want to just jump out the window."

"Despite being shy about my past, I'm a communicator. It's how I deal—dealt with my parents' death. Even if a conversation is hard, it's better to have an open one than assume anything. Like, I might assume this would be weird for you, but instead of thinking it, I'm asking." I moved my hand to her neck and teased her earlobe.

Goosebumps broke out across her body before she huffed out a breath.

"Shit, that felt... mm. Wait., are you insinuating I'm inexperienced?"

I smiled and brought my thumb to her full bottom lip. Her eyes got wider, and I tried to control my breathing. "No. Not at all. I'm assuming this would be weird because you made your stance on rowdy hockey players pretty clear. That's what I mean, Fletcher."

"Back to last name, hm?" she said, but her cheeks were flushed and her chest heaved. I teased her neck all the way down to her chest.

"I find it suits you when you're a pain in the ass," I teased, throwing in a wink at the end. She laughed, like I intended, and she made a raspberry sound with her lips.

"I suppose it'll be weird, but I'm willing to try."

"And we keep it all private, right?" I asked, this one piece important to me. Friends with benefits was a clear agreement. We would be friends, attend games together, and hook-up in private. We wouldn't date. Feelings would be kept safe. Her dad would never find out the truth. I could still have a future in hockey, and she wouldn't get upset about it. It was the best-case scenario I could've asked for.

Plus, sleeping with her once wasn't going to be enough. Not even close. I was damn certain on that.

Her eyes shuttered for one half of a second before she nodded. "Of course. No one finds out about us."

"And if one of us is done, we say it. Deal?" I said, still not believing that this conversation was happening. It felt like we needed a contract or something to make it final. Her tits strained against her shirt as she breathed deeper, and I oh-so-slowly ran my hand over one of her pebbled nipples.

She bucked off the couch. "Deal. Definitely deal."

I grinned so hard my face hurt, and then I pulled her onto my lap. Her thighs landed on either side of mine, and I rubbed my hands up her sides, under her large shirt so I could feel her skin. She trembled on top of me, and my cock swelled in my jeans. She must've felt it because she ground against me, making me release a loud groan.

She ran her hands over my shoulders and pecs as her breathing quickened, and I finally gripped her ass and kneaded my fingers into it.

"Mm," she said, closing her eyes and moaning.

I was done with this. I needed her mouth on mine, right fucking now. "Kiss me, Naomi. I'm losing my mind."

She let out a cute giggle before lowering her mouth toward mine and *finally* kissing me. It seemed important to let her initiate it, but now? I wanted to fucking devour her. I bit her bottom lip and pulled, watching her eyes go wide as I sucked her lip into my mouth.

"Michael," she panted, her fingers running through my hair.

"You drive me wild, Naomi," I said, using my hands to pull her as tight as possible against me. She was perfectly petite in my arms and fit against me like she was made for me. I dragged a finger down her spine as I kissed from her mouth to her neck. My dick was hard as a fucking rock as I bit her earlobe. She tasted like salt and sweetness, and I nipped her neck, making her groan.

"Does this feel good?"

"God, yes."

She ground her ass on my lap, rubbing against my erection, and I stilled. Fuck. It'd been months, enough that the mere heat of her body on mine would do me in. I almost growled at the two dimples at the base of her back. I wanted to lick those dimples. I kneaded them with my fingers as I bit her collarbone over her shirt. She might be sitting on me, but I was in charge here.

I tilted her head back, yanked her tighter against me, and captured her mouth with mine again. This kiss was urgent, fast, messy. Her teeth hit mine as she pushed me back onto the couch harder. She tasted like cinnamon and coffee.

She moved her hands toward my hair and gripped my shirt hard as she kissed me deeper, like she couldn't get enough of me too. It was addicting. Sweet, smart, sexy Naomi let out a moan and grunt as I flipped us over so her back was on the couch. I broke the kiss only for a second to make sure she was okay, and she stared up at me with *hungry* eyes.

"I want to fucking lick you," she said, her face wild with passion. "Everywhere."

Jesus. I crawled on top of her and kissed down her neck, her collarbone, and lifted the edge of her baggy shirt up to kiss her chest. I easily flicked my tongue against her pebbled nipple, and she bucked beneath me.

"Unnh, Michael," she moaned, pushing her chest out more.

"You like when I do this?' I flicked her nipple again, then sucked down on it until my mouth made a popping sound. She squirmed, and I repeated the action with her other breast. I took my time, tasting her salty skin and teasing her perfect pink nipples. Her tits were perfect. *She* was perfect.

"Again," she begged, the desperation in her voice matching my own. If she wanted more time on her tits, then I'd be a gentleman and give her what she craved. My dick throbbed so hard it hurt, and I was seconds away from losing control. I needed to be inside her.

I swirled around the tip and blew air on it, then bit down

just enough to have her yelp in pleasure. "That day in the bathroom," I said, moving to do the same thing on the other one. "Your shirt was soaking wet, and your perky nipples strained against the fabric."

"I remember."

I sucked, and she moaned, letting out a needy little whine.

"I've been fantasizing about doing this since then."

She shivered. Once her nipples were wet and warm from my mouth, I moved down her body and lifted her shirt so I could kiss her stomach. So soft, curvy, and sexy.

Something thudded from somewhere in the apartment, but my goal was on getting Naomi off. I *needed* to know what she sounded like.

"Shit. Shit!" Naomi pushed me from her and smoothed her shirt down, her face getting redder than a tomato.

"Uh, what?" I asked, dazed and very fucking confused. My dick throbbed against my jeans. My mouth had been on her skin point two five seconds ago.

"We can't do this *here*. You should go."

"Leave?" I couldn't possibly get up and walk out the door.

"Yes, Michael." She frowned at the hallway that went further into the unit. "Leave now. I'll call you. Uh, thanks for the coffee. And the food. And the kiss."

She jutted her chin toward the door. This was a first. Being dismissed when I swore she was into it. My dick throbbed, and my entire body tensed with regret. I didn't want to leave, but Naomi pleaded with her soft eyes and worried expression. I *knew* this pushed her outside of her comfort zone. Friends with benefits.

Wait. The sound. *Someone else was home.* My lust-fueled brain took a second to catch up with reality. *That's* why she shoved me away. We would've gotten caught.

I groaned as I wiped a hand down my face, lost for words because what did I say? That I didn't want to go? Because I didn't. I understood why I had to but fuck, I needed her bad.

Horny, hurt, and embarrassed, I didn't look at her again before making sure I had my keys and my phone.

It was risky enough thinking about doing anything with the coach's daughter, and we almost got caught.

I walked out without a word.

CHAPTER
EIGHTEEN

Naomi

There wasn't a to-do list that could save me from myself. Not a single special on serial killers could pull me from overanalyzing what just happened. I couldn't stop thinking about Michael.

And not just one part of him. All of him. The good bits and the problematic ones. The way his mouth felt on my body, the absolute confidence of a man who knew how to please a woman. The ease in which he shifted from friends to *this*— whatever this was. I wanted him. Naked. And yet, one small sound that could've been Mona walking into the kitchen had me jumping back like he was a criminal.

It was his rule, but I could've taken him to my room. Done a normal thing instead of getting all weird on him.

My face flushed, and my pulse raced something fierce as I walked back and forth across my room. I ran my hands through my hair and took deep breaths, unable to stop replaying the moment. His hands on my body, his tongue on my nipples. My nipples! They were always an afterthought with my past boyfriends but not Michael. They tightened when I imagined his mouth on them again.

I sighed and fell onto my bed, annoyed at myself, my reaction to him, and at Mona for no other reason than she was right. Because despite my attraction to him and the fact he was a decent guy, hockey would always be his priority. Staying friends was safer.

But you agreed to be friends with benefits.

Then I kicked him out right after—basically doing the same thing he did to me the week before after our first kiss. Being a hypocrite didn't sit well with me.

"Fuck." I sat up and stared at my phone, hoping the right words would come to mind. I needed to say something to him. It'd been an hour. That was enough time, right?

Utter panic gripped my throat. What if he thought the deal was off? No, that couldn't happen. My fingers shook, and I channeled all the badass parts of myself to take action. I could own up to my freak out and hope we were still on. Maybe I could go to his place?

My phone buzzed, and Cami's name popped up, throwing ice on the inferno of emotions brewing inside out. I ignored her.

She called again.

Okay, that was...weird.

The turmoil about Michael shifted in a blink, and I answered, afraid of a worst-case scenario. That had to be the only reason she would call me multiple times in a row. "Uh, hello?" I asked, chewing my lip and preparing myself for bad news.

Someone was sick. There was an accident. Something along those lines.

"I need you."

Every muscle in my body tightened as I prepared myself for war. Aggressive, *protective* feelings coursed through me, making me stand straighter as I scanned the room. "Of course. What is it?"

"A ride. Soon, please," Cami said, her voice shaking and lacking her usual luster. She sniffed, and that sound sent alarm bells off in my head. Cami didn't cry. She didn't show sadness. She was the happy one, the bubbly dancer. The one with so much confidence I swore she could sell it and make a profit.

"Are you okay?"

"Yes. Just, can you get here fast? I texted you the address."

"Of course. I'll leave now." I slipped on sandals and an oversized sweatshirt left over from my ex last year and grabbed my keys. "Do you need anything?"

"A ride out of this shithole." She sighed, and my own soul ached. My sister was hurting.

"Are you safe? Should I call Dad?"

"No!" she yelled. "Don't, no. Don't tell anyone. Please."

"Sure, yeah." I got into the car I'd spent four summers saving to buy. Benny B the Blue Bug wasn't shiny and new, but he was sturdy and my guy. "Getting in and pulling up the GPS."

Something loud carried over her end, and it sounded like shouting. Angry shouting. It reminded me of a party, but it was eleven a.m.? I wasn't judging because I was a firm believer of *you do you,* but a rager at eleven a.m. was a new one for Cami. She might party a lot and steal guys I dated, but she took dance seriously.

"Shit, I gotta go. Please honk when you get to the address." She hung up before I could say a word, and I put the car in reverse.

"Watch it!" someone yelled, a deep familiar voice. I winced, horrified I almost hit a human, and Michael's large body appeared at the driver's window. I hit the button, on autopilot.

"Fletcher, of course it's you."

"What are you… why are you…you're here," I said, not providing any evidence of my intelligence. I sounded demented. "Michael," I said, my face tingling from mortification.

"Trying to hit me, hm?" He bent low, smiling and looking way too relaxed after what we almost did an hour ago. His face was a few inches from mine, and his lips stole all my focus. They were so full and soft and talented. Goosebumps broke out from my neck to my toes, and I shivered.

"Whoa, hey, you're pale as fuck. What's wrong?"

"Uh." Right, Cami. "My sister. She needs my help." I lifted my phone like that made it all clear. "She needs a ride from." I paused and squinted at the address. "Shollock. Damn, that's twenty minutes away."

"Shollock?" Michael's brows raised, and he frowned. "That's not a great town. Why is she there?"

"No idea. She called me upset, and I'm going to help."

"I'll head there with you," he said, not even bothering to wait before he walked around and got into the passenger side door. He was in my car, buckled and staring at me, before my brain caught up to the moment.

"Wait, no." I shook my head, so flustered with *everything* that nothing made sense. "You don't have to come."

"From what I know of that town, it's not a great place for you or your sister to be. I won't say anything if you want silence, but I'll feel better knowing you're safe."

"You don't need to watch out for me," I said, annoyed at feeling incompetent. He did this. He rattled me.

"You're right, I don't, but I'd like to." He narrowed his eyes and flexed a hand at his thigh before he sighed. This one felt like disappointment. The sun hit his face at the right angle, making his blue eyes darker. Like the sky right after a storm at dawn. My breath caught in my lungs at how beautiful he was, and for a moment, I forgot my task ahead of me.

I could only stare at him, at the shape of his jaw. The way his brows were thick and brown. The hair that was still a bit messy from running my fingers through it. Wait. Him... us... "Why are you here?"

"Ah well, someone… meaning me, left their wallet here." He

gave a goofy smile. "Then you tried to hit me with your car, *and* now I'm tagging along to get your sister. Which, you didn't ask for my opinion, but I'm glad you're helping her. Those without siblings don't understand the *I love them but don't like them* argument. You might not like your sister, but you'll do anything for her."

"That's exactly it." I shook my head a bit and settled myself by gripping the wheel and wiggling my toes in my sandals. "You hit it perfectly. She called, and my stomach dropped. Of course I'd help her."

"And I'm coming with you because I've heard that town is rough. If I'm assuming anything about your sister, my guess is she might've gotten into trouble, so having wonderfully strong male backup isn't the worst idea." He winked and leaned back into the seat.

"Tuck your ego in, Reiner. It's hanging out."

"Just the truth, baby."

I snorted, and just like that, there was no weirdness between us. I didn't have the paralyzing worry about what happened or didn't happen. It felt normal. A beat of silence passed as I got onto the main road that took us out of town. Worry ate at my stomach the longer the silence went on, but not because of us. We could talk about that later. It was Cami. "Do you think she's in trouble?"

"I don't know her, but the fact she called you is good." He turned toward me, and I swore I could feel my face heating from his attention. "Does she do drugs? Is she an adventure-seeking type of girl?"

"No to drugs, or at least I'd be shocked by it. She takes dance seriously, but we're obviously not close." My palms sweated. *Ten minutes out.* "Can you text her from my phone to ask if she's okay?"

"Sure thing."

I pushed on the pedal to go faster, and he clicked his tongue. "She sent back a *yes.*"

I didn't know a lot about the town, but my mind was already overactive. Instead of thoughts about partying, they turned darker. Drugs. Sleeping with married men. What if a guy beat her up? Hurt her? My jaw ached, and I got off the highway and pulled into a parking lot with a large gray building.

The blank building had one large word painted on it: MICKIE'S.

"Ah, Mickie D's makes sense now," Michael said, jutting his chin toward the building. "Strip club."

"My sister is stripping?" I frowned, hurt that I didn't know this, but then again, why would she tell me? There was zero judgement in my body if she was in fact stripping. Hell, my freshmen lab partner made a shit-ton of money getting subscribers to her Onlyfans. I respected that hustle.

But in this town?

When I thought she had a better life… and had everything? I honked like she asked, and not two seconds later, a black door swung open, and she marched out. She wore short shorts and a black crop top and cowboy boots. She looked good, and my eyes prickled with relief.

She's safe.

She jogged to my car and threw herself in the backseat before slamming the door. "Go."

I was on the road again in ten seconds, and her perfume flooded the car. It was way too strong and, if I was correct, had a hint of vodka mixed in. "So, you going to—"

"No," she said, her tone fierce. I met her eyes in the rearview mirror for a second before she looked down. She crossed her arms over her chest and kept her face neutral as I tried to think of what to say.

I wanted to demand answers, but we weren't there. I wanted to tell her I was so happy she was okay, but that made my tongue feel too big for my mouth. Instead, I turned on the radio and took deep breaths. This sucked. Too many unsaid words and emotions threatened to overcome me, and I was seconds away from losing it when Michael reached over and placed his hand over mine.

He squeezed my hand and left his there, the weight of it soothing in an odd way. It was just his palm on my fingers, but that support, the silent *I'm here,* was enough to get me through the ride. The air was thick enough to cut with a knife, but I could breathe because his presence helped.

I barely pulled onto campus before she said, "Here's fine."

"I can take you to your place," I said, confused and angry and upset. "Can we please discuss what happened?"

"I've been trying to talk to you for weeks, Naomi," she said, fury lacing her tone like sharp knives to my chest. "You don't get to give a shit now."

"Hey," I fired back, glaring at her in the mirror even though she wasn't looking at me. "I do care. I'm glad you're okay."

Michael's grip tightened on me, and Cami looked up, the hurt so clear in her eyes. I wished I could go back in time to when we were close. When we told each other everything and had trust between us. When we'd shared more than half of a last name.

"Cami," I said, my voice clogged with emotion I wasn't prepared to handle.

She met my gaze, and for one second, her eyes, just like mine, softened. But then she got out the door and slammed it. I winced and leaned back into my seat, completely spent.

Michael, my dad, Cami. My once normal and uneventful life was filled with all sorts of feelings and complications, and my analytical mind preferred the former. Without all the emotions. When my brain overworked, I shut down.

"Hey," Michael said, his voice laced with enough sympathy for me to break. The moisture in my eyes pooled over and dripped down my cheeks. Shame flooded my face, and Michael's strong grip gently tilted my chin his way. "You did the right thing."

"You don't know that," I said, sniffing and trying not to lean into his hand as he cupped my face. "I just... my dad wants dinner tonight, and Cami did... what she did. I'm confused."

"I probably don't help either, huh?" he said, laughing and wiping away one of my tears. His mouth was so close to mine, and his breath tickled my skin, causing that weird swooping sensation in my gut to grow.

"No," I admitted, feeling safe in the brief vulnerability. "You're thrown in there too."

He dropped his hand, and the only indication he heard what I said was a slight frown on his lips. It went away quick, and he flashed his grin my way. "Tell me what you want. You want a buddy? I'm game. You hoping to distract yourself with my body? I'll do it. Want me to get lost? I'll bitch about it, but I'll listen. Whatever you need, I'm here for you."

I could feel the strength and truth to his words, and I nodded, unsure what I was agreeing to. He seemed to understand though.

He patted my hand and slowly opened the door. "I'll wait to hear from you, Fletcher."

He shut the door, and without even realizing it, he seemed to give me the exact thing I needed. Time, space, and control. It was getting harder and harder to *not* fall for him. And honestly, I was afraid it was already too late.

CHAPTER
NINETEEN

Michael

"What are you doing for parents' weekend?" Freddie asked me, three days later.

It was a simple question. A normal question for one roommate to ask another.

Yet, the impact of his words made me stumble. I dropped the glass I was drying into the sink, a loud clunk echoing in our place. "Shit."

The glass broke, and I picked up the pieces and started carrying them to our trash. My heart thudded against my ribcage, and each foot felt a million pounds heavier. He had no idea about my past. Why would he? I kept that shit locked up.

"Dude, you alright?" He stood from the couch and entered the small kitchen. Our unit was simple with two sides of the place that we each took up—our own bathroom and room—then a shared living room and kitchen area. Comfortable. Clean. It reflected the life I imagined here, free of the messes I left back home.

"Yeah, sorry," I said, my muscles tensing as I braced for him to ask the question again. I hated how I struggled with an answer. The truth wasn't complicated, but saying it out loud felt personal. Too personal. The line I drew around myself to keep out emotions got blurry. Mainly due to Naomi, who still hadn't called me, but I shoved the uncomfortable feelings about her away.

If I was going to ride the hot mess express today, I only wanted to deal with one issue at a time. "Slipped from my fingers," I said, picking up the final pieces and rinsing off a little blood. "Hope that didn't have sentimental value."

"It was a hand-me-down from my sister when she went to school here. Zero value." Freddie leaned against the kitchen wall and crossed his arms. "You okay?"

"Sure, it was a minor cut," I said, forcing my face to relax. His lowered brows told me he saw right through my façade, and I barked out a laugh. "Thanks for checking on me though."

"No, I meant about parents' weekend. I don't want to pry—"

"I'm fine," I said, way too quickly. He raised his dark brows and pushed off the wall. He was the same height as me, just a little leaner, and I wasn't sure if his proximity was supposed to make me feel caged in, but it did.

He held up his hands. "You have anyone coming into town?"

"My parents are dead."

I did it again. The tone. The absolute talent of making the entire room fill with sadness and discomfort. Ryann had a gift of being able to talk about our past without alienating herself. I preferred being on the ice and the protection of the team, a shield from the emotions. Something I didn't have any more. But Freddie's reaction was like all the others. He paled, shifted his weight, and frowned.

The next question would be how, so I answered without being prompted, "From a car accident about four years ago."

"Fuck." He ran a hand over his face. "That's horrible."

"Yeah."

"You want to attend any events with me and my folks? My dad is extra as hell. Has a full matching outfit with school colors and even dyes his hair."

It felt like a hand reached into my chest and squeezed my heart hard. My voice stopped working, and he backtracked.

"If you want," he said. "No pressure."

I cleared my throat. "Thanks for the invite. I didn't realize it was next weekend."

I had a unique talent of blocking out anything that reminded me of home, my family, and their death. Now that he mentioned it, flyers around campus came to mind, but my brain protected me and blurred the words. Now it made sense. The extra energy around campus, the older people slowly showing up everywhere.

"Yeah, with the hockey game and the football team both at home, a lot of parents will be there in their orange and blue. They draw a bunch of fans," Freddie said, clearly uncomfortable if his fidgeting and hand movements were any indication.

My face heated, and I focused on the ground, annoyed that I wasn't like my sister. She brought out the best in people when she shared her grief while I brought out the cringey-awkward part.

"I should—" I said, gripping the back of my neck hard just as Freddie cleared his throat. "Go," I finished.

He sighed, crossed his arms over his chest, and gave me a long look that reminded me of my old coach. Like he saw right through my bullshit and was going to raise the stakes. "I want to respect your walls, Michael, but you don't have to shoulder all of this alone. I know we're roommates, but I view you as a friend. If you want to chat, I'm here."

Fuck, my throat got weird. I nodded. His face relaxed, and he pushed off the wall, leaving the silence not as uncomfortable as it was before. The idea of opening up to him about everything made me break out in hives, but the fact he knew now felt like a weight was lifted off my shoulders. A boulder-sized weight.

I finished picking up the pieces of glass and got a text from Coach—he wanted to grab a drink that night to discuss my classes. I responded right away and instantly thought about his dinner with Naomi. Did they have a good time? Was she happy about it? Did she talk with Cami yet?

I needed to run, to work out the feelings manifesting inside me. I grabbed headphones, put on running shorts, and headed out. It was still warm for an October day, part of the weather holding onto that summer humidity, and I took my shirt off after the first mile.

Pushing my body and making my muscles work hard distracted my thoughts. I focused on breathing. On each step forward. My lungs pumping to get oxygen.

It felt freeing. The music blasted in my ears, and I matched my stride to the rhythm for twenty minutes. My emotions were still everywhere, my anxiety lingering past its welcome.

"Hey!" a voice shouted at me, and I stopped mid-stride, my stomach doing a swoop thing that it had no business doing. Naomi sat on the quad with short black shorts, a bright blue tank top, and a navy hat. She sat criss-cross with some books spread around her, and goddamn, the sun hit her face just right.

She was so pretty, and she smiled up at me with a slight pink tinge spreading over her cheeks and down her neck.

"Hey," I said back, removing my headphones. My chest heaved, and Naomi dropped her gaze to my pecs. Her teeth covered her bottom lip, and she took her sweet time dragging her gaze back up to my face. "Eyes up here, Fletcher."

"Mm," she said with a coy smile. "You're all sweaty."

"Yes, that happens when you run." I placed my hands on my hips and tried to catch my breath, not at all focusing on how tight her tank top was. How it hugged her perfect tits and made me replay the other day in my mind. For the millionth time.

"I've been thinking about you," she said, causing all the

blood rush down my body. I had to be careful, or it'd be uncomfortable with a boner in my running shorts.

"Uh, yeah, me too," I said, losing my confidence and sounding like a teenage boy crushing on the homecoming queen. I wasn't awkward. I was charming. "Is there anything in particular you're thinking about, or did my naked chest distract you?"

"Oh, it distracted me for sure." She laughed, and it came out all throaty. Not a helpful sound to hear. She changed her position so she leaned back onto her arms, thrusting her chest out in the air, and I let my gaze linger on her tits and the little sliver of stomach that teased me.

"You look hungry."

"I am." Shit, I almost growled at her and cleared my throat. Safe. I needed a safe topic that took us away from the fact we still hadn't talked about our potential *arrangement*. I should choose an easy topic. A better one to settle down the almost out of control lust I had for her.

Rubbing the back of my neck, I looked at the sky as I asked, "How did your dinner with your dad go?"

She let out a little sigh that took root in my gut. Then, she pushed her hair out of her eyes, and I swore the brown dulled. She chewed on the side of her lip and focused on something in the distance. "He cancelled on me *after* I started walking there."

"No fucking way." I scratched my chest as irritation at Coach Simpson flared inside me. "Why? Was there an emergency?"

She shrugged her slender shoulders and held her hand over her eyes to shield herself from the sun. It cast a shadow over her. "No idea. I asked if everything was okay, and he said *rain check*."

"Maybe it was serious," I said, really needing her dad to not be an asshole.

"Who knows? Him and Cami got lunch yesterday so…" She shrugged again, and I made a fist at my sides. "It's hard when he does this *and* doesn't respond to my email with another profile. I'm not trying to lay all my shit on you, but sometimes… what's the point?"

"I'm sorry." I meant it too. She met my eyes for a beat, a comfortable silence passing between us where I wasn't sure what to say. I knew she'd been excited about that dinner with her dad badly, and for him to pull this shit? I couldn't fix it for her, but I wanted to. I was still thinking of a response when her expression shifted from sad to *amused*. "Why are you smiling like that?"

"Honestly? You're so hot I can't stand it."

"I feel the same way," I replied, laughing at her candor. "I've had to redirect my thoughts a million times since we were at your place."

"I'm sorry I didn't reach out to you," she said, her voice small and her attention moving toward the ground. Without thinking, I sat next to her, leaving an inch between our bodies. Her shorts showed so much skin, and she'd definitely have little tan lines on her shoulders from her tank top. What I wouldn't give to touch her there and run my finger along her smooth skin.

Fuck, my skin felt too hot for my body.

She said something though, and I should respond. Not ogle her and fantasize about her shoulders. Not when she was still upset about her dad. If flirting with me made it easier for her, then I could stifle my need to fuck her. For now, at least.

"Why are you sorry? You should only do what makes you comfortable." My lips turned down at her hesitation. I didn't want us *almost* hooking up to cause her any issue. I could deal with my attraction to her without hurting her.

"It's not that." She spun to look at me. "You confuse me."

"Ah, yes, I understand that completely." I hit her shoulder with mine. She took a deep breath, her tongue wetting her bottom lip, and I followed the movement as my stomach tightened with an aggressive need.

I'd gone running to take my mind off my parents and ended up next to the other part of my life that I wasn't sure how to handle. How ironic. I snorted to myself, but it caused her to frown.

"I'm being annoying, aren't I?"

"Wait, no." I grinned and melted a bit when she returned the smile with that little scrunched nose. "I chuckled because I went running to clear my head, and here I am, next to you. I can't seem to get *you* out of my mind."

"Are you always so honest?" Her voice came out all throaty and husky, and she leaned closer to me. I wasn't sure she knew what she was doing, but I liked it.

"Yes. I try to be." I stared at her lips. "I'm thinking about your mouth again."

She sucked in a breath and looked at the sky, stretching out her smooth neck and not helping my growing attraction to her. "I can't catch feelings for you."

"I'm not trying to throw them at you."

I wasn't. Not really. I didn't want my heart involved either. Emotions were messy and made my chest feel tight, and I had enough sadness in my life. Light and easy was best, with only a small handful of people getting into that inner circle. Like Ryann. Like the team back east.

Like Naomi.

Nope. I slammed my eyes shut and mentally tossed her from that inner circle. When I opened them again, she looked stressed.

She pinched the bridge of her nose and steadied her gaze with me, a moment passing between us that felt heavier than just sitting and relaxing in the sun. Students were all around the quad, enjoying the Tuesday afternoon and the gorgeous weather. Music blared from a group of people a few yards away, and someone mowed the lawn on the south side. But that all faded into the background when Naomi looked at me with her brown eyes, like she could see into me.

There were a million reasons why I should've been freaked out, but I wasn't. She already knew most things about me. I didn't put on the show around her that I did with everyone else, and instead of running from it, I liked it.

"Do you live far from here?" she asked, her chest flushing. She chewed that lip again, and when her nostrils flared and she eyed my body, I got the message.

Fuck, I wanted to bite that lip until she came.

"Ten minute walk. Shorter if we run."

"I'm not running, but let's walk *fast*."

My blood pumped like it was working overtime as she picked up her books. My fingers itched to peel that tight tank off her body and remind her how good I was with my mouth. I'd start on the couch, then my bed. I'd take her hair down so I could see it all over my pillow. *Shit*. My cock hardened in my running shorts. She was taking too damn long, so I hoisted the rest of the books and shoved them into her bag, not bothering to zip it all the way.

"Wow, look at you being gentlemanly," she said, a mischievous grin on her lips.

"We both know that's not why I did that."

Her eyes flashed with understanding, and she pulled on the hem of her shirt like she was nervous. "Lead the way, Reiner."

She spoke with confidence, and I held out my hand, just to make sure she didn't change her mind. It had nothing to do with connecting with her and everything to do with how badly I wanted to see her body. Saturday was just a tease, and maybe I'd get over this insane need for her after sleeping with her.

A fuck her out of my head plan. That always worked well.

She placed her palm against mine, sending a ripple of electricity up my arm. Just from her skin on mine. We stood there, her backpack on my arm and her hand in mine, and every cell on my body burned with need, want, desire.

We took two steps toward my place when Cami fucking Simpson walked into view from the south end of the quad. She wore a tiny outfit that I could only describe as an overall dress and little else. She eyed our hands and looked at Naomi, her eyes wide and nervous. Of all the fucking times she could've appeared. Right now? When I was minutes away from tasting Naomi again? My dick was hard as fuck, and my left eye twitched with irritation.

What a cockblock.

God. My jaw clenched, and I could feel Naomi pulling away. Not just physically, but emotionally. Her eyes got misty, and she stilled.

"Hey," she said, the emotion in her voice almost too much to hear. Her grip on my hand tightened, like my fingers held the answer.

Cami's attention moved to my chest for a beat before she grinned. "I can see you're busy."

"No, no." Naomi almost jumped away from me. Rationally, I knew it wasn't personal. This was Coach's other fucking daughter. The second most dangerous person to see us *holding hands.* Fuck.

I didn't want Naomi to be in a worse situation because of me, so I handed her the bag. She eyed me with want and regret, and I squeezed her shoulder.

"This is more important. I'll be fine."

She looked down at my waist, and for one second, my dick twitched. She took the bag from me and sighed. "I'll call you to talk about the *project.*"

I nodded, unable to be upset with her when I could feel the hurt pouring from her sister. My goddamn libido was out of control, and I wanted nothing more than to have Naomi naked in my bed for a full day, but her family mattered. With a small wave, I winked and took off in the other direction. I raced home and didn't do more than grunt in greeting at Freddie before going straight to my shower.

I had my cock in my hand a second after the water turned on, and I pictured Naomi's perky tits and the way her skin felt against mine. Her sounds, the way she sucked my tongue and kissed me back. *Yes.* I pumped harder and felt the familiar pleasure start at my spine and work its way up. I came hard just *thinking* about her.

How was I going to survive once I had her?

CHAPTER
TWENTY

Naomi

I shouldn't have watched Michael's back muscles as he walked away from us. It made me regret *not* going with him. Even though I couldn't. Not when we agreed to keep this a secret between us. It was too important to remain friends in public, and worry etched its way down my spine. Cami totally saw us holding hands.

Was this thing ruined before I even got to sleep with him? My intent had been clear until my damn sister showed up. Irritation danced on my spine as I eyed her. She watched Michael's ass and whistled.

"He is *hot*."

Anger reared its head, and I made a fist at my side. "Going to go after him too?"

She scoffed and popped one hip out to the side. While my expressions gave every emotion and feeling I had away, my sister was the opposite. She could be thinking about serial killers or cute babies and no one would know the difference. Still, a part of me, a small part, wanted to make her feel bad.

To see her squirm.

But she didn't. She arched one brow and laughed. "You must think the worst of me."

"I've lost track of the good, Cami." I pushed my hair out of my face, forcing the final thoughts of Michael and the heat in his eyes away. Later. I could worry about him later.

"Could we talk?"

"I mean, sure. Like I've done most of my life, I'll adapt to your schedule." I put my backpack on my back and pointed like I was a freshman tour guide. "Where do you want to go?"

Cami played with a buckle on her outfit, and for one half second, she looked sad, a flash of vulnerability on her ice-cold face. My soul hurt for my twin who had once been someone I shared my entire life with. But as quick as it happened, her regular *resting bitch face* returned, blocking off any hint at what she was thinking.

"Here's fine. I want to feel the sun on my face anyway." She sat on the grass and leaned back, her tiny outfit rising up. When the light hit her, I noticed the bags under her eyes. My sister had a skin-care routine that was intense, so this was a new development.

"Did you walk here to find me, or did you see me with Michael and want to intrude?" I asked, sitting down and looking over my shoulder.

"Our phones still show our locations. I realized you were on the quad and thought it'd be the perfect chance to talk." She still closed her eyes, but there was a lilt to her voice. "You didn't tell Dad about Saturday, right?"

"No, Cami, I didn't."

"Thanks. He's been on my case enough." She sighed and ran a hand over her face and groaned. "He didn't ask you about Gage though, right?"

"He cancelled on me last minute, so we never got dinner," I said the words fast as my face flushed with embarrassment.

"He'll make it up to you, don't worry. He's done that with me a few times and always brought me lunch to apologize."

She grinned, like her words were supposed to make me feel better.

"It was days ago, and he won't respond to a text, Cami."

"Hm." She pursed her red lips as a brief frown line appeared between her eyebrows. "He said he sees you every week for your project though. You're doing a data report for him on game stats? That's good, right? You talk and stuff?"

"By talk, you mean he has me reporting to Michael? Sure. Yeah, it's great."

"Michael is easy on the eyes, Nana." She winked and let out a slow whistle. I didn't know how to respond with all the thoughts of our dad intruding. He cancelled on Cami but made it up to her. He told her my project was game stats? He belittled my project to my twin sister?

My face prickled with the urge to cry. I sniffed and looked at the sun to act like my watering eyes were from the brightness. Cami didn't seem to pay attention though.

She shifted her position and lowered her voice as she asked, "Nana, do you *really* think I go after guys you're into on purpose?"

Ah, we were getting right to it. *Move over, Dad drama, Cami's taking spot one right now.*

I blew out a breath, focused on settling my racing heart, and nodded. "It's happened three times. So, yeah, I do."

"I had *no* idea about Gage. I ran into him at a frat party, and he pursued me. It wasn't until Michael mentioned something at the diner that I realized you two had a past. I swear it." She picked up a blade of grass and ran it through her fingers. "Who else?"

"Isiah from high school. We kissed three times before he dumped me for you. Then, Henry the summer before college."

She winced, surely remembering how she flaunted those guys around. Henry was the worst because he was so out of my league, I knew better than it think it was anything. It was my idea to keep our hooking up private. *Kinda like Michael…*

"Isiah…he said he wasn't seeing anyone, and Henry… fuck. I had no idea, Naomi. None. I would *never* intentionally hurt you."

"You did though, Cami." I took a shaky breath and waited for my sister to meet my eyes. "It's not about the guys, well, not all of it. It's everything that's happened in the past six years."

She sucked in a breath and let her guard down. My real sister was here, not the painted version she put on for everyone else. "The divorce."

"Part of it, yeah." I too, picked up some of the grass and ripped it in half. It gave me something to do with the nervous energy filling me head to toe. At this rate, there'd be no grass remaining in the center of the quad. "You got Dad. Mom got a new family. I was left behind."

"That's not my fault," she said, her voice raising. "I can't help that—"

"I'm not saying it is. I'm telling you where I'm at and how I see things." I swallowed down the lump in my throat. "I lost everyone, so I stopped assuming best intentions. You and Dad have the jokes, and you got the parent to lean on while I lost you all. So yeah, we grew apart which is fine, but what was I supposed to think, Cami? You stopped wanting to hang out with me. You stopped viewing me as an equal. We never did anything just the two of us after we turned fifteen. Not *once*. You stopped our movie nights and milkshake runs. You hung out with your shitty mean girl clique and partied."

"Did you ever think that I didn't want to spend time with you because I was jealous?" she said, saying the thing that shocked me to my core.

My beautiful, popular, had-everything-in life sister was jealous of me? No way. I laughed. "How is that possible?"

"You think I had it all?" She smiled, but it was filled with pain that I felt in my soul. "Dad's terrified I'm going to elope or get pregnant. Mom thinks I'm *too* much and a bad influence on her new kids, so she never talks to me anymore. I have no idea what I want to do in my life, and yeah, I'm pretty and can dance. Those are useless skills, Nana. You have brains and real friends who've got your back. Even in high school, you had genuine friends. I never did. Plus, Dad doesn't have to worry about you. Sure, we have jokes, but we don't openly fight in front of you. Where he tells me he's embarrassed about my actions and that I should be more like *you*."

Cami sniffed and wiped her nose with the back of her arm. My mouth hung open, my mind shattered at her confession. I was utterly speechless. My perfect sister was maybe a little broken.

She cleared her throat and looked at the sky. "I was at a strip club because I needed to feel something other than pity. I went out with this shady as fuck dude, and we ended up there. He went down on a dancer in a private room and wanted me to join. Apparently, they're together and bring in third parties for fun."

"Jesus," I said, exhaling as I tried to analyze her pain, her words, her perceptions. I'd be a fool if I didn't admit I was a little relieved to hear our dad didn't hate me, that my sister's life wasn't all rainbows. We each had our struggles, but the saddest thing about her confession was that she'd truly felt she was utterly alone. I reached over and said to hell with it. I pulled her into a hug, and she fell on top of me.

"What are you doing, you weirdo?" she said, laughing as I squeezed my arms around her. "Nana, stop it. People are watching."

"I don't care. I feel like I have my sister back." God, those words filled me with a sense of home. *Finally.*

She stilled, and slowly, she wrapped her arms around me and returned the hug.

"You're never by yourself, Cami, and I've been jealous of you too. For years. It sounds like we're both a little messed up."

"Yeah, we are." She sniffed again, and we adjusted so we both lay in the grass, our faces up toward the sky. She reached out for my hand, and I grabbed it. "I truthfully never tried to date guys you were into. I need you to know that."

"Okay." I squeezed her hand. "I believe you."

It was weird to forgive her for years of strife that quickly. But seeing her break down changed things. Cami didn't cry. Never in all our lives. My sister was hurting.

"I think we need weekly dates."

"Yeah?" she asked, a little lilt of hope to her tone. "Me and you?"

"Yup. To work on us. To go back to being friends, not just sisters."

"I'd like that."

"Me too."

We sat there, chatting idly about her dance team and about my internship with our dad. Conversation flowed easily when I didn't assume the worst, and the uncomfortable wedge driven between us chipped away a bit. Not all of it. That would take time. But a good chunk had shifted. We parted ways after a good hour with plans to meet at the student union on Thursday for lunch. She had to get ready to dance at the game Friday, and it was the only time we were both free until next week.

After I put my headphones in and headed back toward my place, I realized the first person I wanted to tell was Michael. He'd be so happy to learn we were working on things. I sent him a text.

Naomi: Are you home?

Michael: Yup.

Naomi: I'm coming over.

Michael: Sweet. I hope the talk went well. Really. I know that's been weighing on you.

He meant the words too. Even in our lust-fueled haze, he'd known how much Cami meant to me and left so I didn't have to ask him to. Dangerous territory for me. That was for sure.

Something stung on my lower back as I made the journey there and then again on my side. I scratched at the spot but winced at the continual stings and went faster toward Michael's place. All my thoughts about getting him naked, about confiding in him about Cami evaporated from my mind as the stings grew worse. I slammed my fist against his door, and he opened it not two seconds later.

"Hey—what's wrong?"

"My backpack." I dropped my bag on the ground and lifted part of my shirt. Red dots covered my side and back, and a little black thing crawled on my skin. "What the hell is that?"

"Ants." Michael winced and swatted at my skin a few times. "Shit, they're all over you. Come on, you need to take this off."

I cringed and wanted to throw up. Ants were so gross. SO GROSS. I followed him into his bathroom and started stripping. I had one thing on my mind—getting these little insect fuckers away from me. "I must've sat on them or something."

"They're on your bag too." He cringed and held it up. "Is anything valuable in here?"

My shirt was on the floor. Then my shorts. "My phone. Wallet."

Michael frowned as he opened the large part of my backpack and pulled them out. "I'm setting this outside. Be right back."

He left the bathroom. An ant was in the waistband of my panties, and that was it. I stepped out of them, kicking them across the room and yanking my bra off. This was my worst nightmare. Ant bites. What if they'd crawled *inside me*? I shook in disgust and turned the water on in the shower, not waiting for it to get hot before I went in.

"Here I brought you a—" Michael froze at the doorway. His shower was a clear glass wall, and I stood, naked as hell, three feet from him.

His throat bobbed, and the tube of medicine dropped as he joined me in the bathroom and shut the door. His eyes trailed from my face to my chest, to my pussy, then down my legs. He ran a hand through his hair, and he cleared his throat. "Uh, do you need me to uh, check out the bites?"

"Could you? I can't see on my back." My voice came out strong and smooth, which was the opposite of my insides. He looked at me like I was the sexiest thing alive, and my lower stomach tightened with lust. He swallowed and took a step closer to the shower. I turned, giving him full view of my back and my ass, and he reached out to trail a finger over my bites. The hot water blasted over my already burning body.

"Shit. They look infected." His touch gave me goosebumps, and he *totally* saw me shiver. His fingers lingered on my lower back, then trailed up my spine. "Naomi."

The way he said my name had me closing my eyes. He said it like it mattered, like I mattered, totally shattering the *let's hook-up* plan. I turned around slowly, watching how his gaze heated as he glanced at my mouth. I bit down on my lip, unsure what to do when Michael stepped into the shower, clothes and all. He was getting soaked, but he didn't seem to care.

I didn't have time to react when he slammed his mouth on mine, searing me with a kiss that made me weak in the knees, all tongue and teeth. Holy boner town.

He backed me up into the shower wall and kissed down my neck, biting my earlobe as he groaned. "Fuck, Naomi. You're a walking dream."

I shivered at his words and gasped when he hoisted me up and wrapped my legs around him. He was soaking wet and clothed. That was a real problem.

"This. Off." I tugged at his shirt, unable to form normal sentences now that he was here kissing me, looking at me with the same hunger I felt in my core. He smiled before using his hips to hold me in place as he yanked off his shirt.

His muscles were divine. No other way to describe them. I ran my hands over every curve and bulge, and he groaned into my mouth again. He moved his hands to graze the sides of my breasts before he gripped my waist, hard. He panted when he rested his forehead against mine.

"I should take care of your bites. That was my goal," he said, just above a whisper. The hot water pounded onto us, filling the air with a mist, and the shower smelled like him. His soap.

"Take care of me then," I said into his mouth. He broke our kiss and turned me around, getting a bar of soap from the ledge and running it over my back. He was so gentle, feathering kissing on my shoulder, neck, back as he cleaned the bite marks.

He spent a lot of time on them before returning the bar to the edge. But now, he gripped my ass. He kneaded each cheek and spread them apart before reaching between my thighs. I sucked in a breath, and he stilled.

"No, that wasn't *stop* gasp. That was an *about time* gasp. Touch me, Michael, please."

Still with my back to his chest, he reached between my legs, and I sighed in relief when he slid a finger inside me. The fact I couldn't see him made this better, kinkier. More *friends with benefits*. It fit what I needed us to be, but after a few seconds of his thrusting finger, he slid out and turned me around.

His eyes were hooded and filled with heat as he brought the finger to his mouth. Oh my word. He flashed me a dangerous smile before getting onto his knees. Michael Reiner, who still wore pants, was on his knees in the shower. It was possible I could pass out from lust.

"I'm being selfish right now, but god, look at you." He eyed my legs, running his hands up and down my thighs before spreading them and lifting me. He had my legs resting on his shoulders, my back pressed against the wall, and he looked up at me with water falling from his lashes. "Tell me what you like, okay? I'll start slow."

Oh, start slow he did. He dragged his tongue along my inner thighs, nipping the sensitive skin before moving over to my pussy. I trembled with a terrifying need as he flicked my clit once, twice, then again. He didn't move fast. Not at all. He flattened his tongue on me and stroked like he had all the time in the world.

I saw stars behind my eyes as the water pounded against us. I gripped his hair to steady myself as pleasure built. This was the most intimate act, and instead of feeling worried or self-conscious, I felt safe, wanted, desired. Each stroke of his tongue had me whimpering. Despite his *slow rhythm*, my orgasm ripped out of me like it was desperate to escape. I trembled, tightening my legs around his shoulders as he never picked up his pace. His hands dug into my bare hips as I came apart, and when I caught my breath, he stared up at me with awe in his eyes.

"Delicious. You are delicious." He licked his lips and stood, grabbing the front of my neck and dragging me closer to him. He led this show, and I was happy to let him. My toes tingled from that orgasm, and I wasn't sure which way was up at the moment.

"How's your back feeling?" he asked.

"Um, don't even know where my back is."

He laughed and pulled me out of the shower, turning off the water and handing me a towel. He stripped down, his very erect dick hitting his stomach, and my mouth watered at the sight of him. Strong toned thighs with a dusting of dark hair. His full thick cock jutting out against his washboard abs. His tattooed arms hung at the side, and I couldn't stop staring at him.

"You're beautiful," I muttered, like a drooling fool.

He winked. "I have plans for you."

I literally shivered at the promise of his words. He took my hand and led me to his room, and I wanted so badly to stare at all the parts of him he kept hidden. The photos on the wall, the stickers on his laptop. What did they mean? Why did they matter to him?

I didn't get a chance though.

He backed me up until my knees hit the bed, and he crawled

over me. "You, Naomi Simpson-Fletcher, are distracting as hell. Now, is your phone on silent, or is someone else going to interrupt me before I devour you head to toe?"

I shook my head, my stomach exploding into millions of butterflies. Not just a few. Millions. They swarmed and danced, and my breath caught in my throat when Michael pressed a soft kiss on my mouth. This kiss felt personal, tender, *deep*.

It didn't take long though. Michael's eyes flashed with heat as he took a nipple in his mouth and pulled. It stung at first but then it felt *hot*.

"You're mine for the next hour, Naomi. If you have any hesitation, tell me right fucking now."

"No, none." I meant it too, even though my heart galloped inside at the way he stared at me. Because having Michael look and kiss and touch me like this? It was a fantasy come to life.

CHAPTER
TWENTY-ONE

Michael

More skin. More contact. That's what I wanted. *More.* I teased Naomi's tits until she turned into putty beneath me, squirming and moaning as her wet hair splayed out in every direction. Her pink perky nipples stood on end, and I bit down on one, harder than before, and she bounced off the bed.

"Did you like that?"

"Um, yes?" Her cheeks were pink and her eyes wide, but it was her lips that did me in. Swollen and puffy from kissing me.

"Um isn't a good enough answer. We almost got caught last time I did this." I kissed her nipple again, sucking it until it made a loud pop. "Yes or no?"

She nodded, and I clicked my tongue. "Say it."

"Yes, I like when you do that."

"Don't be bashful on me, Fletcher." I kissed down her stomach and below her belly button, over the silver ring, before I looked up again. I tugged at the ring a bit, loving the piercing on her. "My mouth's been on you, so there's nothing to hide from me."

She quivered, and I licked her nipple long and hard before I reached for my bedside table. I grabbed a condom and put it on, studying Naomi's reaction before going further. Our chemistry was insane, but I was more experienced than her, and I didn't want her to be uncomfortable. "How are you feeling?"

"What?" she asked, snapping her gaze to my dick. "You're asking me that with your massive dick just in the air, swinging around?"

"Yes," I said, laughing as I crawled over her. I held myself up with my forearms. She looked up at me, her eyes wide and manic, and I kissed her quick. "Because I want to fuck you, but I want you to be alright first."

"Michael, if you don't stop talking, I'm going to get pissed."

I laughed again and grabbed her hip as I crawled on top of her. Despite the fun and teasing, I couldn't get enough of this woman. Everything about her squirming body got me harder. She dug her fingers into my shoulders as I kissed her collarbone and the trio of birthmarks on the edge of it. She bucked her hips, impatient as hell, and I smiled against her skin. "Are you wet for me?"

"Jesus, yes," she said, her pleading voice sending a flurry of desire through me. I loved her like this—open and needy and finally *mine*. I nudged my dick into her slowly as I kissed her on the mouth. She gasped against my lips, and something passed between us as our gaze held. It was…surreal.

I thrusted a few times, letting her adjust to me, and I swore I saw stars. She was tight as hell, warm, and I grunted at how amazing she felt. How right. It'd been a few months for me, but man, I wanted to bury my face in her neck and fuck her until I couldn't see straight. She made me get that way. Wild.

"Damn, I swear I can feel you in my throat," she gasped. She brought her hands to my ass and squeezed. "Mm, you're so meaty. I love it."

"Meaty?" I said, thrusting a little faster as I got into a better position. Her legs were wrapped around me, and she arched her hips up just enough so I could tell a difference. I buried my face in her neck, taking in her lemon scent and her warm skin.

"Meaty. Thick," she said, groaning when I went deeper. "Oh, Michael, damn, you're big."

"Do you need me to slow down?" I asked, finding the willpower to stop thrusting. It hurt my raging hard-on to pull out, but I paused and glanced at her.

"Wow, no, please don't." She wiggled her hips against me and pulled me down so my weight was on her. "I like feeling you like this, on me."

She cupped my face with one hand and kissed me deep, making me forget for a second that this was just a friends with benefits situation. This wasn't an emotional fuck, despite all the confusing feelings combining in my head. This wasn't a relationship, even though she knew me so well. I kissed her back and rocked into her again and again, desperate to get off ever since I'd had a taste of her all those days ago.

"Touch your clit for me," I said, my hands digging into her ass and holding on. She did as I said. "Swirl it around. Get yourself nice and prepped."

"For what?"

I continued my pace and showered her with light kisses and nips. As the heat started at the base of my spine, I pulled out and flipped her over. I slid in from behind and reached around from the back to swirl a finger around her clit. She trembled as I thrusted in over and over. She felt so damn good that my thoughts got messy. Her scent, her sounds, her body. Nothing else mattered anymore. Just her, her pleasure, her squirming. She squeezed her legs together, making her pussy feel even tighter, and I growled against her sweaty neck. Her wet hair stuck to my face, and she panted beneath me. The slap of skin against skin, her soft groans, and the sound of me fucking her filled the room.

It was so fucking hot. I took her arms and held them over her head as I pounded into her. She arched her back, providing me the exact angle I needed, and pleasure shot out of me without warning.

"*Naomi, fuck,*" I moaned, my vision blurring as my entire body convulsed with white hot pleasure.

She bucked and thrashed on the bed as she yelled, '*Yes!*' way too loudly. "Michael, oh shit, whoa," she said, her body going limp. Sweat pooled between her skin and my chest, and I kissed the back of her neck before rolling over her. My ears still rang from the joy of being with her, and my god, why hadn't we been doing that the entire time?

"Damn, Fletcher," I said, dragging my hand over her back to end on those damn dimples. "Damn."

"Good damn, right?" she asked, lifting her head to face me and resting on her chin on her wrist. "Because, whoa mama. That was…"

"Yeah. That was," I said, not needing to explain more. I knew what she meant, but since we were keeping this in the friends-only zone, we had to be comfortable with how we talked about us, sex. Like, could I beg to do this every day or four times a week? I wasn't sure about the right protocol for friends-who-bang-like-animals-with-benefits.

Naomi blew out a long breath, let out a little laugh, and plopped back down onto my bed. "I need to catch my breath. Regain feeling in my feet. Then, maybe, I can put clothes on again."

Clothes. I frowned, something nagging at me. *Right.* "Roll over," I said, getting up from the bed butt ass naked. The cream I had to help with cuts sat on my dresser, and I picked up the tube. "I want to look at those bites."

"Oh wow, I forgot about those." She frowned and ran a hand through her hair "Wait, now I can feel them. Ugh, they sting and itch. Why did you mention it?"

"On your belly," I said again, kneeling onto the bed and sucking in a breath at the raised bites. They looked angry and painful. "I shouldn't have kissed you," I said, my voice deep and laced with shame.

"You already regret sleeping with me?" she fired back, her tone sharp.

"No, no, *no*." I ran a hand down her spine, enjoying how her soft skin broke out in goosebumps. "I meant, these damn bites. I should've helped you with these first, not attacked your mouth."

"I didn't mind."

That put a smile on my face. "Yeah, I rather liked seeing you wet and naked in my shower."

I applied some medicine on my fingertips and swiped them over the bites. She jumped a little, and I put my other hand on her hip to hold her steady. Ryann was allergic to mosquito bites, and they could swell into golf balls. These didn't look too far off from that. "Did you lay on an ant hill or what?"

She groaned. "I must've. Can you sex me up again to distract me from the pain, or do you have plans?"

She asked the question so casually, like she was offering up a snack, and I snorted. "I'd very much like to *sex you up*, but how about later? I'm going to grab some ice to see if I can get the swelling down."

She looked over her shoulder to stare at me, a line appearing between her brows. "You're being a real mother hen. It's sweet."

"It can happen." I winked, ignoring the swell of my heart at her words. Taking care of others was easier than taking care of myself. Plus, the little ailments I had from being an athlete all these years? Unless a bone was shattered, I knew basic first aid. "Stay put."

"Yes, sir."

I put on a pair of loose shorts and headed into the kitchen to make an ice pack. Tossing some ice into a plastic bag, I found a clean towel and headed back to my room. I had two hours before I met with her dad—shit. Just thinking of Coach sent my alarm bells on high alert.

I slept with his daughter.

My boss's daughter.

What did I do?

Deep breath in, then out. I reached for the counter to steady myself and thought through everything like a play. Worrying was too late since I'd already slept with her. That line was crossed. We agreed to just be friends, so it wasn't like I would hurt her. Friends with benefits was a thing. We were adults. Consenting, horny adults.

I ran a hand down my face and ignored the growing pang in my chest. I could worry about all that stuff later. I had a mission, and that was to help her bites. I marched back into my room and found her wearing one of my t-shirts. My breath lodged in my throat. Her hair hung down on her shoulders, the large orange shirt way too big for her. A smile lifted her lips as she held a picture of Ryann and me. She must've sensed me because she looked up, blushed, and set the frame down.

"You're not naked in my bed."

She shrugged, but a small smile remained. "No."

I narrowed my eyes and jutted my chin toward the photo. "That's my sister, Ryann."

"I can tell. You have the same eyes," she said, her voice soft and gentle. It was like a warm blanket after spending all day outside. Wait, what?

Was I spouting poetry because I finally got laid?

My eye twitched, and I was irritated with myself. I took the frame from her hand and set it back on the shelf above my desk. The photo didn't face the bed because a) that was weird and b) photos made me more sad than happy. "Shirt up, Fletcher."

"Are you always this aggressive with the ladies?"

"When they're having an allergic reaction, yes." I made a point to relax my face. It wasn't her fault my mind was having a field day. She sighed before going back to the bed and lifting the end of her shirt up. It showed off her luscious ass, and I admired the two dimples at the base of her spine. I loved back dimples. I wanted to swirl my tongue in them and spend an hour teasing her there, but that wouldn't help her.

The bites. I refocused. I applied the cream and smoothed it on her skin, frowning as they seemed to get bigger. "You need allergy medicine."

"No, I'm fine." She moved the shirt back down and rolled over, pushing herself up onto her elbows and grinning at me. "Dare I say, you're being adorable."

"I'm not *adorable*. Watch your mouth, Fletcher." I narrowed my eyes at her, but she stuck out her tongue, and my heart fucking did a cartwheel. "I have some Benadryl you should take. Seriously. They look bad."

"That makes me sleepy though. Like, twenty minutes after, I'm passed out."

"Do you have plans tonight?"

"No, but—"

"Then do it. Sleep here. I don't care." I motioned to the rest of my bed. "Seriously, I don't need that much room, and I have to head out in an hour anyway. Use my bed."

"But what if I find out all your secrets?"

I grinned, wide at that, and swatted her leg. She had no idea that she knew almost everything already. "Go ahead and try."

Her lips curved up, and in that moment with both of us smiling, I could picture what it would be like to be hers. To be with her. To tell her all the things going on in my head and heart. She wouldn't judge me or laugh or downplay it. She'd listen. My smile faltered, and I looked away, needing to break the connection. Relationships were so not my thing.

Plus, her dad.

The dad who upset her countless times. God, this was messed up.

Get it together, Reiner.

With my back to Naomi, I rummaged through my desk drawer to find the little white bottle. I grabbed a pill and handed it to her. "It's settled then. You take this and stay here as long as you need."

"Yes, sir." She mock saluted me, and the urge to *kiss* her had nothing to do with the attraction growing between us. It had everything to do with this pull toward her, the way she teased me like I was just a normal guy. That I wasn't broken and lost on the inside, and I craved that more than air.

"You're a real pain in the ass," I teased, tickling her foot. She kicked me, and I gripped her foot, pulling her back onto the bed. That left me leaning over her, my heart pounding against my ribcage. Her breath hit my face, and she put the pill in her mouth, reached for my water bottle on the side table, and swallowed.

She then sighed and fluffed my pillows around her head, and I just watched her. The way her hair covered my pillow. The way she pressed her lips together to get some of the water that spilled on her mouth. The way her pulse raced at the base of her neck.

"I'm not kidding, Michael, I'm going to pass out in like ten minutes. You sure, you're sure?"

"Sleep. Rest. Relax." I squeezed her forearm. "What kind of friend would I be if I told you to get lost?"

Maybe it was me or the way the light streamed from my window, but I caught a slight frown on her face. I couldn't be sure, but the smile that was there second before faltered. Just a bit. "The worst kind."

"I can't handle being the worst at anything," I teased, needing to see that smile return. I waited, my muscles tightening when her gaze softened. I could breathe again. "I have to head out in a bit. I won't wake you if you're asleep. Should only be an hour. If it takes longer, I'll text you."

"Sounds good," she said, her breathing becoming deeper. I got up from my bed and repositioned the covers so they rested over her. Without thinking, I bent down and pressed a quick kiss on her forehead.

"Be here when I get back, please?"

She opened her eyes and blinked at me. She stared so long I ran a hand over my mouth like I had food there or a weird mole I didn't know about. My stomach sank like I had disappointed her, but then she nodded. "Only because you said please."

I snorted, squeezed her knee, and got ready to go meet her dad. It was a real confusing onslaught of emotions to not want to leave her but to also go face her father. With one last look, I finished getting ready and left her in my room, hoping like hell she would still be there when I got back because things had shifted now.

We'd slept together, and it was so different from any sex I had before. That complicated the *no feelings* thing we wanted to do. It'd have been easier if it was just a hot fuck and not… emotional. I pinched the bridge of my nose on the walk and focused on the leaves changing colors instead of the anxiety itching inside my chest.

Even if I *wanted* more with Naomi, she'd said no. Plus, if she did even think about being more…her dad was legit my boss. So, I had to keep remembering friends was easier and safer for me. I did not have big feelings for Naomi Fletcher, the nerdy goddess who made me feel at home despite being thousands of miles from it.

Liar.

I was in deep shit.

CHAPTER
TWENTY-TWO

Naomi

Why did he have to smell so good? It made everything harder to ignore when all I wanted to do was bury my face in his pillow and blankets. It wouldn't be weird as long as I didn't get caught.

Okay, was that the meds talking because what the hell was I doing? Smelling some guy's sheets? My face burned with embarrassment, and I rolled over in the bed, my muscles relaxed and my mind a little fuzzy. Okay, yeah. That had to be the medicine.

I eyed the clock and bolted up. Whoa. I'd napped for three hours. In Michael's bed. I rubbed my hands over my eyes and used the bathroom before finding my phone. Not a single text waited for me.

Wow, were my roommates the worst or what? Did they not worry about if I'd been kidnapped? I hadn't been at the apartment all day! The audacity of them to not care! I blew out a breath and texted Mona that I'd be home soon just as footsteps thudded outside Michael's door.

He's back!

My heart galloped like a damn racehorse as I tried to look cool. Did I sit up straighter? Pretend to sleep? Gah! I hadn't decided how to pose by the time he walked in, and when his gaze met mine, my entire body broke out in goosebumps. I was intelligent enough to know he looked pleased as hell to see me.

"Hey," I said, my sleepy voice coming out all sexy and deep. I didn't hate how I sounded.

He wet his bottom lip before sitting on the edge of his bed and putting his hand on my leg. "Lift up that shirt."

"I should've known you'd be bossy in the bedroom," I said, unable to stop myself from teasing him. He made me feel audacious and outgoing and wild. His eyes flared, and he clicked his tongue.

He jutted his chin toward the hem of my shirt, and I lifted it up, exposing my butt and lower back. He reached out and lightly touched the bumps. I shivered, not entirely sure if I was chilly or if his touch was the cause.

"Hey, they look better," he said.

"I don't even feel them anymore."

"You able to sleep a little?" he asked, his hands moving from the bumps to my lower back. He dug his strong fingers into the place right above my butt, and I groaned.

"I'm putty. That feels so good."

"I've thought about these dimples every second since I left you here." His voice was gruff and low. My stomach swooped when something warm tickled my skin.

"Did you just… lick me?"

"Yes." He did the same thing again, his tongue swirling around my lower back. "These fucking dimples are my weakness. Fuck, Naomi," he said, a desperate edge to his voice that got me hotter.

No one had ever said *fuck* in that grave way to me before. Just Michael. I hummed approval, and he lifted my shirt up higher, kissing his way up my spine. A horrible intrusive thought burst through my mind—did he do this with all his lady friends? Kiss their spines and take care of them?

He probably did. He was a good guy, but I couldn't let that bother me. Not when we'd agreed on friends. Just friends who hooked up. He kneaded my ass with his hands as he bit the spot where my shoulder met my neck.

"Oh god," I moaned. His touch felt so good.

"What is it about you?" he murmured.

I wasn't sure if he was talking to me or to himself, so I didn't answer. Instead, I closed my eyes and took in everything. The musty scent of the bed, the way he smelled like outside, and the rough pads of his fingertips exploring my ass and back. He was overwhelming in the best way, and my pussy throbbed with need.

"You don't feel sleepy or anything from the medicine, right?" he asked, his lips flirting with the outside of my ear.

I shivered again and squirmed beneath him. "Not even a little bit. Not anymore."

"Good." He lifted me up and turned me around so I sat with my legs spread wide on top of his lap. I still wore nothing under the shirt, and my face flushed with embarrassment.

He could see *everything.*

"You're so fucking pretty, Naomi." He took my shirt off and trailed kisses over my collarbone, over my pebbled nipples. The pressure in my core was enough to kill me.

"Michael," I said in a hazy daze as each one of his touches had me falling a little deeper. He seemed to understand the neediness of my voice, and he ripped his own shirt off. He pulled me close so we were chest to chest, and he kissed me, hard.

It wasn't aggressive like before. This kiss was slow and steady. His tongue slid into my mouth, probing me, teasing me, like he had all the time in the world. I rocked against him, his erection throbbing beneath me, and he growled against my mouth.

"This is insane," he said, pausing our kiss to look down at me. "I just had you, but I need more."

"Me too." My heart stumbled as his blue gaze met mine, his chest heaving with the same urgency. "Me too," I said again, bending down and biting his bottom lip. "Please," I begged, unsure what I was asking for.

To fuck me? To stop teasing me? To not break my heart?

All of the above?

He grinned against my mouth before lifting me and tossing me onto the bed. No more gentle Michael. He looked feral, and holy shit, it was hot. Super hot.

He undid his belt and slid out of his pants and boxers, his massive dick already thick and hard. "Grab a condom, Naomi. Put it on me before you get on top of me."

"On top of you?" I asked, my voice small and shy all of a sudden. I wasn't a virgin, but we both knew I was way less experienced than him.

"Yes." His eyes flashed with heat. He cupped my neck with his large hand, not in a frightening way, but a totally hot, seductive way. He trailed his thumb over my bottom lip, and I whimpered. "Your back is healing, and you might be sore. You can set the pace then."

He spoke so softly I blinked back emotion. He was worried about me. My poor heart.

I took the condom and ripped it open, my fingers shaking as I slid it over his cock. His massive dick pulsated beneath my hand. I'd never done that before, but after a nervous glance at his face, I relaxed at his expression. Warmth. Trust. Softness. He lay on his back, and I carefully climbed over him. His stomach muscles clenched as I straddled him, aware of the light dusting of hair leading to his cock. I could stare at his naked body for hours and find something new. The slight scar under his ribs, the dark shadows of tattoos on his arm. He was dangerously beautiful, inside and out.

He leaned up and took my nipple in his mouth, swirling his tongue around it until he released it with a pop.

My body clenched with need. I positioned myself over him and oh so slowly guided his cock into me. "Damn," I said, feeling full from his length. I was a little tender from earlier, and he gripped my waist, slowly helping me set the pace.

"Take your time, Naomi, I want this to be good for you."

I arched my hips and leaned forward, aware that he could see all of me. Each roll, each imperfection of my body. The insecurity didn't last long though. He touched and kissed everywhere, essentially kissing the worry away. I didn't have time to think about how my boobs jiggled as I rocked on him or if my stomach looked too big.

He pulled at my nipples then touched my clit. His eyes darkened, and his mouth went slack as sweat pooled between our bodies. This slow build up was a special form of torture. I needed more pressure, but before I could reach the peak, he stilled his hand and cupped my head, moving me down to kiss him.

It was weird, holding eye contact while we kissed and he thrusted inside me. Sex had never been this personal before, this *intense*. And we were just friends! Imagine how it'd be if we were—no. *No*.

"Hey, where'd you go?" he asked, his entire body turning stiff. "Your eyes changed."

Did they? I blinked, shocked that he could read me so well. "I'm fine, I swear. This feels… incredible." My throat clogged, and I pushed back up and increased my pace riding him. Each movement got me a little closer. He bit down on his bottom lip, his blue eyes taking everything in, and I clenched around him.

He groaned and gripped my thighs tight as our tempo grew faster. The tingling sensation started at my toes and made its way to my stomach, then to my clit. "I'm right… right there," I panted, needing just a bit more.

He knew what to do and ran his thumb over my swollen clit

three times before I burst. I cried out, rocking harder than before as my orgasm took over. My vision blurred, and my body pulsated with pleasure.

"Naomi, fuck," he grunted, lifting me slightly to adjust the angle. Michael thrusted hard four times before he groaned a long *Fuuuuuck.*

My hand rested on his chest, my heart pounded, and Michael looked up at me like he was drunk. He scanned my face, chest, then my mouth before he let out a small groan. "I had plans to get you food."

"Well, you fed me your dick."

He barked out a laugh and threw his head back. "Holy shit, nice one." He laughed again as he lifted me off him and set me down on the bed. He disposed of the condom in a trash can and sat next to me, sighing.

I felt the weight of that breath, like he was as confused as I was about our situation. Friends with benefits seemed to be the perfect solution for our insane chemistry. But it was more, for sure. At least… for me.

Shit. Self-doubt crept in, and suddenly I was very, very aware of my nudity. I got up and put on the large shirt, avoiding his probing gaze. He could easily see through me, and I wasn't ready to have *that* conversation.

"Hungry?" he asked, no indication that he knew I was freaking out. I snuck a glance at him, and he wore his easy smile. "I have a frozen pizza."

"Hm." I crossed my arms as my stomach growled. I couldn't lie and say I didn't need to eat because he heard the evidence, but I wanted to go. Running away was more of the truth, but I shrugged. "Sure, yeah. I should leave after though."

"Do what you gotta do, but I have questions." He slipped on some shorts, leaving his bare chest on display, and went out into the main area. "Freddie is gone with his friends so we can hang out in here if you want."

"Clark Kent, you mean?"

"Yup. That guy." He snorted and got the pizza from the freezer before preheating the oven. He leaned against the counter, eyed me up and down, and smiled. "We've had sex twice now, but you're acting shy. What's going on?"

Shit. I wasn't doing a good job of hiding my inner turmoil. *Play dumb.*

I shook that thought away immediately. I owed it to myself and Michael to not lie. "We're friends with benefits."

"Was that a question or a statement?" He crossed one foot over the other, and I swore his eyes clouded, like he raised his own shields against me.

Am I making this harder than it needs to be?

Guilt ate my insides. Being more than friends wasn't possible for either of us. Hockey! Coach! Heartbreak! We knew that and had talked about it. So, what good would it do to bring it up? *What if he feels differently though?*

I rubbed my temple and forced myself to relax. "Statement, sorry. I'm in a post-sex haze."

I looked at the ground, and Michael's footsteps neared me. He lifted my chin and frowned at me. His damn scent flooded my senses, and I breathed him in, hating the way he made my body lose control. I jerked my chin out of his grip, and he let his hand fall to the side.

God, that one gesture hurt my heart. The lines around his eyes deepened, and he spoke in such a soft tone I wanted to melt. "Hey, tell me what's going on, please."

That damn please again would kill me. "It's…" I took a breath and thought of the first thing I could. It was better than saying I HAVE FEELINGS FOR YOU, YOU BIG HOCKEY DUDE. "My sister."

Understanding filled his eyes, and he nodded. "I wanted to ask but wasn't sure if the subject was off-limits."

"Is anything off-limits with us?" I asked, my face heating from the hypocrisy of the situation. I was a LYING LIAR. It was my insecurities about hockey and getting hurt.

"I'd like to think not. At least, not after what just happened." He winked and brought his hand back up to my shoulder.

It was that moment I knew I was screwed. I *craved* his touch. Not just in a sexual way either. In a comforting he-brings-me-joy way. I cleared my throat and ignored the erratic patter of my heart, forcing a quick laugh. "My body is still tingling."

"Mine too." He guided us to the couch. "So, Cami. What happened? Are you alright?"

That *are you okay* almost got me emotional. I wasn't quite all right with everything that happened with my sister, but we were on the right track. "We're going to have weekly dates."

"I dig that. Ryann and I had a standing lunch agreement." He moved back and scratched his chest, right where his heart beat underneath. "I miss them. A lot, actually."

"You could do a virtual lunch date," I said, wiggling my brows as he tilted his head to the side. He blinked and let out a tiny humph.

"That's a dope ass idea." He nodded and went back to his room, only to return three seconds later with his phone. "I'm organizing that right now. I can't believe I didn't think of a virtual one!"

His fingers moved fast over his phone before he set it on the table and gave me his full attention. "Forgive me. I miss my sister and wanted to set that up before I forgot."

His intensity often made me forget what I was saying. Like now. I cleared my throat and spoke about Cami again. It was easy talking to him, sharing my doubts and hopes about her. It wasn't until hours later that I got dressed and he took me back to my place. He didn't call me a ride or demand I leave. He walked me back, and god, it was like the guy was trying to get me to fall for him. He was patient and let me set the pace. He made me feel gorgeous. Every time he touched or looked at me, I *felt* his appreciation. He loved his sister and the team, and my heart swelled as I thought about his smile.

I was in deep trouble.

CHAPTER
TWENTY-THREE

Michael

The weekend was the Bermuda Triangle of *feelings,* and I honestly wished I could just make all the thoughts disappear. Not only was it our home opener for the season, but it was parents' weekend *and* Naomi smelled so damn good.

It'd only been two days since she came over, and sitting next to her in the cold rink, hearing her sigh and laugh, was a special form of torture. It wasn't like I could ask her to hang out after the game. She was supposed to have plans with her dad, which he better not cancel again. I hated seeing him as separate people —the coach and her father because he acted two different ways.

But, fuck, at least she could work things out with him at some point. She wasn't going to spend the weekend alone like me. *Sad Express, party of one.* Sue me for wanting to distract myself from the weekend with her.

"So, Hank reached out to me about those motivation tests."

"Hank the guy you have a crush on? About this high?" I held my hand in the air, ignoring the absolutely absurd bout of jealousy.

She rolled her eyes but there wasn't the same playfulness in her expression as before. "Shut up, but yes."

"Well, what did he say?" I frowned, swearing that her dad promised to work on getting the tests to the players. I heard him talking about it the other day. "About the tests?"

"Hank said all the guys on the team took it. The team will cover the cost as long as *the results are actually helpful.* My dad's words, not his." She bit her lip and tapped her nail on the clipboard. She painted her nails blue and orange—just like our school colors. "Do you think it's odd that I'm working with you and Hank on all this stuff when it should be… my dad?"

YES. I wanted to demand answers from the guy about what was going on. It was so clear his daughter wanted to work with him, but the dude either didn't care or didn't want to return the gesture. But that wouldn't be helpful for Naomi. "I'm sure he has a reason," I said, my bullshit answer annoying me. I needed to change the subject. Move on from *this* because it pissed me off. No wonder the woman hated hockey.

"More importantly, have you started going through the results to make the profiles?" I leaned closer to her and fought the urge to push some of her hair behind her ear. It escaped from the hat she wore and looked so soft.

"I've done two players, yes. This project will take… weeks of constant work." She rubbed the back of her neck and looked at me with her light brown eyes. So full of life and warmth. "I was going to ask, and you can say no…"

"Yes," I said, flashing her a grin. "I'd love to get naked with you again as soon as possible."

She giggled, and a light blush crept up her cheeks. "I mean, yes, I've been thinking about that a lot. But what I was saying was about you helping. I know you have your own class assignments and meetings with my dad, but… if you can somehow correlate them… I'd love you to help if you had an interest."

"Help you with the project?"

"Yeah." She frowned, and her tongue wetted the side of her mouth. "If you want. Obviously. I'm not trying to put off work, but it'd be cool to hear your side of things as a former player and potential coach."

Spend more time with her, talk about hockey, and use it for my classes? There was no bad part of this suggestion. "Hell yeah, I'm in."

"Don't make fun of me," she said, but I raised my brows. She elbowed me and kept going. "I have a schedule already set for the next two weeks of when I plan to work on it."

She blushed and closed one eye as she scrunched her nose at me. "Say it. I know it's dorky."

"Not saying a word. Not one." I pressed my lips together to hold back my amusement, but the longer the silence went on, the harder it was. Eventually, I snorted and let the cackle out. "You are such a nerd, my god."

The crowd cheered, loudly, and I jumped up into the air as Erikson scored. I pumped my fist and high-fived the people around us before sitting back down with a new sense of adrenaline. They were playing as a unit this time. Cal Holt, not as much, but the rest of them were a team. A brotherhood. Exactly what a team should be.

My pulse raced, and my knee bounced up and down while Naomi studied me. "What?" I asked, unsure what the sparkle in her eye was for. Was it joy or the end of a joke I didn't know about?

"You're nerdy too in your own way. It's society's fault that sports are *cool* where data is *nerdy*. You guys use data to be better athletes, so honestly, the double standard is annoying."

"Is your schedule color coded like your Gantt charts?"

She pursed her lips but not before I saw a quick smile. I knew her too well, and I nudged her knee with mine.

"Nerd," I said, softer this time. "But I like it."

She rolled her eyes but not with real heat, and we went back to watching the game. At some point in the second period, our hands touched on the armrest. It wasn't anything scandalous, but the back of her hand rested against mine, and our eyes met.

Was she going to move? Was I?

It was dumb, dumb, dumb how my chest felt heavier and my breath caught in my throat from that simple touch, but here we were. I winked and made her smile grow before someone shouted *super fucking* loud. Two rows back, a visiting fan cussed up a storm, and the sound made us jump apart.

"People are so weird over hockey," Naomi said, side-eyeing the dude with her lip curled. "For real. To have the confidence of that guy, standing up at an opposing stadium and not giving a shit about all the death glares he's getting."

"Takes some big balls." I nodded and made sure to keep an eye on the guy. I didn't think he'd throw beer or a punch, but I moved my arm around the back of Naomi's chair. To protect her, obviously. "So, this schedule. When does it start?"

"Hm, probably tomorrow. I know you meet with my dad for post-game stuff, but if you want to send me a text when you're done?" she asked, her tone hopeful.

I nodded, and I swore she moved closer to me. Her shoulder bumped my chest, and I breathed her in, forgetting for a few seconds that we were a few rows away from the team. It was like he could sense this shit—Coach turned our direction. I jumped away from her like she was on fucking fire.

My mouth was too dry, and sweat pooled down my back. Did he see us touching? Was he going to kill me? I didn't get a chance to read his face before he focused on the game.

"Fuck," I mumbled, wiping a hand over my face.

"Why are you stressed?" Naomi asked, her soft voice getting closer to my ear. She put her small hand on my back and rubbed it. God, I was always thinking of ways to touch her, and the one time she placed her cute hand on me, I wanted to shake it off. Her dad could see. Could see *us*.

"Nothing, it's fine." Even I realized my voice sounded off. The rest of the game went like that with Naomi leaning closer to me, a casual brush of our fingers. But the harsh reality was that we agreed no one would know we slept together. We'd be *friends* on the outside, freaks on the inside. This was to protect *me* from Coach. My soul hurt, and I felt like an asshole because she knew something changed. Even after the final period ended, the line between her brows was permanently there.

I wanted to explain I mentally pulled away because of her dad, not because of *her*. She had to understand that. But every time I tried, it was like my voicebox broke or forgot how to work. The words wouldn't come out, and now I worried she thought I was mad at her. Fuck, this was the shit I hated. The emotions. The anxiety. I took a soothing breath as we stood and waited to start leaving the row before I forced myself to talk. "Tomorrow then? I'll come over."

"Yeah, if you want."

"I do." I nodded, hard, like that would explain my inner turmoil. If my nerves were a circus, they were the trapeze artists flipping around and doing weird shit in the air. Messy. Terrifying.

She looked at the ground, and her shoulders slumped, making me feel like an ass again. This was my fault. My reaction to her dad had her hesitant around me. I took her hand, stopping her from walking any further. She met my eyes and tilted her head to the side.

"I'm sorry."

"For what?"

"I had a moment, okay? Your dad looked over as us, and I swore he could tell what we did." There, I said it. I put the words out into the universe. "We're definitely keeping this on the DL, right? Because of him and my internship?"

Her eyes dimmed just a bit, but she nodded. "That's what we agreed on."

"Okay, cool," I said, still unsure about the tension. "There's nothing more to it than your dad. At least on my end."

She twisted her lips into a half smile as our hand still

touched. I wanted to kiss her to make it up to her, but that was out of the question.

"I'm sorry I acted off. You're my favorite person to hang out with here even though my behavior didn't reflect that at all."

Her cheeks pinkened, and just like that, the sparkle was back in her eyes. "Favorite, huh? A compliment like that might go to my head."

"Great, I regret saying it now."

She scrunched her nose and tugged the back of my hoodie with her hand. She pulled me toward her just a bit. "You're on my list too, you know. Like, top ten."

"Top ten favorite people? Wow, hit a guy where it hurts." I playfully swatted at her, and she giggled.

I decided that was in my top favorite sounds. But I wasn't going to fucking tell her that. We pushed through the doors, and I took a deep breath of the chilly fall air, hating that we had to say goodbye. Heading to my place alone sounded as fun as a root canal, but I knew how important it was for her to hang with her dad. "I'll see you tomorrow?"

She nodded and had that same, hesitant look in her eyes. I bent down to whisper in her ear. "I wish I could kiss that fucking mouth, Naomi. Tomorrow can't get here fast enough."

She hummed in response and shoved my chest playfully. "Be good, Reiner."

"Don't trip, Fletcher."

The hesitant look left her eyes, thankfully, and she waved before walking toward the locker room. That meant I was by myself until Coach texted me when to meet in the morning.

I scanned the crowd and saw parents everywhere. It was obvious with their clothes and graying hair. Sure, a couple of moms were hot, but it was the laughter and joy radiating from all of them that snuffed out the fire Naomi lit inside me. Even Freddie was out with his folks.

Fuck it.

I was going to a bar.

I shoved my hands in my pockets and let my grief consume me. Each step took twice the effort as the familiar emptiness spread through my body. My stomach ached the same way it did all those years ago when I was at the funeral. Why did this happen to us? How were we supposed to go on through life like this? Parentless? I took a deep breath of the cold air and fisted my hands at my sides.

I needed a drink to take the edge off. The urge to punch a wall threatened to take over, just to feel something besides grief.

What would my parents think of me now? Would they be proud or annoyed? Ashamed that I never made it to the pros?

No, they wouldn't. I ignored that thought immediately. They always encouraged me to be a good teammate, the best leader, and they had no crazy ambitions for me to go to the NHL. They wanted me to be happy. End of story.

Was I happy though?

I smiled a lot and woke up ready to go, but happy? Like Ryann happy? I wasn't sure. My sister found joy in every moment while I avoided feelings like it was professional sport.

My mind wasn't in any better shape by the time I got to the local bar right next to where I lived. Coop's Stoop was the perfect grunge bar with cheap specials. That way, I could have a few drinks and only had to walk a block. Not bad at all.

Plus, this place didn't have a ton of the parents visiting. This was off the path more, which was what I wanted. I ordered a whiskey and got comfortable at the bar, focusing on the basketball game on the TV. The NBA wasn't my thing, but it was distracting enough to not think about all the feelings.

The fucking Bermuda Triangle again, hitting me hard.

"What the fuck are you doing here?" a hard voice jolted me from a haze. I followed it to see Cal Holt propped up on the stool next to me, his eyes cold and his jaw tight.

I blinked, unsure of why he was in a bar. He was eighteen. And why he was right next to me. "There are ten other places to sit. Move."

"This is my place. You move."

"You're not even of age, nice try," I said, taking another long swig of my drink. "You could get deep shit for this."

"My cousin owns this place, alright? It's fine. Unless you fucking narc on me," he said, his neck flexing as he glared at me.

Glare away kid. I can beat your pompous ass. I said no such thing and kept to myself. This wouldn't end well for either of us. It wasn't my business what the kid did in his own time, and I drank underage when I was eighteen too. That wasn't news. It was just his attitude and entitlement I despised.

"Cally, my dude," a large man with a huge beard walked out from a bar door and held out his knuckles. He had graying hair and had to be in his forties. "You played okay tonight."

"Okay? I did better than okay."

"I swear, if I wasn't your pseudo parent, I'd smack you in the mouth." The man slapped Cal's hand as he tried to reach for a bottle of vodka. "Not now."

"What?" Cal snapped, the icy tone I heard all the time escaping him. "Why not?"

"I know this shit is hard for you, but dude, there are cops everywhere. My job is more important than your pity drunk party."

Keep to yourself. Don't listen. Finish the whiskey. Go home.

"I need a fucking drink, Dan."

"And I need to keep my license to live. If you want to fuck up your scholarship, I'm not helping tonight."

Cal slammed his fist on the counter, and something about the conversation nagged at me. The familiarity of it. The unshed emotions lingering in the words. Why would tonight be hard for him? He won a game… he played well…plus, the guy said pseudo-parent… *Fuck.* I scrubbed a hand over my face and stared at the ceiling for two seconds.

"Come on, Holt." I put my hand on his back, a little harder than I should've, and dragged him off the stool. "You want to get drunk and risk your career because you're having a prima donna moment, then do it at my place. It's next door."

"Don't touch me, Reiner."

Dan narrowed his eyes, and I let go of the kid. "I'm interning with the coach of the hockey team. Former player. I don't like the guy, but if he wants to get drunk, I prefer he does it away from people."

Dan grabbed a card from his pocket and jotted something down. "Give me a call if shit goes bad. I'm here until two tonight."

"You got it."

"Stop talking like I'm a fucking kid," Cal said, the emotion fully escaping his voice now. He sounded hoarse and sad.

"Then stop acting like one," I said, wanting to somehow make his anger at me and not Dan. "You're not the only one with parent issues, alright? So, we're going to go to my place, get drunk, and yell at each other."

He stared at me with anger swirling in his eyes before he nodded. "Fine. Just, fucking lead the way."

"Wonderful manners. Bright kid, I tell you," I said to Dan, making him bark out a laugh as I pushed Cal out of the bar and led him to my place. We marched into the living room, and I got two beers out of the fridge. Before I handed one to him, I leveled my gaze. "You can have all you want, but you crash here. If that's a problem, then you can fuck right on out the door."

He nodded. "Whatever. Going back to my shitty dorm with my weird-ass roommate is the last thing I want to do anyway."

I handed him the beer and waited. He gulped until half of it was gone before he looked at me with a sneer. "Why you staring at me like a fucking creep?"

"Dude, lose the stick up your asshole man. Do you enjoy being the most hated person on the team? Seriously. You can have all the talent in the world, but you suck as a human."

His eye twitched, and he took another long swig, finishing it off fast. He jumped up and went to grab another. I didn't say anything as he sat back down and chugged. I worried he had a drinking problem and debated how to approach this with Coach. Because it was clear this kid might be a prick but something was going on.

Minutes of silence passed by as I slowly drank mine and watched him struggle with whatever was going through his obnoxiously large head—from ego, not physically large.

"I don't love being this way," he said, so quiet I almost missed it. "It's this weekend. I just… I feel like I'm going to burst out of my skin."

"Parents' weekend, specifically?" I asked, my own voice filled with emotion. "It's hard for me too. I lost mine four years ago. It's just my sister and me, and she's back east."

Cal looked up at me, and for the first time since meeting him, he didn't glare. The ice that was always there melted away, and he looked exactly like a sad, lonely teenager should. "So, it's just you."

"Just me."

"How do you…" he started before cleared his throat and leaned back on the couch. His entire body language changed. He relaxed and spread his legs apart, turning into a human form of butter. "Does it get better?"

"The grief? No. You learn to manage it. I'm still fucking dealing with it four years later. I was going to get shit-faced drunk because seeing all the parents at the game tonight almost made me lose it."

Cal set his beer down, and his knee bounced. "Last year. It was just my mom and me since my dad took off when I was born. She wasn't feeling well. Went to the doctor and was told she had three months left. She didn't make it two. I just… Never got to fucking prepare for it. It was the two of us and…" Cal sniffed, and my entire heart broke into a million pieces.

I had Ryann. I had the team. I had my coach and hockey to heal me.

Cal had... Cal. And that guy next door.

I moved from the chair to join him on the couch. I didn't sit too close to him but near enough to show support. "I'm sorry. There aren't enough words in the world to explain how much this fucking sucks. I wouldn't wish the grief on my worst enemy, Cal. But you need to deal with it. Talk to a counselor or therapist. You're letting your grief ruin your future."

He hung his head, and his shoulders shook.

Cal was crying.

My own eyes stung a little at how relatable this was. I'd been there and revisited that grief often. But having people around you... even like Naomi, made such a difference. My voice was rougher than normal when I put a hand on his shoulder. "Want to meet at Dan's once a week? We can talk about this... or not. We could eat or glare at each other. But from my experience, talking about it does help. I had my team help me every step of the way. The guys could be like that if they understood."

"Knew I was a weak pathetic mess?" He wiped his face and brushed off my hand. "No. I'm Cal Holt. I'm already drafted."

"Oh cool, yeah, I didn't know because that's all you mention, ever."

He snorted exhaled. "I'm such a dick. I know I am. I wasn't always like this, it's just..."

"It's easier that way. Why let people get close if they can leave you?"

"That's exactly fucking it."

"We're having a YouTube night." I got up and grabbed the remote. "The guys used to do this out east. Try to find the weirdest video on YouTube. We go back and forth and announce a winner at the end."

"That's the dumbest shit I've ever heard."

"Don't care. You're drinking my beer at my place. We're going to do what I want." I started with a comedy bit about deer, and after three minutes of it, Cal almost smiled. It went on like that all night, six beers in and way past two in the morning. It was the better than my original plan for the night, and after I tossed him a blanket for the couch, my mind went to Naomi.

She'd get a kick out of this. Cal and I being buddies. My tipsy brain refused to acknowledge my own hypocrisy of how being *just friends* with her was mainly about protecting myself. I could worry about that later.

For now, I was a little drunk, but I wasn't in tears after missing my parents all day. It was the best-case scenario for me, and honestly, I might've found another friend.

CHAPTER
TWENTY-FOUR

Naomi

I had to blink twice to make sure what I was seeing was in fact, reality. The asshole hotshot on the team sat by Michael on the bench, their heads together before the start of the next game. I'd spent almost every night with Michael the past two weeks where we talked about the team and hockey nonstop. We'd start at my place working on the project then move to his, where we got naked. But during all these nights, he never once hinted he maybe got along with Cal.

He'd never said it outright, but it was clear he didn't like the guy, so this new development was interesting.

Seeing him focused with his kind eyes and his easy grin, my heart somersaulted. Cal Holt was a dick, and there Michael was, being kind to him. Ugh. Michael Reiner was a dangerous kind of guy. He was one of the nice guys who pretended to be tough and unflappable. He reminded me of Cami in a way, putting on the show for everyone else and only letting a few inside. I was one of those people—the ones on the inside who knew what he was going through. I also realized the feelings I had for him were growing. Exponentially.

And yet, I couldn't say a word about it. Was I afraid? Yes. Was I worried he'd put an end to it? Also, yes. It would hurt bad when we stopped… hooking up, but our friendship was worth it. I enjoyed my time with him too much to try and make it something it wasn't meant to be.

"Naomi, hey," my dad's voice pulled me from the weird trance. He flashed a tight smile at me as he walked toward the bench. *Speaking of getting hurt…* would Michael be like my dad some day? Blowing off his family for a sport?

"Hi," I said, my face flushing red. It'd been weeks into the season, and nothing had really changed between us. The familiar sinking feeling of being an embarrassment had me crossing my arms over my chest.

Michael and I entered the rink early before people arrived to show my dad and Hank the first part of the project—the full analysis of Erikson and Hansen. The project that my dad displayed zero interest in.

"Your sister should be coming to the game tonight," he said, rocking back on his heels as he stared at his phone. "I have her in my seats near the box."

Of course he did. "Cool," I said, unsure how to respond. I was here to show him my project and instead, we talked about Cami. As per usual.

The only difference this time was that my irritation wasn't directed at my sister. It was all at my dad.

The sounds of skating and laughter had us turning toward the ice. Cal and Michael stood, and Michael put a hand on Cal's shoulder. I tensed, waiting for Cal to shove him off or do something stupid, but it never happened. My dad frowned and tilted his head to the side, the exact same mannerisms Cami used when she was confused.

Michael hopped over the side of the bench and made his way to where we always sat. He flashed us a grin. "Hey, Coach, Naomi."

"What happened just now?" my dad asked, jutting his chin toward the ice.

"What do you mean, sir?"

"Cal Holt." My dad put his hands on his hips and leveled his gaze at Michael. It was the dark brows and furrowed lines on his face that made players fear him. Cami and I got scared as kids when he pulled that look, but Michael's grin grew.

"We came to an agreement, Coach. He's going to stop being a dumbass."

"Come with me. Now." My dad put his hand on Michael's shoulders, and they headed down the stairs toward the ice. Michael shrugged like it was no big deal, but a little pink entered his cheeks.

"What about the profiles?" I asked, my shoulders sagging. I spent *hours* preparing a preview of them for tonight.

"Later, Naomi. This is more important. Team stuff always take priority. You should remember that, Reiner, for when you're a coach. Now, tell me what the fuck I just witnessed."

They disappeared from view as they headed toward the locker room, and my stomach twisted. *Team stuff takes priority.*

It sure did over his wife. Over his daughter… at least, one of them.

I went to our usual seats and got comfortable, waiting for Michael to join me sometime later. The interaction with my dad proved one thing *very* clear—this situation with Michael was dangerous. Hockey would come first. The constant worry that I wasn't enough, that I was an afterthought would only get worse. God, it'd be like dealing with dad's shut out all over again. Keeping him at a distance as best I could meant everything. I chewed the hell out of my nail by the time Michael finally returned.

This wasn't a date, but my heart still went haywire when he walked my way twenty minutes later. He wore dark jeans, a Central hoodie, and a backwards hat.

He was stupid hot. The white teeth, the messy hair, the

playful glint in his eyes. *And he's into me.* Well, into my body. It was my job to protect my heart.

"You're blushing, Fletcher. You better tell me what's going on in that pretty, genius mind of yours." He sat down, and his cologne washed over me. Clean laundry, coffee, and musk. He kept distance between our faces, but his thigh pressed against mine, and I loved it there.

"Nothing," I said, way too quickly, and he laughed.

"You're a shit liar. Honestly, might be the worst I've met. Want to play strip poker sometime?"

It was my turn to laugh, and I slid him a glance. "We're thinking along the same lines then, hm?"

"Naomi, you slay me." He put a hand over his chest and pretended to faint. "Don't tease me like that when I have to sit here for three hours in the cold and we both know I'd rather be naked with you," he whispered, leaning back into the seat looking relaxed as hell. His arm dangled right next to mine, so close our fingers touched.

He didn't immediately pull away, and it sent a thrill through me. That maybe he was okay if people knew about us. Wait, did I want people to know we were hooking up? Maybe? Even if he'd crush me at some point?

I frowned, unsure what I wanted anymore. We weren't in a relationship, and I wasn't ashamed of him, but whoa. Sweat pooled in my underboob, and my skin felt too tight for my body. We were literally fuck buddies who got along. We weren't exclusive...well, shit. Mona and Kellie were chill about exclusivity. It wasn't a big deal to them. Monogamy wasn't in their top three priorities where it was for me. Maybe it was my parents' divorce or seeing Cami go through guy after guy, but being with multiple people at one time sounded like a nightmare.

Is he sleeping with other girls? We aren't together.

"Hey," Michael said, nudging my knee with his. He bent

closer to me, so close his breath hit my face. "What's wrong? I wasn't sure if you wanted to talk about your dad or not…"

"No, it's not that," I said, the mention of my dad making everything worse. "I mean, he upset me but that's… it's nothing." I chickened out. Plain and simple.

"If we're going to be friends, don't pull that shit with me," he said, his voice more aggressive than I'd heard before. He pressed his lips tight together as his stare intensified.

"It's… just… well," I stammered, pushing my hair out of my face to buy some time. This was horrible. Why did these thoughts have to intrude now? Why not later, when we were in bed together?

A loud buzzer went off, and the players got on the ice, hip-hop music blasting from the speakers and drowning out my voice. Thank god. It bought me a few more minutes to figure shit out.

I could be honest, but he'd think I was making *this* into something more. What if he did want to hook up with other women? I couldn't stop him. He had all the rights to. I chewed on my hangnail and felt Michael's stare on me through the entire warm up. Ten minutes later, the game started, and sound returned to a normal level.

"Should be a good game, huh? I hope Hank talks to him about using the profiles."

"Please don't change the subject. If something's bothering you, especially if it's me, I'd like to know so I can rectify the situation. You matter way too much to me to try and guess what's in your head."

Fuck. I closed my eyes and pushed out the words. "We never talked about exclusively hooking up. It's been on my mind."

"Oh."

I opened one eye and found him frowning. He pulled at a loose string on his jeans and worried his bottom lip. He ran a hand over his face before clearing his throat. "Are you thinking about getting involved with someone else?"

"What? Me? No."

His gaze snapped to mine, and his lips curved into a smile. "I'm not either, so *why* is it on your mind then?"

My face heated like a thousand suns, and I groaned. "So, we're both not interested in other people."

"Correct, and I don't have any plans to go after anyone else either. I like spending all my time with you, but if you think differently, don't be afraid to tell me."

His words washed over me, warming me all the way to my soul. Even the freezing temps in the rink couldn't stifle the fire in my heat. *I like spending all my time with you.* God, did he not realize I felt the same? He was being so mature about all of this… it threw me off. "You're not like the guys I've been with."

"I'll take that as a compliment, thank you very much," he said, those damn dimples teasing me. He placed a hand on my knee and squeezed for a second before he winked.

If someone asked me *right now* why we weren't dating, I wouldn't have an answer. My dad being his coach? My fear of him hurting me? Those were both bullshit. It'd be so easy to fall into a relationship with him. Even after just a couple weeks of hooking up, we spent every hour together that we weren't in class or sleeping. Sure, we didn't do sleepovers. That was the unwritten rule between us, but god, I wanted to know what it'd feel like to be *with* him.

For real.

I voiced none of that and focused on the game. Hank had provided me with stats from the team data specialist so I didn't need to track in game data, but I still watched and tried to find patterns. I observed behaviors from the guys and added the qualitative information to the profiles. Who punched a wall when they were pissed? Who ignored high fives from teammates? Who led on the bench instead of sitting alone and pouting? All of the information helped form the full profile of the players, and my blood fucking hummed when Cal Holt reached out for a high five to one of the less talented guys.

"Whoa."

"Hm?" Michael said, leaning onto his elbows. It was zero-zero, and he kept mumbling about needing a stronger offense.

"Cal. He's acting different."

"Good. I think I found a way to pull the stick from his ass." He barked out a laugh and *whooped* when Cal passed to Hansen who scored. "Fuck yeah, let's go!"

He jumped up, and his energy was contagious. People all around us cheered and hit his back as he yelled, loudly. If I wasn't mistaken, Cal looked up in the stands at Michael for a second, and Michael nodded at him.

"What did you do?"

Michael sat back down and let out a long sigh. "His past is his to tell when he's ready, so I won't break that trust. But he realized he's not alone in his experiences. No one is. He just needed someone not afraid of him to call him out."

"He needed a friend," I said, the urge to kiss Michael almost unstoppable. He was such a damn good person. Of course he would help out the punk kid and befriend him. My eyes stung just a bit. "You're incredible, Michael."

"Hey, thanks. Two compliments today. My lucky night." He wiggled his brows.

Irritation prickled my spine. "I'm being serious."

His smile fell, and he nodded. "I'm sorry. Praise is hard for me, but I can tell you that your words lit me up inside. Seriously. Coming from you…" He whistled. "It means more than you know."

Shit. The heavy look in his eyes, like longing, had me freezing in my seat. Michael stared at me like he wanted *all* of me, and god, I wanted that too. My throat bobbed with an uncomfortable swallow, and after a full thirty seconds of eye contact, he tore his gaze away from me.

Our easy conversation shifted tonight into something more.

I wasn't sure what it meant, but when the game ended and Michael asked me to come back to his place, I couldn't say no. He'd befriended the worst human I'd ever met. He pushed me outside of my comfort zone. He was such a decent human being with a huge heart, and *damn*. I couldn't *just* be friends with him anymore. Not with all these thoughts and aggressive urges to keep him. I was a moth, and he was the flame.

Even though I knew at some point, I'd get hurt, I couldn't stop myself because even in data, there was always the chance of an anomaly. An exception. It was rare but god, I wanted to be the outlier so bad.

CHAPTER
TWENTY-FIVE

Michael

If I had to pick my favorite scent, it had to be the way Naomi's neck smelled after we had sex. It was a combination of sweat, lemon, and *her*. I nuzzled my nose along her skin, not wanting the night to end. Two weeks of getting her to myself and then she'd leave to head back to her place. I was a gentleman and always escorted her home but tonight, I didn't want her to go.

I wanted to spend all night with her in my bed, but not just for pleasure. For comfort too. To have someone who got my pain and didn't downplay it.

She giggled when I bit down on where her shoulder met her neck, and she pushed at my chest. "I should get dressed. I'm all about *you do you,* but I'm not going to be the girl walking back at night naked."

"Stay with me," I whispered against the shell of her ear, enjoying how her body shivered beneath mine. I'd kissed and tasted every single part of her, but she still reacted to me like it was the first time. That was an addicting feeling.

"But Michael," she said, her muscles tensing. "Our rules."

Yeah, I knew that. I thought about them over and over. I'd even talked to Ryann about it extensively who laughed at the irony. I gave her major shit for dating a teammate, and she hid it from me to prevent me from lashing out. This was different, but the situation was still similar.

I was a grown man, and it was getting harder to hide my feelings for Naomi. Should I be into her? No. Not at all. Her dad was my boss. But none of that mattered. When she laughed with me, listened to me, and moaned when I slid into her, all those thoughts went the fuck out of my head, and I kept hoping for more.

"What if I wanted to be together-together?" My chest felt too tight as I buried my face in her neck, smelling her lemon hair and avoiding her gaze. I already gave too much away, and she needed to take a step toward me. I thought maybe she was into it too after she mentioned the exclusivity thing, but I couldn't be sure.

Plus, I'd take whatever Naomi would give me, so I wouldn't push. I had shit to figure out—mainly, how to tell her dad about us before this was a real thing. They had issues, and I refused to cause even more strife between them.

Naomi didn't answer nor did she move. She remained stiff for so long I pushed up on my elbow and stared down at her. Her eyes were wide, and her pillow lips slightly parted. God, I loved her mouth.

I kissed her softly as my heart flip-flopped. It'd been so long since I had real feelings for someone that I forgot what it was like to have a giddy, almost terrifying pull toward another human. All I knew was that life was better around her, and I was selfish enough to want more of it.

The flip-flop settled as another possibility took root. She could *not* want to be together, which would be fine, probably. Her silence grew, and unease itched down my spine.

"Fletcher, I asked you a question."

She moved her fingers to the back of my head and ran them through my hair. It felt fucking good, and I closed my eyes, relaxing against her touch. It went on for a minute before I studied her.

She narrowed her eyes before saying, "Are you sure?"

"About being with you? Yes. There are a few things I need to do before we release a sex tape—"

"Shut up," she said, swatting at me as her face turned pink. "We are *not* doing that."

"It's a joke, Naomi. Come on now." I scoffed and kissed her forehead real quick. "I want this. To give this a genuine chance. These feelings are new and scary for me, but they're unavoidable. I like you. I trust you. I want you here all the fucking time."

She gulped and blinked a lot, her hands stilling on my head. "Are you always so honest about everything?"

"Yes. It makes no sense to lie or talk in circles. Makes my messy emotions easier to deal with. I want this with you if you're interested." I moved down her chest to kiss the center of her breastbone and flicked her pink nipple with my tongue. God, I loved her tits. "I'm confident that you're into this." I took one between my teeth and pulled.

She let out a strangled moan and grabbed my face, yanking me up to her. She kissed me hard and sloppy, and I loved it. I loved how she was so organized and neat in her professional life but not with me. I got all her different sides, and I cupped her head to kiss her back.

Making out was always a fun way to pass time until I fucked, but with Naomi, it was an art. A foreplay that sank into my skin. The strokes of her tongue started rough but smoothed out, like she kissed me without a plan or because she could. She tasted like mint and sex, and she hummed into my mouth when I matched her pace.

I'd kissed a lot of women, but I couldn't remember a single one right now. Not with Naomi's tight body and perfect creamy tits in front of me. Not with her soulful eyes and beautiful heart. My chest felt heavier as we kissed and kissed. My lips got swollen, and I was unsure if minutes or an hour had passed, but I pushed up onto my elbows and glanced down at her. "Stay over."

"Okay," she said, panting with a wild expression in her eyes.

"Want to try being together-together?" I asked again, my lips curving up before she answered. She looked so damn good with red lips and flushed skin.

She giggled and nodded. "Yeah."

"Thank Christ," I said, every cell in my body coming alive.

She reached down to my dick, already hard again from our make out session, and she pumped it a few times.

"Woman, I want to lick every inch of you right now."

"I want to lick you too, Michael." She moved from under me and put a hand on my chest to shove me onto my back. "Your body is a temple, I swear. Just looking at your muscles makes my knees weak."

Shit. I gasped when she dragged her nails down my chest with a wicked expression in her eyes. Not an evil look, but an *I'm going to sex you up* one that had my cock twitching. She licked her lips before taking my dick in her hands and sliding her tongue around it.

"Oh hell," I said, groaning at how hot her mouth was. She sucked and took me all the way back to the point my hips bucked off the bed. "Naomi, god."

She winked at me, my dick in her mouth, and I might've fallen in love. She was a playful sex goddess who was also smart as hell. I should propose. *Especially* when she deep throated me and used her hands on my balls.

I'd been inside her an hour ago, yet the familiar tingling sensation started at my spine. I put a hand on her head and stilled her. "Baby, slow down, I want this to last."

"If I'm spending the night here, we're not getting a lot of sleep. You're a walking fantasy, Reiner, and I want to enjoy you," she said, her voice deep and husky.

"Well, fuck me," I said, laughing. "That might be the hottest thing ever."

She grinned before she took me in her mouth again, humming against my cock. My eyes almost rolled in the back of my head at the way she sucked me. I tried to fight it, but it was no use. "Naomi, I'm—"

She went faster, sucking me deeper as pleasure pulsed through my cock. She swallowed as I came, staring into her eyes. She grinned wide and looked mighty proud of herself, but I couldn't move. I was spent. A noodle.

"Holy balls," I said, breathless and half-way in love with her. "Get your ass over here *right* now."

"Why?" she asked, scrunching her nose and being cute as fuck.

"Because I need to kiss you again."

She climbed up my body and did just that. We kissed and fooled around all night until we fell asleep, her back to my chest. There were no more excuses or bullshit reasons why we couldn't be us. To give this a real shot. I wrapped my arms around her tight and held her close, finally fucking happy that I wasn't lying to myself anymore.

After keeping people at a distance for years, letting *her* in felt right. She was the one.

It was the best night's sleep I'd had in a long time.

The last thing I expected to wake up to was a text from Coach saying we needed to talk ASAP. My stomach sank because here I was lying naked next to one of his daughters. *Fuck.* Did he find out about us somehow? We were careful, but sure, we flirted at the games. It was impossible not to.

I stirred in my bed, trying not to wake Naomi. She slept with her body pressed against my side, her head on my shoulders and her leg thrown over me like she couldn't get close enough. I knew the feeling. I ran my nose along her hairline and pressed a kiss on her forehead, hating how the text weighed me down.

ASAP. What would warrant talking ASAP? We won big last night. Cal played less like a dick. Yeah, Coach cornered me after the game asking why I got along with Cal, and I almost told him the whole truth.

Fear clutched at my throat as my mind spiraled. Could there have been an accident? Memories of getting *the call* four years ago came in full force, and I closed my eyes, letting the anxiety fade away. Sweat beaded on my forehead, and Naomi ran her hand over my chest.

"Morning," she said, her voice sleepy and perfect. I tightened my grip on her and pulled her even closer to me.

"Why haven't we been doing this the whole time?" I asked, hoping to tease her to forget about my worries. It didn't work. My voice came out gruff and scratchy.

She looked up and frowned. "Hey," she said, that soft word breaking whatever shield I had around my heart. "What's wrong?"

I could lie or deflect, but that'd make me a hypocrite. I took a deep breath and rubbed my forehead. "Your dad said to call him ASAP, and my mind went from zero to fucking sixty imagining all the things it could be about."

Her brows lowered in understanding, and she pressed a kiss against my chest. "I imagine texts like that remind you of your parents."

"Exactly." My throat was on fire at this point. I hadn't talked about this, ever. "I was at practice when it happened. I fucked around with some guys, laughing, not having any idea that Ryann was going through hell. I had fifteen missed calls and texts from her to get a hold of her ASAP. That something had happened. Even now, seeing those letters together sends a chill through me."

She didn't say anything, but she rubbed her hands up and down my chest and held me tighter. It was the best response, and after a minute of her soothing me, my heartbeat went back to normal.

"I won't tell you that your worry is silly because it's not. But with the way my dad operates, hockey is everything, so my guess is that it's related to the team."

She's probably right.

"I'm going to call him in the other room." I pushed myself up and tossed on some shorts. She ogled my thighs, and seeing her blush made me smile. "You stay there."

"Yes, sir," she said, stretching her arms over her head and thrusting her tits out into the air. Goddamn, she was a sight.

With one last glance, I marched into the living room and called him. It rang three times before he answered. "This is Simpson."

"Coach, it's Michael."

"Can you meet me at the cafe next to the rink in fifteen minutes?"

"Um," I said, thinking about Naomi in my bed. This was all sorts of weird. "Yeah. What's going on?"

"Rather talk to you in person. Be there in fifteen." He hung up, and I stared at my phone, my stomach twisting in knots. What the fuck was going on?

I went back into my room and shut the door. Naomi sat up in bed with a line between her brows.

"He wants me to meet him in fifteen minutes."

"Did he say why?"

"No, just that it'd be better in person." I scrubbed a hand over my face and got dressed. Jeans, long-sleeved shirt, hoodie. Hat. "I need you to know that I planned on spending all morning with you in bed. Please tell me you understand this."

"I do," she said, her voice soft. She gave me a half smile, and I cupped her face, dragging my thumb over her bottom lip.

"I'm glad we're doing this. You and me."

She blushed, and I kissed her. It was a sweet, comforting kiss that didn't last nearly long enough. She broke apart and put on her clothes, the silence cutting through the air. "Let me get dressed so we can head out together."

"Shit." I made her jump. "I don't have time to walk you to your door."

"Michael, that's okay. You have every single time before. This is different. Just let me know what's going on, alright?" She slipped on her clothes, and soon enough, we were outside and into the cold morning air.

The chill did nothing to tamp the worry growing in my gut. Things were *just* right in my life. School was going well, Ryann and I had weekly calls, and Cal and I were even… friendly. Naomi and I were together. So, this meeting had me on edge. Like it would shift everything after it had just gotten good. We came to the intersection where she headed north toward her place and I went south. She wrapped her arms around my waist in a hug, and my god, I adored this woman.

"It'll be okay, Reiner, I know it." She squeezed me hard, like she was giving me her strength, and I fell for her even more. I kissed the top of her head before we parted ways, and I went toward the cafe.

Puck Pastries smelled like coffee and sweetness, and the warmth flooded my face once I walked in. Coach was easy to find with his large frame and dark hair. He sat in a corner with a steaming cup of coffee and his laptop. He didn't look distressed, like something horrible happened, so that was a decent sign.

"Coach," I said, my voice scratchy as I sat in the chair across from him. He lifted his chin in greeting and whistled for the waitress.

"Get what you want. It's on me."

"Uh, just a coffee for now, thanks." I leaned forward so my elbows were on the table. "Gotta be honest, Coach, I'm on pins and needles about this. What's going on?"

Coach leveled his gaze as he took a deep breath. "To put it frankly, I need you to be my new assistant coach."

"Like next year?"

"No. Starting today."

CHAPTER
TWENTY-SIX

Naomi

Mona, Kellie, and Lilly all wore grins way too large for their faces when I arrived back at our place. My entire body burned with embarrassment because yeah, we all knew I spent the night somewhere. If this was Kellie, none of us would bat an eyelash, but it was me. The *good* girl. The boring one. It was a big deal.

"Stop staring at me," I mumbled, tossing my keys onto the side table.

"Where were ya last night?" Mona asked, wiggling her brows to the point she reminded me of a cartoon character.

"Michael's. You all know this." I huffed out the awkward need to laugh and poured myself some coffee. "I've been there how many times the last few weeks?"

"Naomi has a regular booty call, and I don't. This isn't fair," Kellie said, falling back onto the couch with an exaggerated groan. "He's so hot too."

I sat in the recliner and tucked my feet to the side as we all positioned ourselves in the living room. This was the best part of sharing a place with these girls. The way we could just sit and hang out. We had our own spots, and even now, I was dying to tell them about Michael and me. "Listen, he asked me last night if I wanted to be together-together."

"Shit," Mona said, wrapping her arms around her knees. "Didn't think the guy had it in him."

"Shut up, Mona. You're just cranky because your vibrator ran out of batteries," Kellie fired back. Kellie smiled at me. "What did you say? You seem happy with him."

"We agreed we were a thing. Exclusive too." God, the room was hot.

"We're happy for you, really. Now we don't have to pretend we didn't know you two were hooking up on the reg," Lilly said, flashing me her cheeky grin. "Bring him over sometime so we can grill him."

"Absolutely not." I shook my head and tried to picture how that conversation would go. No way. They knew too much about me and had potential to embarrass me. "Hell no."

"That's no fun for us. Seriously. The last guy you dated was a dweeb, and now you have Michael and we can't interrogate him? This seems like a breach of the friend contract."

I flipped Lilly off. "I like him," I said, voicing the thought that had been swirling in my mind the past week. "A lot."

"He's an easy guy to like, but just be careful, alright?" Mona said, her tone softer than all the teasing before. "I'm glad you're putting yourself out there and he's treated you well. I just... have this feeling. I don't know. He's still a hockey guy."

The need to defend him surged out of me. "Hockey's not so bad, Mona."

"Okay, okay." She put her hands up in the air and blushed. "I'll say no more."

The conversation skated away from Michael and me to Kellie's latest dilemma. I couldn't help but check my phone every thirty seconds to see if Michael had texted me or not. There was nothing. No news of what my dad wanted to ask him, and the longer the radio silence went on, the more my nerves frayed at the edges.

Maybe it was something about his internship. That made the most sense, but the weight in my gut grew as the morning stretched into lunch. I'd already texted him once, but there was no indication he'd read the text yet. I didn't want to be needy and ask again, but shit, this was a lot.

Kellie and Lilly went to the library to get a head start on homework, and that left me and Mona at the apartment. I didn't like the way she studied me, like she knew something about the future I didn't. Michael was honest to a fault, and I had to trust that.

"I'm going out," I said, craving some fresh air. Maybe I'd stroll toward the rink. Just to see if they were still there. *That's creepy.*

"Oh yeah, to where?" Mona asked, essentially calling me on my bluff.

"To walk. It's beautiful outside."

"I'll come with you."

"Oh, you don't have to," I said, not sure what reason I could give her. "I just need to clear my head. Alone."

"No worries." She frowned for a beat. "Hey, I'm sorry about earlier. I didn't want to stress you out. I love you to death, Naomi. You know that, right?"

"Yeah, I know." I smiled at her, and that eased some of the tension in my gut. I couldn't shake the feeling that last night and this morning were just a dream. It had to be my nerves creating fake scenarios because of how much I was into him. I had it bad.

"Let's watch How to Get Away with Murder later, yeah?"

"You got it."

I left the apartment in the same thing I wore last night, but it was cold enough I didn't care. Plus, the sweatshirt smelled like Michael's place, and I was probably a little lovesick.

LOVESICK? Love? Did I love him?

I stared at an old oak tree that had been around for decades as I contemplated the answer. I thought about him all the time. I wanted to take his pain and make it my own, and my heart beat twice as fast when he was around. If I wasn't in love with him yet, I would be very soon.

He had to be feeling something similar with all the things he said. He was an open book, and maybe it was time I attempted that too. I got my phone out and texted him.

Naomi: I hope everything is okay. I'm trying this new "Reiner" thing where I'm honest as hell. I want you to know I'm falling for you, hard.

Wow. I sent it and shoved the device into my pocket. That was exhilarating and terrifying. But it was worth it. I wandered around the quad for a good thirty minutes before heading into a different cafe. Still no response from Michael and I was hungry.

"Nana?" Cami's voice startled me, and I spun to see her right in line behind me.

"Hey, hey," I said, pleased at the surprise.

"How are you doing?" she asked, her brows coming together in a way that had me on edge. That made no sense. Why would she assume I wasn't doing phenomenal?

"Um, good, why?"

"The sudden change with Michael? I assumed y'all were hooking up, but this'll have to shift that dynamic, I'm sure. Dad won't let him have a moment of free time." She snorted and squinted at the menu on the wall. "Have you had their salads? I shouldn't eat carbs, but fuck, I'm hungry."

"What change, Cami? What are you talking about?" I asked, the metaphorical shoe dangling from a cliff, ready to drop and ruin my momentary bliss.

She winced. My fearless, ballsy sister winced. "Hank quit. Something to do with family out west."

"Okay?"

"Michael's the new assistant coach for the team. Didn't he tell you? Did dad not send you a text too?"

My head spun, and I gripped the counter in front of us. Assistant coach. To my dad. For the school team.

No one told me.

Not either one of them. How could they ignore me over something so important? My eyes stung, and my stomach cramped with pain from betrayal, disappointment, and resignation. Keeping this from me was an active decision.

"How is that possible? He's a student," I said, trying to grasp at straws.

"Not sure." Cami narrowed her eyes again. "Want to split a parfait?"

"How do you know this?" I asked, my voice tense. "Did Dad tell you?"

"Yeah." She picked up a bag of chips and an apple before she met my eyes and shrank back. "Dude, why are you paling?"

I swallowed down the pain in my throat. This changed everything. Us being *together-together*. I was sure. The lack of response from Michael confirmed the shift between us. One night of bliss. That was what we had before *hockey* came between us.

I should've fucking known.

And one of them should've fucking told me.

"Thanks for telling me," I mumbled, my own voice sounding off to my ears. Cami nodded and ordered a salad before looking at me with wide eyes. "Oh um, just a tea please," I said.

"Not hungry?"

"Not anymore."

We got our food and made our way toward the back of the cafe, my stomach absolutely in tithers. My phone sat upright, my texts unanswered, and I chewed my lip. How was it even possible to have a student be an assistant coach? There had to be rules against that.

"Having Michael as an assistant is a huge gain for dad.

Hank was fine, but Michael only left the ice a year ago, right? He has clout and charisma."

"Spend a lot of time with him?" I snapped.

Cami held her hands in the air. "No, I don't. Dad does and talks about him constantly. An assistant coach can make or break the team. Hank didn't add anything for the past three years. Sure, decent guy, but no player would go to him for shit." Cami took a bite of her salad and groaned. "I hate that I have to *keep my figure* for dance. Sometimes, I just want to eat all the fucking carbs on campus."

"Eat the carbs then," I snapped, my body tight as a rubber band. I was seconds away from breaking. My breathing wouldn't settle as a huge wave of betrayal hit me.

Michael chose my dad.

My dad chose Michael.

No one ever chose me.

"Okay, you're being a real dick. Talk me through it." She set her food down and propped her elbows on the table. Her makeup was perfect, her lips red, and her hair styled in a way I couldn't do if I tried. And yet, her gaze softened, and the look was enough for me to release my fears.

"We just decided we'd give a relationship a shot and then this happens? He was going to find a way to tell dad we were together, but now as an assistant coach? I know what it's like to try to love someone when the ice always comes first. Should I assume we're over? This could lead into next year or a full-time coaching job. We've already seen one marriage end over that."

"Okay, first off, marriage? Chill out, girl." Cami laughed, but it wasn't filled with joy. "You gotta figure out if you trust the guy. Either you do or you don't, and that'll be your answer. Sure, it could get weird or complicated, but all this assuming you're doing isn't a good call. Talk to him about it. See what he wants to do."

"And if he wants to end it?" A fist took my heart and squished it at the thought.

"At least you'll know, instead of playing this fucked up game in your head. I doubt he wants to break it off. I've seen how protective he is around you. And yeah, it'll be awkward with having dad as his boss, but what's the rush?"

My heart. That was the urgency. I'd already fallen for the guy, and I didn't want to fall more because I'd be second place. I was always second fucking place.

This was why friends with benefits was better. We would've at least still been friends, and after he opened up to me about only being close with me, I didn't want to leave him. He needed a friend. Maybe that was the answer. I could take a step back. See how things played out. Give myself a little time to put up some walls.

Yeah. Maybe.

My phone buzzed, and I answered it way too fast. Cami raised her brows and smirked, but every cell in my body was tense. "Hey, hello?"

"Fletcher, god, sorry I'm just now calling you. Everything's… okay. I'm getting pulled into something all afternoon, but I'm hoping I can stop by later?"

"Right. Yeah. What did my dad want?"

"To talk about opportunities. It's not anything bad or too crazy," he said.

He lied. Being an assistant coach was huge. "Nothing crazy?" I asked, my control snapping. "You weren't just named assistant coach of the team?"

"Naomi," he said, his voice firmer than before. "I didn't lie to you. I would never do that. A lot is going on, and I'd like to talk to you about it tonight. I'll text you before I head over?"

"Sure." God, I sounded bitchy. Cami's knowing glare told me I did too. "See you later then."

I hung up, hating myself for acting so childish. I almost-loved the guy, and I shouldn't have acted like that. This was why feelings were messy. They made people do stupid shit. I rubbed my face with my hands. "What's wrong with me?"

"Hm, that feels like a loaded question I'd rather not answer."

That made me snort. My sister was back in my life, and I didn't want anything ruining it. "Probably a good idea."

"But," she said, arching her brow and leaning closer to me. "It's clear that you're scared."

"I am."

"Of what? Getting your heart broken? You'll be fine. Mom's fine."

"Yeah, with her new family. She calls me once a month now, but they're getting shorter and shorter."

"I get a few texts, so be thankful about the calls. Maybe that wasn't the best example, but you get what I mean. If you're scared of him picking hockey instead of you, you'll have to get over that. Is this his dream? What young athlete gets a chance to be an assistant coach before they graduate? Don't jump to conclusions and hear him out, Nana. If you really care for the guy, you'll listen."

Wow. My sister's words were like a sucker punch to the gut. How could I be upset with him if this was his dream? He mentioned feeling lost without hockey, and now he had a chance to make a difference. Find a new home. I had to wait and let him explain. I closed my eyes and nodded. "You're right."

"I know, but it feels good to hear you say it."

We changed topics after that, but her words stayed with me all afternoon. The day wore on, but each time I looked at my phone, without a text or call, my stomach hardened. At nine, Cami checked in on me, and the buzz of my phone sent butterflies through my gut. *Not Michael.* I texted her back, but the weight in my stomach worsened.

I tried to rationalize all the things that could've happened. He was busy, obviously, but to tell me he'd stop by? I sighed, the hope of *us* disappearing more and more. The same, horrible feeling that I wasn't worth it came back full force. Like all the times my dad made promises and backed out.

It wasn't until eleven that I got a text from him.

Michael: I'm so sorry. Tomorrow morning, I'll be over.

Dad: Gotta reschedule the project thing again. Hank quit, and the team needs me. Hope you don't mind.

I stared at my phone the next morning, unfazed by my dad's second attempt at *not* meeting with me. The first time—Michael and Cal stole his attention. This time... Hank. Sure, the *team* was always more important. Not his daughter. Never me. There was always going to be *someone* or something else that mattered more. What if he needed Michael? What if Michael turned out to be *just* like him? Cancelling plans. Not realizing how much he'd hurt me. The first couple of times I'd forgive him, sure. But then how long would it go on?

I rubbed my temples and tried not to let my fingers tremble.

Three things were clear after getting a shitty night's sleep and waking up to my dad's text. I couldn't be upset with Michael for figuring out his dream or future. He deserved the world. The second thing that became clear was the fact hockey would be his main priority. It made sense.

But I wasn't sure I could handle that. I knew what it felt like after watching my mom, and as the leftover daughter, I found out the hard way about coming in second place. Protecting my heart was important because it had never really felt whole. The third thing was the fact I didn't want to lose Michael. If we were *together,* there was a large chance we'd break up and it'd be awkward and horrible.

Staying friends was safer. Easier.

A soft knock pulled me from my thoughts, and I let Michael into the apartment, trying not to cry at how badly I wanted to pull him to me.

"Hey," I said, my voice scratchy.

"I brought you coffee." He set a cup on the counter and bent down to kiss the top of my head. "Man, it has been a fucking weird twenty-four hours."

"Michael."

He stilled and looked at me, his blue eyes narrowing and frown lines forming all over his face. God, he was so handsome. I gulped, finding my courage to do what I needed to.

"What is it?"

"Are you the new assistant coach for the Central Wolves?"

"Yes, I am." He sucked one of his cheeks in, and his shoulders stiffened. "I think we should talk about what it means for us."

"We both know already," I said, leaving the coffee on the counter and pacing near the kitchen table. Lilly's textbooks sat out, and I focused on those instead of Michael's face. I had one question to ask before I did what had to be done. "Did you tell my dad we were involved yesterday?"

This was the chance to prove that I'd come first because last night felt too familiar. My mom waiting up for my dad to get home and eventually giving up. Me, pacing after school because he was supposed to pick me up and forgot. My mom, Cami, and I always boxing up food at restaurants because *something* happened on the team.

My breath lodged in my lungs, waiting for the inevitable no.

"Naomi, what are you doing?"

God, he sounded sad.

"Why won't you look at me?"

"Because we can't be together, okay? Not now." I put my hands on my hips and faced him. "You coach for him. I know what it takes, and you'll be pulled into that world even more. Plus, you're still a student, which I'm not even sure how that would work. Do you still go to classes? Are you getting paid? Either way—"

"Hey, take a breath. You're talking too fast." He moved to

stand closer to me, but I stepped back when he reached out to touch me. That seemed to break the warmth in his eyes, fast. "Do you or do you not want to be with me?"

"It's not a simple yes or no question," I said, my watery voice not helping the situation at all. I could practically hear my mom's voice from all the fights her and my dad had for years. *Why didn't you marry the fucking sport then? I can't be with you if hockey is in your life. It's me or hockey.*

He *always* chose hockey. And look at them now…

"Yeah, it is. Because if it's a yes, then we'll figure it out together. Sure, it's not ideal that I'd have to tell your dad I'm sleeping with his fucking daughter, but I will."

"You could've yesterday," I said, fighting tears at this point. "You could've accepted the job *after* you told him the truth. But no. Hockey will always come first."

"Naomi, I'd like to give us a shot. It'll take some time to adjust, but I want to be with you." He ran a hand over his jaw, suddenly looking very tired.

I'd be a fool to believe him. To think he wouldn't fall into the same patterns. *Next time will be better. I swear.* I heard my dad promise my mom things would be fine and not a month later, it was back to hockey everything.

Just a weekend game. Just a sick player. Just a quick coaching thing.

Michael saying we'd adjust… no. We wouldn't.

"I think… I think we should be just friends for a bit. Like we originally planned."

He blinked and flexed his jaw a few times. I wasn't sure what I wanted him to say, but the silence dragged on, and I fought the urge to throw up. Then he said, "For a bit? What does that mean?"

"Just that with this change and the new pressures you'll face, it'll be easier to remain friends." *And when he chooses hockey every single time, it won't hurt as badly.*

"So, you're too scared to give this a chance." He backed up a step. The distant look I saw him wear when he talked to others replaced the tender gaze he used on me.

And as always, he cut right to the chase.

"Maybe, maybe not. But this is the right move. You have so much to balance now."

"And you get to decide for me. Okay, cool." He shook his head and pinched the bridge of his nose. "Well thanks for thinking about *me* and what you think I want."

"This is hard for me too, Michael."

"Is it? Because you're the one making all the calls right now." He exhaled and sliced me into pieces with the coolness of his blue eyes. "I should've known better," he said, just above a whisper.

He spun around and walked out my door, and the absolute devastating realization hit me in the chest.

No more Michael.

No more touches and late night conversations. No more holding hands and laughing with him. Those blue eyes wouldn't look at me and crinkle on the sides, and *fuck*. My stomach coiled tight, like I might throw up. I covered my mouth with my hand as a sob broke through. I *hurt* him in trying to protect myself. The guy who had already suffered so much loss.

My soul ached, and my heart shattered into pieces as I sank to the ground. If this was the right choice, then why did it feel so horrible?

CHAPTER
TWENTY-SEVEN

Michael

Cal shoved fries into his mouth and chewed with his mouth open.

Disgust rolled through me. "Close your mouth when you eat, Jesus."

"Just cause you're a coach now doesn't mean you can boss me around." He smirked like he had the best zinger in the world.

"I'm saying this as a human being who likes food, not as your assistant coach. If I wanted to boss you around, then I would. You can't do shit about it." I took a slow sip of my water and rolled my shoulders, wishfully thinking it would ease the pain there.

One week since my life shifted. One week since seeing Naomi. She wanted to be *friends,* and we hadn't talked once. *Friends* sure felt like a death sentence. I scratched my chest as the pang flared there, and I focused on Cal. I stayed true to my word about not telling a soul about the nights we drank together, but we had to change things now that I was on the staff.

God, an assistant coach at twenty-four. It didn't seem real. But again, a lot of moments in my life didn't feel real until they happened. The nagging sensation in my gut disappeared and was replaced with something like peace. Like *this* was what I was supposed to do.

Even my sister was thrilled for me. *You found your place in the world. You're meant to lead others on the ice like you always have. Enjoy it, bro.* Her words helped ease the pain of losing Naomi, but the ache remained there.

It didn't seem fair that getting an opportunity for my future came at the cost of the first person I'd opened up to in years. What sucked was that I understood her hesitation about me coaching. I did. I just... assumed she knew I'd be different. Or I'd hoped she'd give me a chance.

I fisted my hand and powered through the pulsing in my temple. Focus on the good. The coaching opportunity. On learning from Coach Simpson. On the fact I got a salary. A decent one.

Even as I listed all the good news in my mind, the one glaring *bad* moment remained fresh. Naomi deciding it was too hard to try and be together. I scrubbed a hand over my face and regretted it because I had ketchup on my fingers. Annoyed at her, myself, and Cal's loud chewing, I groaned.

"Dude, you're grumpier than normal," Cal said, grease dripping down his chin. He wiped it with the back of his hand, and I snorted. He was uncivilized.

"Yeah, that can happen."

Cal furrowed his brows and set his food down, leaning onto his elbows and frowning at me. "Your parents are cheering for you, you know? With you getting this job. They'll be proud."

My throat tightened, and for the life of me, I wanted to cry. The absolute understanding in Cal's eyes was enough to set me over the edge. Suddenly, I had to move. To run. To do something other than sit here and feel and think. "Let's go."

"Uh, I'm not done."

"Fine, stay and finish. I gotta get out of this place." He had like four fries left. I stood and tossed a twenty on the table. I didn't wait to see if he followed before walking out of the cafe and breathing in the crisp fall air. The chilled temperatures always soothed me in a way that some people talked about the summer heat.

The cold was less personal and comforting than warmth, I knew that, but I preferred the sting in my throat, the way my nose tingled from the wind. It was familiar and safe like back home. I stood at the edge of campus and focused on things to ground myself. The leaves changing color since Thanksgiving was right around the corner. The fading colors of the bricked buildings with the clouds covering most of the sky. The throngs of students walking to or from class.

I wished I could call my dad and ask for advice. For him to tell me what to do or how to get these feelings to go away. I wanted to hear my mom's voice.

I called Ryann.

"This is Ryann's phone," Jonah answered, and my first instinct was to yell at him for picking up her phone.

But they lived together, had been together for years, and he was good for her. I didn't have a complaint about him except for the fact *they* figured out how to make it work when I couldn't. "Hey, J.D."

"Everything good? Your sister's in the shower, but I can get her if it's urgent."

"No, it's... not." I sighed and scratched my chest again.

"Cool. Congrats on getting the coaching job, by the way." He sounded like he genuinely meant his words. "Can't think of anything better suited for you."

"Nice words, coming from you," I said, a sliver of my *old self* returning.

"I mean, damn." He cleared his throat. The guy was horrible at compliments and general conversation unless it was with Ryann, so I cut the guy some slack.

"I appreciate it, Jonah, I really do."

"I'd play for you in a heartbeat," he grumbled out, and the weight of his statement made me nod. There was no higher compliment coming from a laser-focused guy like J.D.

"Thanks, man." I coughed to clear the feelings creeping into my voice. "Hey," I asked, nerves exploding in my gut. "Back when you were with… my sister and were afraid to tell me and the team, what made you change your mind?"

He sighed, and I pictured his dark eyes widening in panic. We didn't discuss this stuff, ever. I talked with Ryann about it, but J.D. and I had a mutual understanding that if he hurt my sister, I'd hurt him. However, the parallel of their relationship and what I had with Naomi was too similar to ignore.

"Picturing life without Ryann wasn't something I ever wanted to do. That meant… well, when you found out before I could talk to you, it scared the fuck out of me."

"What would've happened if I said I hated it and didn't approve?"

"I wouldn't have cared, Reiner. Ry would've been upset, and we would've worked through that together, but it was about us. Ryann and me. Look," he said, his tone shifting to a softer one that I hadn't heard before. "Whoever she is...because let's be honest, this isn't about me and your sister. Don't let someone else determine what the two of you want."

"Right. Thanks," I said, emotion clogging my voice, and my face burned. Despite *how* we got to this point, I trusted Jonah. He was a part of our family now. Even if he and Ryann never decided to get married, he was part of our circle. "Just have Ryann call me later, please."

"Sure thing."

We hung up, and something hard and sharp formed in my heart, like an icicle. Piercing, cold, and painful. Jonah's words repeated, and the meaning of them took root. I wasn't the problem with Naomi. It was her dad. Her baggage with hockey. She was the one letting the past determine us being together.

Only, it was my new job. She never once mentioned her dad in her reasoning.

It seemed that I was more invested in her than she was with me, and it stung because I knew better. I told myself to not get too involved, but it happened so easily. Effortlessly, even. The way she understood me and talked to me about life. The way she laughed and smelled.

Fuck.

"You always such a dick?" Cal asked, moving to stand next to me.

His sudden appearance had me snort. I shrugged. "Don't you have something better to do than bother your assistant coach?"

"Not really. My roommate's an asshole, and what else could I do on a Friday morning?"

"Not bother me," I said, laughing to take the sting out of the words. "Come on, if you want to continue annoying me, let's make use of the time. We can watch some old games and discuss your ego on the ice."

He groaned, and *that* made me cackle for real. "No need to be a bitch about it since you're in your feels."

"Oh, I'm not. This is for the team, Cal. It has nothing to do with getting back at you."

He could've walked away, but he followed me to the rink, talking about nonsense. The number one thing I learned since that night in the bar was that Cal wasn't as shy and quiet as I thought. What I mistook for arrogance and attitude was, in fact, a kid struggling with his life and not knowing what to do.

He wanted attention—which I understood.

But sweet Jesus. The kid liked to gab, and I refused to be legit annoyed by it. I had a handful of mentors who helped me when I was younger, and it was not only the right thing to do but also something that mattered to me. Giving back to the hockey community. Paying it forward. And hell, if guiding Cal was a part of that, I'd see it through.

We approached the block the rink sat on, and I stopped, dead in my tracks. *Naomi.*

The sight of Naomi walking with her dad and sister felt like a punch to the sternum. I hadn't seen her since Sunday when she decided being with me wasn't worth the risk. This had to be heartbreak.

I'd heard about it. I'd seen teammates go through it, but fuck. It was worse than I thought. My stomach cramped when she smiled at Cami, and then her gaze moved toward me. We had to be at least a hundred feet away, yet I felt her stare in my soul. *You ended this. You did this.*

Cami stopped walking and elbowed Naomi, the two clearly whispering.

Cal cleared his throat. "Is there a reason we're in a mini stare down with Coach's twin daughters? Which, can we talk about the fact Coach has twin girls? Like, what the fuck, man? Twins! They don't even look like him."

"Shut your mouth." I shoved my hands in my pockets and took a deep, cold breath. My heart hammered in my chest, and everything got hotter. My neck, my face, my fucking palms.

"Coach, good to see you again," Coach Simpson said, his voice loud and cheerful. He held out his hand, and I shook it as I forced a tight smile.

"You as well. You heading out?"

"Sure thing. Naomi crashed my standing lunch with Cami, and I lost track of time. Gotta run to my condo." He put his arm around Cami in a hug and did a watered-down version on Naomi. "See you in a few hours, Reiner. Tonight's your debut, officially."

Shit. I didn't even think about that. My first night as the assistant coach on the bench. My tongue felt too large for my mouth, and he must've known.

He reached out and squeezed my shoulder. "Hey, you're made for this. Things work out for a reason. But I have some gear for you later. You gotta represent Central."

"Of course, sir."

He slid his gaze to Cal and then back to me. "Keep him in line."

"Always do," I said, earning a scoff from Cal. "We're about to watch some films."

"Good. Good. Okay, I really need to go. Can't get talked into hockey stuff now, or I'll never get there on time. Bye." He took off toward the parking lot, leaving the four of us standing in a weird circle. It reminded me of high school. Awkward.

Naomi took a step closer to us with a hesitant smile.

How dare she *smile* at me after she made me fall for her? The nerves about the game and the lingering heartbreak shifted to anger, and that icicle in my soul guided me. "Naomi," I said, not happy at all. "Cami."

"Hey, Coach," Cami said, winking at me before approaching Cal. "Can't wait to see you on the ice tonight. Holt, you ready for the game?"

He nodded, and the same serious face I was used to seeing replaced the relaxed one that was just there. Interesting.

"Walk me to the coffee shop, would you?" Cami asked him, holding out her arm in an obvious attempt to leave me and Naomi alone.

No thank you.

"He's with me." I shook my head and ignored Naomi's large brown eyes pleading with me for *something.* What did she want? To hang out? To pretend like this past week didn't fucking suck? That I didn't lose my best friend here?

"It'll be quick. He'll be back in five minutes." Cami's tone was a little harsher, and she took Cal by the arm and dragged him down the sidewalk.

He met my eyes for one second, his brows scrunched together. I nodded. Something melted inside me that this punk ass kid was worried about me. He didn't know a thing about Naomi or me. I hadn't told a soul about us, but it was clear the air was heavy.

Tense as hell.

I watched Cami and Cal get smaller as they walked farther away, and I slid my gaze to Naomi. My heart fucking hurt seeing her this close. Her hair was pulled into a bun, and her large brown eyes looked anxious. She kept moving her attention to my face, then my shoulders, then my face again. She wrapped her arms around her Central State sweatshirt and rocked back on her heels.

"Hey," she said, her voice husky and nervous. "How have you been?"

"Naomi," I said, anger seeping into my tone. "What do you want to say? We don't need to do *this*." I waved my hand between us, motioning it left and right. Jonah's words came back to me. He'd known the risk about being with Ryann but chose it anyway.

I knew it with Naomi and chose it anyway.

She just didn't.

She chewed her bottom lip and sniffed. "I thought… Michael, look." She gulped and blinked a few times before glancing up at me. "Could we talk or something?"

"About what?"

The wind picked up, the cold breezing sending a chill down my spine. It was a good reminder to step back. To *never* let someone tear my guard down and cause me pain.

"Us." She shivered and reached out to touch me but dropped her hand. "I miss—"

"We're *friends* now, right? That's what you wanted. That it'd be easier *for you* now that I'm an assistant coach," I said, my voice getting louder. "Well, it's not easier for me, okay?"

She tilted her head to the side and scrunched her cute nose. "What does that mean?"

"It means that this… it's done. All of it. I can't…" I shook my head and wanted to punch a wall. With one final look at the girl who'd gotten into my soul and sliced it open, I cracked. I couldn't go through this again. "I would've risked it all for you."

"Michael," her voice broke, and her eyes got watery. I didn't wait to see if she had more to say though. I went into the rink and focused on the only thing that had always been there for me. Hockey. It's what I knew and did best.

CHAPTER
TWENTY-EIGHT

Naomi

I wasn't a pretty crier. My face became puffy, and my eyes stayed red for at least a day. Plus, my voice got scratchy, and my throat hurt something fierce. Two weeks post-Michael, I was a mess. He wouldn't answer my texts and didn't look back at me once the last two games. I knew I fucked it all up, but *why* did it feel like I couldn't breathe? My laptop had two percent battery, and my wrists hurt from working at this awkward angle. Given my inability to sleep or be happy, I threw myself into the stats project.

Numbers were therapeutic and didn't have feelings. Someone knocked on our door, and for a split second, my heart leapt in my throat.

"Want me to get it?" Mona said, reaching out from next to me and running a hand over my shoulder. She'd been watching season five of How to Get Away With Murder. We both had insane crushes on Viola Davis and the guy who played Dean Thomas, and focusing on fake drama was what I needed.

"No, I'll get up." I brushed crumbs off my shirt and knew as I walked toward the door that it couldn't be Michael. It was

Saturday. Post-game. He'd be with my dad *all* day doing hockey business.

I ground my teeth together at the *third* time my dad blew me off on the project. He dissed me in front of Cami, refused to spend time alone with me, and I was sick of it. Speaking of Cami… I opened the door, and my sister stood there wearing an overly large white cut off sweatshirt.

"You look like shit," she said, frowning as she walked right into my apartment. "God, your place is great. Smells like cookies."

"Because I made some," Mona said, pausing the show and eyeing Cami with a protectiveness that made me almost smile. "We're still in the moping phase if you'd like to join us."

"Absolutely. I'm great at moping." Cami flashed a grin at Mona and situated herself on the single chair to the right of where I was sitting. "You've avoided my calls the past two weeks, and I remembered how you got in junior high. Pouty. Recluse. I figured I needed to come over to pull you out of it."

"It's not that simple."

"Yes, it is." She leaned onto her knees, and a dark, intense stare crossed her face. No trace of the beauty-pageant sister. "Fix your issues with Dad, then talk to Michael."

"She's right," Mona said, wincing as I turned to her.

"Excuse me?" My heart raced, and my face warmed. "Issues with Dad?"

"Look, I love you. Things have been weird with us, and we're working on it, but I'm sure Mona would agree. Your shit is with dad, not Michael. Not hockey. Dad was a horrible husband and a crap father to two girls. I know you think we have a special bond, but there's a lot you don't know." She pushed her hair out of her face. "Dad is a dick, and I see it more and more since you told me how you felt. Confront him. Demand an explanation. Because girl, you're not ever gonna be able to open your heart if you got all this drama in there."

Mona put her arm around my shoulders and squeezed. "You

started this internship because of your dad. Has it gotten better?"

I shook my head.

"Worse?"

I nodded.

"And that's okay with you? The Naomi I know would *never* let a middle-aged man make her feel inferior. Who cares if it's your dad? Stand up to him. Outsmart him. Show him that you know you're worth loving." Mona sniffed and hugged me tight. "I think you need to let the idea of you two healing go and instead, work on showing him the real Naomi. Because if he doesn't want you in his life, then why are you trying so hard to stay in his?"

Fuck. I hung my head as a heavy, deafening silence followed.

They were right. One hundred percent right. My sister and my best friend. Another wave of tears hit me, and the taste of salt rolled into my mouth. Was this heartbreak with Michael because of my issues with Dad? Was I the reason this had fallen apart? The truth hit me in the side of the face, hard.

I'd fucked up.

"So, are we thinking uh, now? I need to talk to my dad today?"

"No." Cami patted my knee, awkwardly. "When you're ready. But… the sooner, the better. I've seen a really grumpy and sad assistant coach walking around."

Michael. The guy I loved.

I let him down. The guy who'd been through so fucking much. The guy who told me I was his best friend here.

I squeezed my eyes as pain radiated through me. The thought of confronting my dad scared the shit out of me, but I'd do it for Michael. I owed Michael that—to open up this wound that made me drive him away. Maybe this would be enough for him to forgive me.

"Today. I'll do it today."

My dad always wore a polo on game days. It was that way growing up and no different now. He muttered something to himself as I stood outside his office a few hours later. I wore my favorite jeans and hoodie along with an orange beanie. It was getting colder outside, and my teeth shook from a horrible combination of chills and adrenaline. I knocked on the doorframe hard, and he looked up.

"Naomi, what are you doing here?" He glanced at his watch. "We didn't have a meeting, did we?"

"No, because every time I've set one up with you, you've bailed. Which, you're really good at bailing on me. You've been doing it my entire life."

He stood straighter than I'd ever seen and set the papers down on his desk. "Something on your mind, kiddo?"

"Clearly," I said, crossing my arms and refusing to sit on the chair he pointed to. "Do you know why I wanted this internship?"

"Uh, for your class project, right?" he said, his face flushing as his eyes moved back and forth from me to the doorway. "Should we shut the door for this or…?"

"Jesus. Worried about the team? Of course you are. That's legit all you care about. The fucking hockey team." I pinched the bridge of my nose as my eyes stung.

"Naomi, look—"

"I took this internship because I was sick of hating you. I wanted to fix our relationship before I graduated because then we'd just do the awkward holiday calls. But you know what? I don't care anymore. You're selfish and cruel. You dismiss me every chance you can. Not with Cami though. No, you make time for her."

He blinked and swallowed so hard his throat made a clicking sound. "I-I don't—"

"I'm not done," I yelled, my face almost on fire. "I worked

my ass off for this project. The player profiles and team dashboard are next level."

"I know that," he almost shouted. "Michael walked me through them. Told me how good you are and how incredible they were! I made a change last week on the line up because of the one you did for Erikson!"

Michael showed him? Told him how good I was? A thrill went through me, giving me some extra courage.

"Which you should've. Told. Me. About," I said, my teeth clenched together.

The mention of Michael caused my stomach to ache, but I powered through. This was the mother of confrontations, and it was like a dam of emotion unleashed. My head pounded and my palms sweat. My hands shook, and I paced the room, gripping the back of a chair as anger wrapped itself around me. I couldn't stop my thoughts and feelings toward my dad.

"You *pawned* me off to Hank or Michael. You cancelled plans. You've let me down so many times that I can't recall the last time you haven't." I laughed out of sheer adrenaline, not that there was anything comical about the situation. "I used to think I hated hockey, but the truth is you're a shitty dad."

"*You don't think I know that?*" he yelled back, his eyes almost popping out of his face.

"You know that you're a shitty dad?" I asked, completely dumbfounded. I blinked a few times, repeating the words. There was no way he admitted it. None. My heart raced like I went up five stories of stairs. I could feel my heart pound against my ribcage in a painful way as I stared at him.

"Yeah, fuck." He ran a hand over his face a few times, causing his face to become redder. "I don't know how to act around you because I'm so terrified of making things worse, so I avoid you."

"But with Cami…"

"Your mom always made me go to Cami's things. As a kid until now—because your mom hates sports. All of them.

Blames them for our divorce and her unhappiness. Athletics is how I know to bond, and honestly, Cami doesn't look at me like she hates my guts. I don't have to... Look, Naomi. I'm sorry. I'm sorry for what I did to your mom, to you. If I could go back, I'd change *everything*. But when the marriage ended, I had nothing else *but* hockey. Do you see that?" His eyes were wet, and his voice shook. I was so used to the stern guy or the charismatic coach, but this... the absolute shame and regret etched onto his face was a lot to take in. I nodded before he continued.

"I got a do-over on the ice. I could guide these kids without them despising me. I get guys like Michael who look up to me and don't see a failed husband and father. They see me like a good coach."

"I never hated you. Not really," I said, my voice weak and quiet. "I lost everyone. Mom, Cami, and you. I just wanted someone to care about me."

"Fuck, come here." He shoved a chair out of the way yanked me hard against his chest. He smelled like stale coffee and stiff laundry, and my eyes stung as he hugged me so tight I couldn't breathe.

"I'm so sorry, Naomi. I'm so fucking sorry you felt that way. Of course I love you. I'm so proud of you. I just didn't know how to talk to you."

The dam broke. All the hate and anger... all the regret and wondering if I was enough. This. This was why I wanted to intern with him. Sure, I didn't envision us screaming at each other, but we finally had the confrontation we needed. I cried against him as relief rushed through me. He held me and patted my back for a good five minutes before we broke apart.

His brown eyes looked a little misty as he gave me a half-smile. "Do you want to get some food? Or not, if you have plans. I just... I'm so happy you came here and yelled at me."

"I can't believe I did." I wiped my nose on the back of my sleeve.

"I can. When you're passionate about something, you go all

out. I remember once you were intent on saving this family of ladybugs, and you wrote an entire rulebook for the family on how to take care of them. You made us all sign an agreement page, and you were eight, maybe nine?" He laughed, the lines around his eyes deepening. "I promise you, right now, that I will never put hockey above you again. There might be emergencies, but *us*, this… this matters more. I want to be in your life, kid. Could I have another shot?"

I nodded before he even finished the sentence and pulled me into another hug.

"Yes. I think I'd like to try again."

"So, about that dinner?"

While the thought of us eating together was appealing, I had another person in my life who deserved the truth. "I can't tonight. There's something else I need to do."

"Okay, then before you leave, let's check my calendar to make sure we get something down."

He pulled out his phone and clicked his tongue as his fingers moved across the screen. "Tuesday night work for you?"

I nodded, nervous about this new arrangement but willing to give it a try. My dad had work to do to get me to trust him, but our relationship already felt different. Yelling at him and clearing the air gave me peace of mind, and I chewed on my lip as he finished putting the details in his phone. While the wound was still fresh, the motivation behind this confrontation still hadn't left my mind. *Michael.*

"Um, how has Michael been doing the past few weeks?"

My dad's gaze snapped to mine, wide and full of understanding. "On the ice, fine. I have a feeling that's not what you're asking."

Okay, we were getting right to it then. I put my hands on my hips and exhaled all the nerves. "We were together, kind of. I ruined it before we had a chance to try." I cleared my throat as emotion clogged it—I had a hard time accepting the fact my heartbreak was my fault. Yes, he chose hockey because it was an amazing opportunity. But it was my beef with my dad that had me too scared to give him a chance.

Love meant taking a risk, and I'd been a damn fool. Michael had too big of a heart to intentionally cause me pain. He communicated openly, where my dad *never* did. I hated knowing I hurt him. "I love him. I'm in love with him. He works for you, and we have issues we need to deal with, but I can't let those excuses rule me anymore. You can hate it, but frankly, I don't care."

"I can't think of two people better suited for each other, Naomi." He gave a hesitant smile and lifted one shoulder up in a shrug. "I figured something was going on. Look, you're human. We all make mistakes. I do constantly. But don't be like me. Don't be afraid of admitting you fucked up. If I got over myself and my self-pity, we wouldn't be where we are now. Talk to him."

Don't be afraid. He was right. I didn't want to be like my dad or be a hypocrite. I'd been so afraid of falling for Michael and coming in second place that I ended up putting him second. Second to my fears. Courage was a weird thing that I rarely felt because I always considered myself the opposite of brave.

But that was false. I'd opened my heart to my sister. I let Michael in. I confronted my dad. I *could* be bold, and it was time I used it to repair the relationship with the guy I wanted to be with—hockey and all.

"I gotta go, but... I'm glad we're... okay."

"Me too, Nana." He used my childhood name. Hearing it made the stinging in my eyes come back again. "We'll start slow and figure out how to be in each other's lives again. I promise, alright?"

I nodded and was already out the door. The brief flare of courage morphed into fear, paralyzing fear as I marched toward Michael's place. Each step weighed a million pounds, and the unanswered texts from him had me questioning everything.

Was I too late? Would he forgive me? Did I hurt him so badly that he hated me now?

Cars raced down the busy road, the loud sound of their engines giving me a focal point. Logic helped me. So, I made the plan in my head.

Not talking to Michael wasn't a choice. So, no matter my fear or the outcome, I couldn't hide back at my place and pretend I was fine. I'd go to him and put it all on the line.

And if he tells me to fuck off?

Then I'd deserve it.

I tripped over a curb from my shaky limbs. Even though my toe stung, I smiled. I'd have to tell him to add another point to my klutz score. My mind played the horrible *what if* game the rest of the walk, until all too soon, I stood outside his apartment door.

I should call him. See if he was even home. He could've been out or—a woman laughed.

Someone was inside his place. A female.

It could be Freddie's sister or mom or friend or…

The door opened, the sound of the door handle turning as the female voice said, "Michael, my god, you're too much right now."

Here I was, standing with my fist in the air about to knock when the door opened all the way, and another woman stood there.

CHAPTER
TWENTY-NINE

Michael

I couldn't believe Ryann and Jonah surprised me. My goddamn sister *knew* I was in a funk and borrowed Jonah's dad's car. They drove thousands of miles to cheer me up for Thanksgiving weekend. Getting the call from her yesterday morning was exactly what I needed to get out of the shitty mood I'd lived in the past two weeks.

"I don't like the fact you drove here in a day. No humans should have that many energy drinks. It could destroy your body," I said to my sister, who rolled her eyes.

I'd never been in love before, and this part of it sucked. How unfair was it that getting my dream job meant losing the girl I fell for? I scratched a hand over my chest as Jonah came out from the bathroom.

"You sure your coach won't mind if we skate?"

"He'll love getting to meet you." I already texted Coach Simpson and asked permission. It made zero sense to me that this honest, hard-core guy was such a horrible father. While I wished Naomi had taken a chance on us, I understood why she didn't. "I still can't believe you're here."

"Well, the guys are stoked that you're coaching. I'm not the only one who'd play for you, Michael." Jonah's intense eye contact might've put some people off, but I knew what it meant—that he was serious. He adjusted the strings on his hoodie as my sister stood at the open door, not moving or saying anything.

"Ry, what are you doing?" The cold air blew in, and while we were supposed to head to the rink, we weren't in a hurry. I had nothing to do on weekends besides hockey, and we'd already played last night.

"Uh, someone's here to see you."

"Cal?" I said, taking a few steps toward the door and glancing over my sister's shoulder. I frowned. Cal wouldn't be here. He had plans with Dan. Then who could it…shit.

Naomi was outside my place wearing a large sweatshirt and beanie, looking terrified. Her cheeks were pink, her eyes wide, and she clasped her hands in front of her stomach. Her knuckles were white, and my instinct was to take her fingers and give them warmth. Her beautiful face had dark circles under her eyes, and there was evidence she'd recently cried.

God, I wanted to hug her, but that moment passed. It wasn't my job to comfort her, not after she broke my heart. A few beats of silence passed between us, the sound of cars the only thing audible besides the rush of my pulse in my ears. *Say something.*

"Why are you here?" I asked, my voice gruff and deep like I hadn't slept great. Which, I hadn't.

"You're busy." She blinked a lot and took a step away. "I can… come back?"

Ry put a hand on my arm and squeezed. "We can keep ourselves entertained for a while if you need space, Michael."

"No. Naomi's running away again anyway," I said, my eye twitching at her slumped shoulders. For one second, I thought… maybe she was here because she missed me. Or realized we were amazing together. But if that were true, she wouldn't be trying to leave the first chance she had.

"I'm not *running* away. You have a visitor," she fired back, the redness in her cheeks growing toward her neck. I loved her blush, and I made a fist at my side.

I opened my mouth to say something when she interrupted. "You miss your sister like crazy, and she's here, obviously far from home. You deserve to spend time with her. We can talk later."

Whoa. I *liked* that fire brewing behind her eyes. The girl afraid of confrontation had grown some courage.

Ryann narrowed her eyes at Naomi and pursed her lips. "Jonah and I are going to grab food. We need real sustenance after that road trip. Maybe you'll be here when we get back, maybe not. If you are… well, I hope we can get to know each other."

My damn sister walked past Naomi, stopping a few feet away and looking back up as Jonah followed. The guy didn't even glance my way before putting his arm around Ryann and walking on the sidewalk.

That left Naomi and I here, and I was nervous.

"Can I come in?" she asked, her voice small and lacking her usual zest. I missed that *N-energy* and her jokes and her anecdotes about data and murder shows.

"Right, yeah." I moved out of the way as she headed inside my place. I was confused that she was still here and not running. Maybe it was the fire I saw in her eyes. Either way, I was glad she was here even if it was for a short time. Her familiar scent filled me with an aggressive longing for home. I ran my hand through my hair as she paced the living room. Everything about her was fucking cute. Her orange Chucks, her little steps, the way she held her hands behind her back. I guess being in love made me a little insane. "Stop pacing, Naomi. Why are you here?"

"Confrontation is really tough for me."

"I know," I said, my voice softening just a bit. It hardened though when I asked, "Are you planning on yelling at me?"

"No. No, Michael." She stilled and looked at me with *love* in her big brown eyes, I got that weightless feeling of hope again.

I wanted to grip that feeling, but I held off. Naomi had hurt me. I cleared my throat and waited her out. Yes, I'd stopped us from being friends because it was too painful. Wait—was that why she was here? To push for friendship again? Fuck. I wasn't sure I could do that. My pulse raced, and my stomach felt like it was filled with rocks as I raised a hand. "Look, if you're here about ending our friendship—"

"I love you, you wonderful, gentle man. I fucking love you, and I messed up, and I had this entire speech planned out, and my brain went to shit," she said, blurring the words together so it came out in one breath. Her face went fire engine red, and she tossed her hands up in the air. I was stunned, unable to move, speak, or breathe.

"I'm sorry. I'm sorry I was too scared. I'm sorry I let my issues with my dad interfere with us. Am I too late? Do you hate me now? If you do, I get it. Maybe we can be friends again? I don't know, I just… I want to hold you and see how you're doing. I want to watch hockey just so I can talk to you about it. I never want you to feel alone again because you're not. I'll be your person, and you can be mine." She sniffed, and tears rolled down her cheeks.

My brain went in overtime to digest all her words. She said a lot, but the biggest thing that stuck out was that she loved me. She fucking loved me. "You love me?" I asked, needing to hear it again to be sure.

She nodded and bit her bottom lip. "It snuck up on me in the best way. But I do. I love you, Michael Reiner."

She walked up to me, nervously, and cupped my face with her small hands. My limbs went into shock because I couldn't move. I wanted to tell her I felt the same way and kiss her, but nothing happened. I remained still, like a cardboard cutout.

She traced her soft padded fingers over my cheeks, lips, and rested her hands on my shoulders. "Before you say anything, I went to my dad. I confronted him about *everything*. It scared the shit out of me. I yelled. I cussed. The old me never would've done that. Ever. I would've lived my life secretly hating him and wondering why I wasn't enough."

"Naomi, baby," I said, covering her hands with mine. This woman had my whole fucking heart. "God, *I* love you. You must—"

"No, shh, please." She smiled, her watery brown eyes pulling me in like a damn magnet. "You inspired me. I knew I needed to confront that part of my past to be with you. It wouldn't be fair for me to hold onto these thoughts and blame hockey. You're going to be such a fine coach, and I can't wait to see you grow and mentor players. You lead with your heart and soul. But it was your openness and willingness to have tough conversations that helped me find the strength."

A ball formed in the back of my throat at her words. I'd been praised on my leadership, my charisma, my looks, but Naomi's affirmation hit me in my soul. "Are you alright?"

"Am I okay?" she asked, recoiling. "You're asking me if I'm okay when I was the one who fucked this up?"

I couldn't wait anymore. I had to have her, hold her against me and kiss her like I'd thought about every second of every day since she left. I cupped her face, dropped my mouth to hers, and kissed her. I hoisted her up and wrapped her legs around my waist, sliding my tongue into her mouth so I could taste her. Breathe her in. Be with the woman who loved me back.

"Michael," she said, grinning against my mouth.

"Shh," I said, mocking her from earlier. "Let me kiss the woman I love."

"I was groveling though." She kissed my neck and ran her fingers through my hair over and over. She pulled back and looked down at me with love all over her face. "I want to be with you, Michael. Please, am I too late?"

"No. No more groveling." I walked her toward my bedroom and kicked the door shut with my foot. Feeling the weight of her words, her hands on me… I was turning into putty. "You're not too late. I've fucking missed you."

She pulled back, cupped my chin with her small hand, and stared at me. "I'm sorry I hurt you. I was so worried you'd pick hockey over me that I ended up doing it to you."

"You were scared," I said, kneading the dimples in her back. "You're not anymore. Why?"

"Because not loving you wasn't an option. Because my issue was never about hockey. And because…" she said, stopping to kiss me slowly. She slid her tongue into my mouth and groaned, sending all my blood below my belt.

My heart felt put together again, and this sexy woman ground her hips against me. I wasn't going to last long at all once I had her naked. I cupped the back of her head and deepened the kiss, showing her without words that all was forgiven. We all had our baggage, and if she was willing to communicate about it more, then we'd work through our hurdles together.

She pawed at me like she couldn't get close enough, and when I set her on the bed, she looked at me with flushed cheeks and a pretty smile. "I never finished my thought."

"I'm not stopping you." I winked as I reached for her button. She wiggled her hips as I slid her pants off her body and moaned as I ran my hands up and down her thighs. "Fuck, I love your body." I kissed her inner thigh. "And your heart. Your mind. I love all of you Naomi, baggage and all."

She squeezed her eyes shut and pulled me back up to her face. "I won't mess this up again. I need you to know that. I might be an idiot sometimes, but I never want you to question how much I care for you."

I kissed her, softly, before running my hands under her shirt and placing one over her heart. It beat fast under my palm, matching my own erratic pace. "I never doubted how you felt about me. I saw it every time you laughed with me. Every time you held my hand in yours and rubbed your finger over my palm. Every time we shared things with each other that were hard. Love isn't enough sometimes, which is a scary truth. But I know it was your fear holding you back, not your emotions, and I'm so proud of you."

"Of me?"

"Yes." I grinned at her and let my hand wander toward her nipple. I pinched it, and she bucked on the bed. "For fixing things with your sister. For standing up for yourself with your dad. For giving us a chance…love is terrifying, but I want to try, with you. We each have our own shit to deal with, but we can do it together. That's all I wanted. I've suffered a lot of loss, which makes finding joy rare. *You* are my joy, Naomi Fletcher."

She sighed and gave me a huge, heart-stopping smile. I scooped her up, intent on kissing her. She had her own ideas though. She crawled onto my lap and traced her finger over my chest. "Your relationship with Ryann inspired me to be a better sister and maybe even a better daughter. You have such a good heart, Michael. I want to prove to you I'll take care of it."

I kissed her, hard, and she let out a deep moan. Her words took root right in soul, where I wanted to keep them there forever. *This* feeling had to be what life was about. Two puzzle pieces that fit together, that formed a team. After being a lone wolf for most of my adult life, her words were reassurance, promise, and hope. My throat felt tight and rough as I stared down at her, unsure how to relay how much she meant to me.

"You are my person, by the way." I kissed her softly. "If you weren't sure, you are." I pressed my lips against hers again. "Damn, I missed your mouth."

"What about your sister? She must hate me," Naomi said, trying to scoot away from me. I traced the outside of her damp panties, and she stilled.

"She'd never hate anyone I loved." I ran a finger down her slit, watching how her pulse raced. "And I've been talking about you for months, Naomi. Now, enough chatting. I want to devour my girlfriend before they come back."

"Your girlfriend?" she squeaked out, her eyes going wide again.

"Yes." I slid her panties to the side and inserted one finger into her. She panted and wet her bottom lip before I nipped at it. "We're together. Exclusive and together. You and me. You got any problems with that, Fletcher?"

"No, none at all." She gave me a breathless smile as I added another finger. I was going to get my girlfriend off twice before finally having her again, and after, we could go hang out with the other two people in my circle.

It wasn't large, and yeah, the thought of getting hurt again worried me, but life wasn't filled with guarantees. I knew that the hard way. So, I was going to enjoy every second I could with the woman I loved, the one who had snuck past all my damn walls. The girl who saw the real me, the grief and sadness and happiness all mixed into one and wanted me anyway.

She said she was going to prove to me that she deserved my heart?

Well, game on, Fletcher. I would prove to *us* that we were meant for each other.

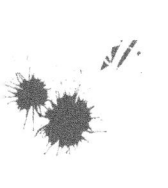

EPILOGUE
EIGHT MONTHS LATER

Michael

The middle of summer always sent an energy through me that meant *get ready*. Not just for school to start but also for practices to get more intense, for workouts to be more regimented, and to start mentally preparing for the season. It felt weird as fuck to still have all the same hockey thoughts but none of the school ones.

I had a masters in sports management. I had a full-time job I loved that consumed me to the point I wasn't convinced this was adulting. Adulting was supposed to be bills and laundry and stress… but this was different. I was happier than I was sad, and I was hopeful about the future. Sure, there were bad days still, but the future didn't seem as daunting. Not with my girlfriend by my side and filling the void in my life with her dorky jokes and contagious laugh.

Plus, my sister and her partner were getting a fucking house together back east, and wow…my life had changed a ton this past year. Freddie and I met once a week to catch up like we were buds. Which, we were. It was still odd to have casual friends who weren't a part of my hockey world. We even met with Naomi's friends for trivia nights. I eyed my desk and the huge to do list I just started staring up at me.

I had a to-do list that was all hockey. My dream scenario.

It was moments like this that made me smile up at the sun, silently thanking my parents for watching over me. Some would say it was weird or what not, but I knew deep in my soul that I had to go through the hard stuff to finally reach the place where life was good. Better than good. I still missed my parents something fierce, but I wasn't as sad.

Or alone.

God, I was rarely alone.

"Ay, Reiner," the familiar voice of Cal Holt at my doorway making me groan. "Don't do that. You love me."

"I don't."

"Yes, you do." He sat down across my desk with a piece of beef jerky hanging from his mouth. I met his confident smirk, and even though he was right, I refused to give in to him. I had a soft spot for him that I was sure went both ways.

The young kid had needed someone, and I'd become that person. I was still his assistant coach, but there was a relationship now that would span beyond the college team. We both knew it, but there was no sense talking about it. "Is there a reason you're in here stinking like teriyaki, or am I just special?"

"Coach said he's ready for you." He wiggled his brows and scarfed down a huge chunk of the food.

Still an uncivilized punk with all the talent in the world. After he swallowed, the weight of his words hit me. *Coach.* Naomi's dad. She was still working on their relationship, but it was better. There were a few times where I was awkwardly in the middle, but honestly, it felt right helping them navigate their miscommunications. The fact I had a part in them fixing their past made me insanely happy. I knew my mom and dad would be proud too.

I rubbed the back of my neck, and Cal picked up on it instantly. He leaned forward with wide eyes and a stupid smirk.

"Oh, you're anxious. Why? Naomi?"

"Wow, way to mind your business." I sighed and eyed the hallway, unsure what I was nervous about. Sure, talking to Coach about my intentions after Naomi's senior year was difficult, but it was time. It'd been almost a year, and we'd only ever talked about our relationship once.

The day I confessed everything. He stared at me, nodded, and said *You're both adults. Handle it that way.*

"Bro," Cal said, and I held up a hand.

"Call me Reiner or Coach."

He rolled his eyes and leaned onto my desk. "For real though, you two get along. You're a decent guy. You and Naomi are annoyingly good together."

"Decent guy? I'm sure every father wants to hear their daughter is dating a *decent* guy."

Cal's ears turned red, and he held his palms up in surrender. "Don't make me compliment you."

I snorted and stood, ready to do this. Whatever it was…if it was hockey related, he'd send me a text that said *let's chat*. This formalized invitation to come into his office made the entire situation weirder. "If you hear any crying, bring me tissues."

"Whatever man, you'll be fine. Promise you'll invite me to the wedding."

I ignored his comment as I walked toward Coach's office, but Cal's words took root and grew. Wedding. Marrying Naomi. Being her husband and sharing every moment of life with her. I could picture it—my small family blending with hers. Hell, her dad was already a mentor to me. Naomi Reiner.

Reiner-Fletcher-Simpson.

I had a smile on my face thinking about all the ways she could hyphenate her name, if she even wanted that, when I tapped the door to his office.

"Get in here. How many times we gotta talk about this?

You're not a player. You can walk in." He grunted and waved me over. "I'm thinking about adding mandatory study tables this year. I'd like your thoughts on implementation and scheduling before everyone comes back."

"You got it." I cleared my throat, nervous and waiting. Still hockey business, but the buildup was there. The squinted eyes. The puffed-out chest. He was in dad mode.

He put his hands on his hips and eyed me. "You've been with my daughter for a while now. She called me last night going on about how much she misses you. So, I have one question for you, Reiner. Just one."

Fuck. I wiped my hands on the side of my pants and nodded. "Alright."

"If I told you right now that you either get this job or my daughter, what would you say? And I know this isn't correct or legal, but from a father to the guy my daughter is in love with, tell me."

It'd be easy to just say *I'd pick Naomi* because this was a hypothetical situation. I knew that, but my answer still mattered. "If this were a real situation, then, sir, I wouldn't only tell Naomi about it, but I'd discuss it with her. I want a life with Naomi, and jobs are going to come and go. There are a lot of situations that could factor into this choice too. If we were together and had a young kid and I was the only one with a paycheck, could we afford for me to quit? Or, what if—"

"Enough. Jesus, you two." He rubbed his temples, but his face broke out into a smile. "I think of you as a son already, Reiner. Don't make the mistakes I did, alright? She's not along for the ride for *your* life—you're in it together as partners."

I think of you as a son. Those words settled over me like a warm blanket. "I know, sir, and I plan to keep it that way as long as I can."

He narrowed his eyes, held out his hand, and I shook it. "Okay, now about these new ideas…"

While I was proud of my girlfriend who got a kick-ass internship for the summer, I missed her. I could only handle jerking off over the phone so many times. But after working with her dad all day, I just wanted to see her. Hold her. Get her naked. Picture what life would be like with her if we did get married.

Three weeks left. Then she'd be back.

Three weeks was nothing in the span of a lifetime, but it sucked. I adjusted my backpack from one shoulder to the other as I made my way toward my new place—sans Freddie—where I had nothing but cold pizza and Netflix to keep me company. But something caught my eye.

A very pretty figure sitting outside my door. "Fletcher?"

No fucking way.

My girl was here, wearing a bright red dress and a huge smile. "Surprise!"

I ran to her and picked her up, slamming my mouth against hers. She kissed me back as she gripped my collar and sighed into me. She tasted like mint and *her,* and my heart raced in my chest. *She's here. With me.* "God, I missed you."

Naomi ran her hands over my shoulders, back, sides, and pecs. "Clothes off, please."

"Needy, huh?" I laughed, picking her up and wrapping her legs around me before I got my keys out of my pocket. She looked up at me through hooded eyes and had the perfect pink smile. My heart stumbled in my chest with how much I loved this woman.

She undid the button on my polo. "You have no idea."

"Oh, I think I do." I opened the door, shut it, and pressed her back against it. "I'm so proud of you for taking this opportunity," I said, kissing down her neck and biting her ear lobe. "But I want you all the time."

"Michael," she moaned, reaching for the hem of her dress

and taking the whole thing off. She went without a bra—my favorite Naomi, and I immediately put a pebbled nipple into my mouth. Perfect breasts. Not too big, not too small. Just right. She arched her back as I teased the edge of her wet panties.

"I have something to talk… to talk to you about," she said, her voice trailing off when I pushed the fabric to the side.

"Mm, what's that, baby?" I slid a finger inside her and about lost my mind with how warm and tight she was. One month of distance was enough to kill me. "Fuck, I need you."

Her eyes darkened, and after a frantic display of removing clothes and moving toward my bedroom, I laid her on the bed and barely got a condom. Then I slid into her. She sighed, and that deeply contented sound warmed my chest. She felt right, like *home*.

She gripped my ass and pulled my face down to hers where she kissed me so hard and for so long my lips felt chapped and I could barely keep thrusting. She hadn't come yet, and I needed her to. I stopped, stared down at her, and was dumbstruck. The way her hair fell across her face, the way her long lashes fanned on her cheeks… the trio of moles on her collarbone that drove me wild. Her smooth skin and perfect lips. The way her eyes closed half-way when she laughed and the deep sound of her contented sigh situated themselves right in my chest.

"What's wrong?" she asked, her throaty voice filled with emotion. She reached up and pushed my hair out of my face.

"Nothing. I just love you. This is the best surprise ever." I kissed the center of her sweaty chest, then her stomach. She pulled me back up just before I could lick her thighs, and she scrunched her little nose.

"No, I want to come with you like this. Our chests touching. I miss it, you, us." Her voice shook, and I cupped her face, pressing a soft kiss on her.

I slid back into her and adjusted my pace to go slower. At first sight, I wanted to devour her, but now I wanted her to know how much she meant to me. How much I loved her.

She, too, changed the pace. She rolled her hips slower and kissed me longer. We'd had soft sex before where it was without hurry and all about touches, but *this* was different. More profound, and when her legs tightened around me and her moans grew deeper, I went harder. It was the pressure she needed, and Naomi didn't hold back from screaming my name. Her release triggered mine, and I held onto her tight as pleasure shot through me. Head to toe.

"Damn," I said, panting as I rested my weight on her. "Just, damn."

"Every time, I swear. I'm obsessed with your body." She giggled as she slapped my ass.

I disposed of the condom and got back into bed, holding her in my arms as I played with the ends of her dark hair. She snuggled against me, and everything felt right again. "I hate to ask, but how long are you in town?"

"The weekend." Her body tensed. "Then I'm done."

Her tone was off, and I looked down at her to find her chewing her lip. "Are you not excited to be back for your senior year? This should be the best one yet, Fletcher. You and your friends should go crazy before adulthood kicks in."

"No, I want that. I do. It's just… Michael." She sat up, her gorgeous body still very naked. Her face was serious, and she took my hand and held it between hers. "I don't know how to ask this, and I'm nervous and sweating."

"Just ask." I shrugged and couldn't do anything but wait her out. Naomi wasn't dramatic and didn't cause shit for no reason. We talked about everything, and I always assumed good intentions.

"Um, do you… want to maybe live together?" Her face flamed red, and she pulled the blanket up to hide.

Live with her? My god. I could think of nothing else I wanted more.

"Uh, no, don't cover your face. You ask me, your boyfriend,

to *move in with you,* and then you hide? No, no way. I want a real ask."

"Michael Reiner, would you do me the honors of living with me so we can see each other every morning and do naked stuff all the time?"

"What about your girls? Cami?" I didn't want to get my hopes up too much since I knew how much her friendships meant. Plus, senior year should be wild. I could wait until she was ready. I wanted marriage, the house, the kids, coaching a team that became like family, and maybe a dog. One year was *nothing* compared to that. "There's no rush, Fletcher. I'm in this for the long haul. You and me… one school year doesn't make a dent in our life together."

"Stop being so considerate! I keep thinking about breakfast dates and laundry parties and cooking naked and sharing a bed with you. Do you want that?" Her cheeks were bright pink, and her pulse raced in her neck.

It was so cute.

"All of it except cooking naked. That could get dangerous." I picked up her hand and kissed the back of it. "If you're ready, then yes. Move in with me. I don't want you missing out on an experience though. So, you're sure?"

"Yes! I'm sure, you big, handsome idiot!" She jumped onto me, and I ran my hands up her bare back. She shivered, and I grinned up at her, so goddamn happy it didn't seem fair.

I knew, without a doubt, I was supposed to meet Naomi, and it had never been clearer. She was going to move in. Her dad gave his blessing. Ryann loved her. The next step? Getting her to marry me.

But no rush. We had a lifetime together.

ALSO BY JAQUELINE SNOWE:

Coming soon!

From the Top, Central State Book 2

CLEAT CHASER SERIES

Challenge Accepted

The Game Changer

Best Player

No Easy Catch

OUT OF THE PARK SERIES

Evening the Score

Sliding Home

Rounding the Bases

SHUT UP AND KISS ME SERIES: INTERNSHIP WITH THE DEVIL

Teaching with the Enemy

Next Door Nightmare

HOCKEY ROMANCE

Holdout

STANDALONES

Take a Chance on Me
Let Life Happen
The Weekend Deal

ABOUT THE AUTHOR

Jaqueline Snowe lives in Arizona where the "dry heat" really isn't that bad. She prefers drinking coffee all hours of the day and snacking on anything that has peanut butter or chocolate. She is the mother to two fur-babies who don't realize they aren't humans and a new mom to the sweetest baby boy. She is an avid reader and writer of romances and tends to write about athletes. Her husband works for an MLB team (not a player, lol) so she knows more about baseball than any human ever should.

You can find her posting photos of her sweet baby on Instagram or rage tweeting. She tries to update her website as often as she can so feel free to poke around. www.jaquelinesnowe.com

Printed in Great Britain
by Amazon